Moonshadow's Guardian

Book one of the Moonshadow Rising duology

Dianna Gunn

Fictional Worlds Publishing

For Astrid, the love of my life.

Cover and Interior Design by Éric Desmarais

978-1-7752798-3-9 (Paperback)

978-1-7752798-1-5 (Ebook)

Chapter One

Naomi

Something jolted my body forward. I tightened my grip on Ma's waist, squinting into the sunlight. The canopy of leaves had thinned while I slept; the trees here were younger and more spread out than in other parts of the forest. I wanted to lift my hood to block the brightness, but I was too scared to fall off our horse. He had broken into a near-gallop, driven by another of Ma's spells.

The forest gave way to a large grassy plain with a deep crater in the centre. Only thin, yellowish patches of grass grew near it. Inside, the ground was pitch black.

All the tension disappeared from Ma's back, and when she spoke I swore I heard her smiling. "We're going there." She pointed at the pit.

I blinked. What could Ma possibly want with a giant hole in the ground? And why was it so important that she had pushed our horse almost to death rushing here?

I knew better than to ask. Ma would tell me when she was ready.

She brought our horse to a halt at the edge of the slope. I stared.

Someone had carved a flat path down the side, leading to a small cabin made of black stone that gleamed in the fading sunlight. Runes of protection and containment were painted on the wooden door in a similar shade of black. The house didn't have a single window, nor a chimney.

"What is this place?" I asked.

Ma shot me a look comprising equal parts annoyance and sadness. "All in due time."

I glared back at her, but she had turned her head toward the cabin.

"We'll have to lead the horse down."

I groaned. After several long days of riding, my legs were a series of cramps. The last thing I wanted to do was walk. Still, it was a break of sorts.

"And then we don't have to go anywhere for days," she said. "You can rest all you want."

"*All* I want?" I grinned. "I'm going to sleep for a week."

I dismounted and grabbed the horse's reins, so Ma could do the same. She glanced at me, and for a moment I saw something behind her eyes—a deep melancholy I had seen many times before. Over the past few days it became more pronounced. I realized that her secret sorrow had something to do with me.

"Ma, why are we here?"

She leaned forward and brushed a stray curl away from my forehead, tucking it behind my left ear. "I'll tell you everything over a cuppa once we get inside, all right?"

I jutted my chin. Usually I was happy to let Ma keep her secrets, but this one was bigger than usual. And it had something to do with me. It had to. Why else would she have dragged me all the way out here, right before my birthday?

"I'm not moving another step until you tell me."

Ma sighed. "Please, Naomi. I just want to sit in a chair instead of a saddle."

Part of me wanted to hold out, but the thought of a real chair was far too tempting. "You'd better tell me when I get inside."

"I promise."

I beamed and handed her the reins. "Then let's go!"

Overcome with a sudden wave of energy, I skipped down the path ahead of her. The air was strangely still, but I barely noticed, too wrapped up in my own thoughts.

I went to push the door open and blistering heat rushed up my arm, hitting my chest with such force that it knocked me backward. I yelped and stumbled, my eyes stinging with tears.

Ma rushed forward and knelt beside me, her eyes filled with fear. "This house is special. Only I can open or close this door."

I held my arm close to my chest, tears flooding my cheeks. My hand had already swollen to twice its usual size. "Dammit Ma, this is why I want you to talk to me! How am I supposed to know—"

"I didn't know either," Ma said quietly, glancing at the door. "Let's get the horse tied up and then I'll get you healed, all right?"

This time I didn't even bother glaring at her. I was too busy blowing cool air on my hand, trying to soothe the throbbing heat.

Several moments later she led me into the house. A heavy wave crashed into my shoulders, almost knocking me over as I crossed the threshold. I had never sensed magical energy the same way everyone else did, but here it was overwhelming.

Ma, seemingly unaffected by this heaviness, led me to an ancient wooden chair with threadbare cushions. I sat gratefully, already exhausted from breathing in the magic of this place. This couldn't be how mages felt all the time, could it? How Ma felt?

My gaze caught on a gleaming black line along the floor, growing larger as Ma rolled up the rug that covered it. The line met with another line, then a series of miniature runes, and the outside of a circle. Curiosity turned to dread. I recognized those lines.

A demon circle, complete with dozens of variations on the standard protection and containment runes. Dozens more filled the margins, though I could only imagine what they were for. They didn't bother teaching nonmagicals about these things. Everything I knew, I learned from stealing Ma's books when I couldn't sleep.

But summoning a demon required human blood, and there was nobody else here.

New questions surged into my mind, but they got tangled in my throat and only one word came out, so tiny that I didn't expect her to hear it. "Ma..."

She crouched in front of me and cupped my chin in her hands. "Remember when I told you that your father would take you away if he ever found out about you?"

Something clicked in my mind. The dread in my stomach solidified. "We didn't come here to summon a demon, did we?"

She shook her head. "Your father is a god. You are a demon. On your birthday your true form will show itself."

All the aches and pains in my body vanished, replaced by a cold, numbing sensation that spread outward from my heart.

"On your birthday, you will sit in that circle," she gestured at the floor. "It will contain your transformation, protecting you from yourself—and your father."

"But he's a god." The word tasted foul in my mouth, like the worst kind of lie; still, it made sense. Demon children didn't show magical talent until they transformed. It hid them until they were ready for the cursed realm. "How are you going to protect me from him?"

She smiled and kissed my forehead. "I'm not the first woman who wanted to keep her immortal daughter. What do you think this place is for?"

The bell hanging around Ma's neck rang out, the little sound barely loud enough for me to hear, and her face darkened.

"It's time." She grabbed a small cloth bag from the table and ushered me into the demon circle.

I moved to the centre and then sat cross-legged. Ma had walked me through the ritual a dozen times since we reached the cabin, but my body still shook with fear.

Nobody knew much about what happened to demons during their transformations, and the scenarios playing out in my mind grew more gruesome by the moment.

Ma leaned forward, precariously hanging across the salt circle, and kissed my forehead one last time.

"Whatever happens, I love you," she said, her eyes shining with tears.

"I love you too, Ma."

"I know, sweetheart."

Ma straightened and took a large handful of red rock salt out of the cloth bag. She opened a small hole between her forefinger and thumb, letting the salt drain out as she walked around the demon circle. The clumps melted into the gleaming black paint, making it glow an eerie almost-white.

"I call upon the power of the great goddess Magdalene," she said, her voice rising slightly with each word. "To contain and confine the beast within, to let the mortal live."

She dropped a final, large clump of salt onto a rune I didn't understand. It solidified instantly, then cracked apart with a sound as violent as lightning hitting a tree. Blinding white light poured out from between the cracks, and the circle around me grew brighter to match. I threw my hands up to cover my eyes and screamed as scalding heat filled my veins. The skin on my hand began to boil and bubble. I forced my eyes closed. I tried to push back a wave of bile, but I couldn't. My body was too hot, and filled with... something. I was bursting at the seams.

I exploded out of my skin, becoming something different, messier, almost without form. My mind lost its connection to my body and I drifted up to the ceiling, watching the red mass that used to be me fill the demon circle. Ma stood on the other side, her body shaking but her expression calm.

The red stuff that used to be me hit the walls of blinding light, crashing against the demon prison again and again. Each time the circle grew a little darker. Some distant part of me felt the magical barrier weakening, the new me growing stronger as it absorbed Magdalene's magic.

That thing, the thing that used to be me, if it got out—

I tried to scream at Ma, tell her to run, but she couldn't hear me. I couldn't even really scream. The demon was too powerful, too visceral. It had already destroyed me, and Ma would be next.

The red mass pulled back from the edges of the circle, forming into a tight ball. Had it changed its mind?

No. That ball was a weapon, growing tighter with every moment only to—

This time the explosion crashed against the shimmering magical barrier, like a thousand simultaneous lightning strikes, engulfing the entire cabin in a red glow. It went straight through Ma, tearing out her insides, and continued on to rip at the cabin walls, blasting away chunks of stone.

A giant of a man with bright red hair appeared by the door. He spread his arms apart and opened his palms, then pulled them together, whispering as he did so.

Something yanked me back into my body, only this body was entirely different. Solid, now, or at least solidifying—and changed. Red, and bigger, and stronger, and filled with a deep, burning power. Every inch of my skin still burned, but now the fire felt good, like it gave me life instead of taking it away.

Taking it away—

I whirled to stare at Ma's body. The red mass—me—had punched a hole through her chest, and her heart lay several feet behind her in a growing pool of blood.

I fell to my knees and heaved, but nothing came out. There wasn't even bile left in my stomach.

The man grabbed my shoulders and brought me roughly to my feet, spinning me to face him. He chewed on the left side of his lip like it was a piece of straw and squinted at me. I stared back at him, wondering why he looked so familiar.

Of course. I had seen him in books, in paintings, even statues.

"You're Loki," I said, with a voice that sounded entirely too grown up to be my own.

He smiled, but there was a deep bitterness behind that smile. "And you, my dear, are one of the Cursed Children."

"Cursed... Children?" That was much nicer than anything they called demons back home.

He tightened his grip on my shoulders. "You have to come with me now. Hold your breath."

A burst of magical force grabbed our feet and dragged us into the ground. My body compressed as thousands of tonnes of pressure forced it through thousands of feet of solid rock, and pushed the wind out of me on the way.

Then the crushing stopped, and I crashed into a solid stone floor. I took several shuddering gasps, filling my lungs and gathering my strength. My arms trembled like they were made of jelly, but after a few tries, I managed to sit up.

I gaped around the room. It was easily the largest structure I had ever seen, made of bright red rock. The same colour as my new skin. Several pillars shaped like harpies held the ceiling up, their clawed hands piercing it in several places.

Each harpy also had a looped metal ring piercing its belly, and a pair of black manacles hung from the rings. They were covered in ancient blood, but nobody was locked into them now.

"Wh-what—"

"You still have several stages of transformation to go." Loki grabbed my arm. "This is the safest place to do it."

"This place looks anything *but* safe."

Loki chuckled. "That word will have a very different meaning for you soon."

The first thing that struck me was a cold so intense it burned, spreading outward from my wrists and ankles. It should have come with pain, but I was beyond agony now. The past few days—weeks, maybe, it was impossible to tell down here—blurred together, a whirlwind of torments, each more imaginative than the last. The cold, emanating from special cuffs made of demon-proof metal, was blissful in comparison.

I could hardly remember what came before. Even my own name was difficult to recall. The only thing I remembered clearly was Ma standing on the other side of the demon circle, the creature that used to be me tearing her apart and Loki dragging me to the demon realm.

My eyes snapped open. Four talons were embedded deep into the ceiling directly overhead, each one part of a different harpy's claw. The talons were intricately carved, with hundreds of little scales on each one. At first I tried to count them, but I couldn't focus long enough to get past thirty. I had given up days ago.

Something popped audibly on my left. I twisted my head—sending fresh waves of pain up my neck—to face Loki. He grinned at me and I recoiled, pulling at my restraints. If only I could escape from whatever torturous spell he planned to inflict on me next.

"I'm glad you're awake," he said. "This next ritual requires consciousness."

"Please," I croaked. "Please let me die." I didn't know how much more of this I could take, how long it would be before the agony stripped away the last of my memories, of myself.

"I can't simply let you die," Loki said, with the tone of a parent scolding a young child. "Demons are immortal. I could leave you here, but you'd be stuck to the floor, alone, for centuries."

"You're a god. Surely you can kill me." Once I had read about a mortal who managed to kill a demon, but I was too far gone to remember the story now.

Loki shrugged. "I could destroy this entire realm if I wanted to. But you don't really want to die."

I narrowed my eyes, pouring all of my pain and hatred into my glare. "I've never wanted anything more."

"You're so dramatic about everything. Still thinking like a mortal. What you want isn't death, it's an end to the pain."

"I want my humanity back." I wanted to shout, but my throat hurt too much. "I want Ma."

A flicker of emotion, gone too fast to recognize, passed across his face. Icy coldness replaced it, without any of his usual mischief. Then suddenly he was beside me, kneeling.

"Some water will do you good." A wineskin appeared in his hand and he offered it to me, then glanced at the cuffs still biting into my wrists. "Right." He opened the wineskin and held it closer to my mouth.

I shook my head. "Just kill me."

"Oh, but you're so close to the end. All you need to do is survive this ritual and you'll be free to roam the entire demon realm."

I broke out into laughter that sounded insane even to my ears. My body might survive, but would there be anything left of me, the real me? "Why would I trust you? The god of lies?"

Loki rolled his eyes. "God of lies is a little simplistic."

"Is it? They told me if I left you offerings every month you would leave me alone, so clearly somebody lied to me. You want me to believe it was them?"

"Mortals can only understand so much of a god's nature," he said. "Now, are you going to drink, or am I just going to perform the ritual anyway?"

I wanted to curse him, to reject him and his water, tell him I hoped the ritual killed me. But I leaned forward. He put the wineskin to my lips, and I drank.

Maybe he was right. Maybe I didn't want to die. Maybe all I wanted was freedom.

Chapter Two

2,769 Years Later: Riana

I spent a lot of my youth in dungeons, rat-infested basements and torture chambers with dried blood for paint. I hated this one more than any of them.

Loki had mastered a new form of torture, something that seemed antithetical to his nature: boredom. Walls of grey stone surrounded me, without any discolouration or even creases to count, or weak points to take advantage of. The door was made of the same grey stone, and it disappeared into the wall between uses.

Instead of a painted or carved light charm, the walls glowed, keeping me in perpetual twilight. Even worse, these walls negated my magic. I couldn't even transform here. That meant no chance of entertainment or escape. Not that I wanted to escape.

For the first many hours—I don't know how many—I had paced in circles and torn my mind apart thinking of all the reasons why Loki might have brought me here. He must intend to punish me for my crimes, but why do it himself? The inner family had many creative ways of punishing demons who broke the rules.

But too many hours had passed, and even my body needed nourishment eventually. I could barely keep myself sitting upright. My red hands shook as I braided a tiny section of my hair for the hundredth time. I was too exhausted to do my whole head—my thick, wavy black hair hung almost to my hips—but the familiar movements calmed me. They reminded me of better times, back when I still believed I was human. When I didn't have magic to transform my hair on a whim. When I had a mother—

Stop it, self. How long did I have to mourn her? How long did I have to feel guilty?

A small, repetitive sound caught my attention. Footsteps, coming this way.

I jumped to my feet, one hand on the wall to steady myself, the other furiously wiping at my tears. With a deep breath, I pulled away from the wall and shifted my feet apart, almost into a fighting stance. My head spun, but I stayed balanced as the footsteps reached my cell. I would not show my weakness. I didn't want to give Loki the satisfaction of knowing he had once again reduced me to almost nothing.

The footsteps stopped, and the outline of a door appeared. Stone ground against stone with a terrible sound as it swung open, revealing Loki. He pulled a ridiculously tall hat off his head and bowed dramatically. He always did like to make a show of things, especially when they concerned life and death.

He straightened and deposited the hat back on his head, still grinning. Today he wore a male form with dirty blond hair and a chip in one of his front teeth that made him look even more troublesome than normal.

"How do you like my dungeon, Naomi?" A faint smile played across his lips.

I tensed. Why in all of the five realms had he used that name?

"My name is Riana now." My mouth was dry as parchment, and my voice sounded hoarse even to me. Weeks had passed since I last spoke out loud, but I was damn well going to give Loki a piece of my mind. "You chose it for me, remember?" To mark me as a demon.

He shrugged. "Yes, Riana, of course. And you didn't answer my question—how do you like the dungeon? It's new."

I glared at him, wishing more than anything that looks could kill. Or that I had any power at all to kill a god.

"Did you come here to poke fun at me or are you finally going to tell me why I'm here?"

"Well, first you're going to eat." He waved a hand, and a giant leg of mutton appeared in the air between us.

I grabbed the mutton and ripped off the biggest bite I could. It was still warm and seasoned with many of the mortal realm's best spices. My stomach rumbled happily as I wolfed the meat down.

Loki chuckled and gestured at my stomach. "Once the beast is satisfied, you will participate in a Raising."

I swallowed hard and lowered the leg of mutton. "A Raising?"

"To become a Guardian-class demon."

I took a step back. This was too good to be true. I failed my last summoner's request, refusing to participate in the mortal war. The penalty should have been death, or at least a century of imprisonment in the demon realm. Not being sent right back to the mortal world.

"Who will I be guarding?" I asked. Guardians were usually bound to a noble family, for so long as that family survived. "And what's the catch?"

"King Jacob Vonstone VIII asked for you specifically," he said.

My heart leapt into my throat, torn between joy and fear. The Vonstones ruled Moonshadow, the only place I had ever truly felt welcomed. I loved it, and I longed to return, but there were so many memories, some of them—

Stop, Riana. Don't put yourself through that again.

"The King has—rather selfishly—bound you to himself," Loki said, speaking even more casually than before. As if he was telling me what he ate for breakfast. "But if you save Moonshadow from the current threat, I'm prepared to offer you freedom."

I stared at him. This conversation kept getting stranger. Loki was never this generous to anyone. Certainly not to someone who broke as many rules as I had.

"What's the catch?" I repeated.

He broke out into that terrible grin again. "If you don't succeed, you go straight back to the inner family. Now, let's go. You'll have to eat on the way."

That still didn't sound right. It was too simple for Loki. He had to be hiding something. Maybe he had chosen this job as punishment because he believed I would fail. Yes, that sounded like Loki. Humiliation was his favourite form of torture.

"What am I saving Moonshadow from?" I didn't bother trying to keep the wariness out of my voice.

"You know the rules. The summoner will explain the details of your job upon your arrival."

True, but those were the inner family's laws. Loki hated the inner family. "When did you start following rules?"

"When it suited me." He started walking back up the corridor, leaving the cell open.

I liked that answer even less than the last one. "What if I refuse?"

But he was already halfway down the hallway, and I wouldn't have refused anyway. How could I turn down a chance to spend more centuries in the mortal realm? Maybe even an eternity, if he was being honest about freedom. It was the only thing I really wanted, the one faint hope I nurtured through all of these years. The idea that kept me alive.

I was stuck doing what Loki wanted, again.

I cursed, tore another bite of mutton off the leg, and hurried after him. We turned a corner and climbed a flight of steps, ending in front of an ancient red door with a dozen runes on it. The iron-tainted stench of blood magic emanated from the room beyond. My stomach churned at the strength of it.

Loki opened the door with a flourish. "Ladies first."

I stepped into a dark room. Black floor, walls, and ceiling surrounded a blue ball of light hovering near the centre of the ceiling. Ancient runes of protection were carved on the walls in gold, alongside four symbols I didn't recognize. I took those to represent the elements.

A ritual circle was painted on the floor with Loki's symbol—three daggers and a gold coin—in the centre. The gold coin was mostly covered by a marble pedestal on which sat a silver bowl, wide and shallow. The door closed behind me, and I jumped away from Loki. I didn't like this place at all.

"This will be far less painful than your original transformation," Loki said, gesturing for me to follow him into the circle.

"That doesn't say much." My first transformation killed my mother and caused me three weeks of sheer, blinding agony.

"Are you in or out?"

I moved into the circle. "I'll do it."

He instructed me to stand on the opposite side of the pedestal from him, close enough to easily reach the bowl. It was filled with black blood, powerful stuff, probably taken from a greater demon who had outlived his usefulness. Their blood would unlock the hidden power within my own.

My stomach churned again. "Is this really necessary, if the king bound me to himself?"

"They performed the Guardian summoning ritual. And he is a Vonstone."

Which meant I could be protecting him for a millennium. "Then let's get it over with."

Loki dipped his hand in the blood and then drew something onto my forehead. It was warm, like blood still in the body, and it soaked into my skin, releasing a power that throbbed throughout the length of me.

"Drink the blood. Feel its strength fill you," Loki said. "Let it unlock the power residing in your veins, and bring out your true potential."

I braced myself and took a big gulp. It tasted awful. I held my breath and took another gulp, then another, and another, wondering when it would end, shuddering with each taste. I finished the bowl and the pain hit me. Burning, searing, filling my veins, mixing with my own blood, activating it—

Dark spots filled my vision and I collapsed. A pair of strong, warm arms wrapped protectively around me, and a gentle bumping motion carried me into darkness, as if I had gone to sea.

Chapter Three

I opened my eyes to a green ceiling with a simple light charm carved in the centre, giving off a soft glow. The bed was soft, the blankets fluffy. Someone had changed me into a soft, loose tunic and matching trousers.

A large window to my left showed open sky and empty ground. Somewhere in the hallway outside two women argued about how much to feed someone whose name I didn't recognize. Beyond that I heard a faint sound, almost like massive wings beating against the wind, but before I could be sure, one of the women in the hallway started yelling.

Pain spiked through my head and into my neck. I groaned and curled into a ball, raising my hands to my ears. But now I could hear even more: the sound of running water and clinking dishes, servants whispering to each other in distant corridors, and yes, those were wingbeats outside.

"Good morning," Loki said, appearing beside my bed.

I flinched. "Do you have to talk so loud?" I whispered.

He wore a new face today, an old man with a scar trailing down one cheek into his auburn beard—a braided monstrosity that hung almost to his waist. The teeth exposed by his usual troublesome grin were bright yellow, and his breath stank like a brewery.

"I'm not being loud," he said. "You have better hearing now. If you want my voice to hurt less, focus on something else. Like the sky. Or your own thoughts. You do think, right?"

"At least as often as you do," I said, holding my head. I could hear a small group of women—three or four—talking and giggling somewhere in the castle's bowels, farther away than the women who were arguing.

"Can you walk?"

"Of course I can." I pulled myself up from the bed and took a step toward Loki, trying to ignore the throbbing in my head. My legs shook under my weight, but with sheer determination I took another step before I collapsed, landing on my knees. My limbs felt heavy and distant, as if the ritual had severed their connection to my mind.

"Not a bad start," Loki said. "Try again."

I shot him the dirtiest look I could muster and used the bed to pull myself back into standing position, wincing as I straightened my knees. I focused on walking and took a shaky step forward. The blood in my veins vibrated with power, but my muscles ached from the change.

I can do this, damn it.

I put a hand on the nearest wall and took another step forward.

"You're a natural," he said. "I hope you're ready to fly."

"Fly?" I wasn't even sure I could walk out of the castle, let alone fly. Even if my new blood had made me powerful enough to grow functional wings.

Loki laughed. "You didn't think I'd give you time to recover, did you?"

"Of course not." I rolled my eyes. "That wouldn't be any fun."

I stumbled after Loki, following him through a maze of corridors to what I presumed was the castle's main entrance. Two great sets of double doors stood opposite each other. One led farther into the castle and one led outside, or so I guessed from the sunlight filtering through the stained-glass window above it. Loki escorted me across the hall and opened the outer doors with the lightest of touches. Sunlight flooded the room, blinding me.

I blinked several times and lifted a hand to shield my face from the worst of it. As my eyes adjusted, and the cliffs came into view around me, I knew exactly where Loki had brought me.

Dragon's Keep, mythical home of the gods.

The keep sat in the bottom of an enormous round hole in the ground. The surrounding cliffs were pockmarked with caves, the dragons' homes. Flying above us were massive, colourful shapes that could only be the dragons themselves. They shone brilliantly in the sun, so much so that it hurt to look at them, but I couldn't bring myself to look away.

The sounds I heard earlier must have been the wings of dragons, carrying them into the sky. Now, listening carefully, I swore I knew what direction they were about to turn. Sure enough, a moment later they pivoted, flying back over the keep.

I took a deep breath—hot air, thick and stuffy with a hint of salt, but clean. "It's just like the stories."

"All stories are somewhere rooted in truth," he said. He took my hand and pulled me toward the nearest cliff. I let him lead me, too fascinated by the dragons' glittering scales to care where we were going.

I tripped on a rock and landed at the foot of the cliff, hissing at the stinging sensation in my knees. Loki chuckled as I got up.

"Is something the matter?" he asked. "You seem awfully distracted."

I stared up into the sky. Two dragons spiralled around each other in what appeared to be a mating dance. They arced through the sky, into the sparse clouds and out again. One made a peculiar sound, halfway between a city cat's purr and a mountain lion's roar, and the other responded in kind.

They disappeared beyond the ring of cliffs, and I turned back to Loki.

"They're magnificent," I said.

"Wait 'til you see them up close."

"Wha—"

He grabbed me by the waist and tapped the ground with his foot. A moment later the ground fell away from my feet and we were floating. Floating became hurtling through the sky, wind pounding on my head and howling in my ears. A gust of wind launched us into a cave and we landed with so much force, it knocked the air out of my lungs.

Loki tried to hold me steady, but I shoved him away, almost falling over in the process.

"Thanks for the warning, asshole." I muttered the last part, distracted by a silver gleam in the corner of my vision.

I spun to face a silver-furred dragon with bluish-green eyes. The creature was a full head taller than my entire body, and three times as large around. Two horns grew out from directly above those eyes, curving back toward its body, which trailed all the way to the back of the cavern, perhaps fifty feet away. A line of shiny blue spikes adorned its tail, culminating in a spike that must have been twice my height.

I had never seen anything like it. This creature didn't even have wings.

"What kind of dragon is this?"

"My kind of dragon," Loki answered.

He created me, after all.

I jumped backward, bumping into Loki. The voice came from inside my head, but it certainly wasn't me. It was too deep, too male. to be mine.

I gaped at Loki. "Is that... him?"

"Probably." He shrugged. "Dragons do have mindvoices."

"They do?" It made sense, of course—that must have been how Shalinor's royal family controlled them—but it wasn't mentioned anywhere in the lore. *Or perhaps the Shalinorans hid it.*

"Yes. Now stop being rude and say hello."

"All right." I turned back to the dragon, trying not to think about the size of his jaws or the teeth hiding behind his furry muzzle. "Hello."

Hello. My name is Rolf.

So you are a male. I tried thinking back to him. *That's an unusual name for a dragon.*

His lips stretched back in what was probably meant to be a smile, revealing two extensive rows of fangs, each one almost as tall as I was. *I'm an unusual dragon.*

I glanced back at Loki. "Why Rolf?"

"I wanted him to be a friendly dragon."

I rolled my eyes and turned back to Rolf. *Is this how you communicate with other dragons?* I asked.

Of course. Our growls and snarls are to inspire fear in our enemies.

Fascinating. What other secrets had the Shalinorans hidden?

You can come closer, you know. I won't bite.

I laughed. *That's comforting.* I doubted Loki's creature was much more trustworthy than the god himself.

Rolf's eyes narrowed at my sarcasm, but I approached him anyway. As I came close enough to touch him, I realized his fur was emerging from a series of cracks between his shiny silver scales. It came out diagonally, hiding these scales. His breath stank of rotting meat.

I held my breath and reached out to touch Rolf's muzzle. His nose was cold and wet, like a dog's. I stood beside it and gently rested my hand on top of his snout. He had the softest fur I'd ever felt, smoother even than silk. When he didn't object, I buried my face in it and breathed in. Rolf's fur smelled better than his breath, like freshly washed linens. Odd, but comforting.

After a moment, I pulled away and smiled. He smiled back at me, all teeth and bad breath. I held my smile in place, suppressing a shudder.

See, that wasn't so bad.

You're softer than I imagined. I thought back to him.

Thank you. I don't get many visitors.

"I hate to interrupt," Loki said, "but you really ought to be on your way."

My heart sank through my stomach and settled somewhere in my ankles.

"Today?" My limbs still felt clumsy, heavy. How was I supposed to help anyone like this? "You can't be serious."

His signature grin vanished, replaced by a disturbingly straight face. "Oh, but I am. *Dramlech*."

A massive leather belt appeared around Rolf's body, fastening itself directly behind the joints of his wings.

"Rolf wants to see the human world, so he's going with you. The saddle is enchanted to appear on the command *'dramlech'* and disappear on the command *'aramleech*.'"

I looked at the leather contraption on Rolf's back. There appeared to be some kind of seat and straps attached to the top of the leather belt, but it didn't look like nearly enough to keep me safely on the back of a dragon. Besides, my stomach ached and my whole body was shaky. Flying now sounded like a terrible idea.

"Don't just stand there," Loki said, "you have a job to do—oh, I'm forgetting something, aren't I?"

He snapped again, and a sheathed bastard sword with a gleaming silver handle appeared in the air between us. How appropriate. The sheath hung on a bandolier, making it easy to strap the weapon to my back.

"This sword's metal is particularly suited to your—talents." He waved, and the sword flew closer to me.

Talents? Rolf asked, his tone filled with the genuine curiosity of a child.

You'll see.

I grabbed the sword and yanked it free of its sheath. The metal had a blue tinge to it, a faint shimmer of magical power, but no obvious markings. I closed my eyes as its power surged through my skin, connecting to the magic in my blood. Yes, this blade would be easy to reshape. Was almost begging to be reshaped.

I traced a line down the centre of the blade with two fingers, letting the line curve slightly as I reached the sword's end and passed it. The metal warped to meet my fingers, creating a mild curve at the end of the blade. In my other hand the sheath pulsed, then changed its shape to match the new sword. The ease of transformation was delightful, but it only increased the uneasy feeling in my bones. Why would Loki give me such a weapon? What kind of enemy would I face in Moonshadow, to require a blade like this?

That's amazing. Can you do more? Rolf asked.

Rolf's astonishment brought a smile to my face, but I ignored him. There would be plenty of time to show off my talents on the road.

For now, I needed answers. I glared at Loki. "Why are you helping me?" I had never been given a weapon before my other summonings, let alone something so powerful.

I clenched my teeth, fighting the urge to curse. *You used your mindvoice?*

What's wrong? All I did was say hello. And he's such a nice boy.

Marcus was beside Rolf now, stroking his snout and watching me reproachfully. As if he could hear our conversation too.

Most humans don't have mindvoices. They aren't used to communicating like this. I glanced at Queen Isabella. If Marcus told her about the mindvoice, we could be thrown out before we even got started. *You'll scare them.*

But how am I supposed to make friends if I can't talk to them?

I'm your friend, and now Marcus is too. Just make sure he keeps your secret. I'll explain everything later.

"My son's ill," Queen Isabella said, bringing my mind back to the courtyard. "It's been some time since he smiled."

"He can visit Rolf whenever he wants." Hopefully that would be incentive enough to keep the boy quiet about my dragon's mindvoice.

She pursed her lips. "I'm sure he'll be happy to hear that. Now, go get washed up. You remember where your old quarters are?"

My old quarters. A chamber of long-buried memories. "I remember."

Queen Isabella's lips curved upward in an attempt at smiling. "You will live in those chambers for the duration of your stay. My husband expects you in the advisors' chamber at sunset."

"Thank you, your Majesty."

My quarters consisted of a large bedroom, a den, and a bathing room with a flushing toilet, an amenity found only in the wealthiest of homes. I entered through the bedroom door, and immediately came to a halt.

Everything was exactly how I left it. The bed, still adorned with my favourite blanket, took up most of the room. A half-written note sat on the nearest bedside table, the parchment somehow untouched by time. Beside it lay a raven feather quill. Here, at least, time showed: the ink on its tip was dried out and crusty, making the quill useless.

I had left this place in a hurry. The wardrobe door wasn't even properly closed, implying that nobody else ever entered, but there should have been dust, decay. Some sign of abandonment.

Perhaps the Vonstones had always known I would be back. Maybe this was part of some destiny nobody bothered to fill me in on. Or simply part of Moonshadow's obsession with preserving its past.

I sighed and went to the wardrobe. Several modified Slayer uniforms still hung inside. Blue surcoats with loose sleeves to accommodate the daggers on my leather arm bracers, sleeveless black shirts made of thick canvas to prevent chainmail from chafing against my skin, breeches made of similar material, leather boots. A single chainmail shirt hung on one side. Like everything else, it appeared untouched by time.

The Vonstones probably intended to make me comfortable by keeping everything familiar, but the stillness bothered me. The mortal realm had always been defined by change. That was part of what made it so charming, so much better than the demon realm.

But also so much harder. My gaze caught on familiar words carved into the top of the wardrobe door. A message from Jacob III, my beloved, who carved the wardrobe for me himself.

My saviour,
In more ways than one
~J.M.V.

Tears formed in my eyes, and memories surged into my mind—

"How do you like it?" Jacob III—Morgan, I was supposed to call him now—asked, moving forward until I felt his breath on the back of my neck.

I touched the engraving. Such sweet words. More than I deserved. "You didn't have to."

He wrapped his arms around my waist and pulled me close. "I wanted to. You've done so much for me, and I can't exactly give you land."

"I suppose not." In a decade or two, he would be dead, and I would return to the demon realm, possibly forever. Besides, my place was here, with him. I didn't want to go elsewhere.

"I thought about getting you jewels, but—"

I shook my head. Jewels would be too obvious, exposing our affair. "You made this. That makes it more precious than the largest emerald in the land."

He kissed the base of my neck, his lips trailing a line toward my jaw. I shivered, and he nibbled at my ear lobe.

"Not as beautiful as you are," he whispered. His hands were moving up now, unfastening my surcoat—

I shook my head, forcing myself back to the present. Morgan died hundreds of years ago, and I had a job to do now. Confronting my memories could wait.

I changed as quickly as I could and hurried out of the room, making a mental note to ask for new furniture. I didn't want to relive my past every night. Not even the good parts.

At least my new abilities gave me plenty of ways to distract myself. I closed my eyes and listened to the castle, searching for a specific voice. There were dozens of people to filter through, servants and guards and a handful of visiting nobles. Most blurred together, discussing the mundane aspects of mortal life. Supplies that needed to be replenished, items and rooms to be cleaned. Nothing of interest to me.

Then my attention settled on Queen Isabella, speaking in a strained, high-pitched tone.

"Do you have any idea how we're supposed to feed this dragon of hers?" Isabella asked. There was a faint sound that might have been her pacing around the room.

"No," Jacob II responded, his baritone voice thick with amusement. "The dragon is a new development."

I chuckled. Yet another thing in Moonshadow that remained unchanged. Jacob II always did have a way of understating things. But I should sort this out. I headed in the direction of the voices, staying focused on their conversation.

"New development? How can you be so casual? Nobody's seen a dragon in millennia. And we aren't equipped to feed something that size—!"

"It's a dragon," Jacob II said. "I'm sure it can hunt for itself."

"It's my guest. Feeding it is my responsibility."

How long are you going to be in there? Rolf's mindvoice burst into my head. *I want to explore.*

You can explore soon, I promise. They'll freak out if you leave without warning. Or if he returned without warning. Or if he did pretty much anything else without warning. They weren't exactly used to dragons here. *Once I've talked to them, you can explore and hunt, so long as you stay away from farm animals. But I'll be stuck here a while.*

Very well. The words rode a strong wave of impatience, making my hands twitch.

I sighed. I couldn't decide if Rolf's childish nature was endearing or irritating. Both, perhaps.

A green sign with a silver engraving—"J.V. II"—in the centre of the door marked Jacob II's office. Both the door and the plaque were new, although identical to the old ones.

I rapped on the door three times. Someone on the other side, likely Queen Isabella, cursed under their breath.

"Enter," Jacob II called.

His office hadn't changed much more than my chambers. The walls on either side of me were lined with bookshelves. Most were filled with leather-bound journals, the living history of the Vonstone family, recorded by Jacob II himself. His desk, an elegantly carved mahogany beast that took up most of the room, hadn't changed either.

Even the art behind the desk was the same, the wedding portrait from his human life. Traditional marriage paintings showed the couple standing together, as they would at the altar. Jacob II's showed him and his wife sitting together, watching a roaring hearth fire. Jacob II was born with a twisted foot that magic couldn't repair. He couldn't stand long enough to be painted.

The only significant change in the office was Queen Isabella's presence in the chair across from Jacob II. She gripped the armrests fiercely, as if struggling to keep herself upright, and offered me a wan smile.

"Excellent timing," she said. "I was just wondering how we're supposed to feed your dragon."

"Please, dear, let me at least be courteous to my guest." Jacob II gestured at a second wooden chair beside Queen Isabella's, indicating that I should sit. He hadn't physically aged a day since our last meeting, but the sadness in his eyes was deeper now. "Riana, do sit."

I ignored him, locking eyes with Queen Isabella. "Once again, I do not own him. We work together. He's a sentient being. He can hunt his own food."

"You are certain?"

"Dragons can mind bond with their chosen riders," Jacob II said. "They've likely spoken about this."

I barely managed to keep myself from gaping at him. When did his knowledge of dragons outstrip mine? Then again, it could have been any time, really. Almost six centuries had passed since the last time we spoke.

"We have," I said. Hopefully I wouldn't have to explain that Rolf's mindvoice could speak with others too. "He'll be off to hunt soon, in fact."

Queen Isabella nodded and rose unsteadily. "I'll inform the guards."

She looked about ready to faint, but I said nothing as she left. Humans didn't like having their weakness pointed out. Especially royal humans.

"So, what really brings you here?" Jacob II asked.

I took the seat he had offered earlier and ran a hand through my hair. "It's been almost six hundred years. I have some catching up to do."

He raised a single, bushy black eyebrow. "You don't really expect me to tell you everything that's happened in six centuries?"

"Only the basics. Like, when did Moon Spire start growing beyond the wall?"

He reached under his desk and pulled out a flat slab of transparent green stone, adorned with a grid of silver lines. "I sense we're going to be here awhile. Care for a round of Kalchen?"

I scoffed. "You know I hate that game."

"You won't humour an old man?"

I couldn't help grinning back at him. "You don't *look* any older."

"Oh, but I am. And you haven't even paid me a visit."

I threw my hands up in a show of defeat. "If it means that much to you, I'll play." I was terrible at Kalchen, but it would keep my hands busy. "But I expect details."

"Yes, yes." He grabbed a handful of carved ebony figurines from another drawer. "People started building outside the wall ten years ago. The curse has been fading for almost fifty."

"That long?" A lifetime, for most humans.

He nodded. "The dead only rise in the farthest reaches of Moonshadow now, and in many ways, our kingdom prospers because of it. But the number of mages born grows lower every year. Even Jacob VIII doesn't possess the gift."

I accepted the figurines he offered me, three horses and four people carved out of white wood. One of the people, the Chieftain, had a thin silver band painted around his head. I turned it over in my hand, trying to digest what Jacob II was saying.

"There are only a few thousand mages left in the kingdom, and most aren't long for this world. By the end of this decade, we will have less than fifteen hundred mages throughout the entire kingdom, most of whom can only perform object magic."

"But..." I trailed off. If they lost their magic, and the curse with it, Moonshadow would be easy pickings for the other nations. For Estefar. "Everything in Moonshadow is powered by magic."

"We're trying to change that." He finished his wine and started pouring us more. His kind didn't get drunk any easier than mine. "But it's slow going. Our people have relied on magic longer than Moonshadow has been a nation."

"So you called me in? I can't exactly restore the magic of an entire nation." And I didn't want to be anywhere near here if the enemy was Estefar.

His face darkened. "That's not why we brought you here. But the king wishes to explain that himself, over dinner."

I rolled my eyes. Damn royalty and their formalities. I wanted to start my job now, if only to get out of playing Kalchen. "Is there anything else you can tell me now?"

He leaned forward. "What did you want to know?"

"Who I can trust, for starters."

He laughed bitterly. "Right now? I don't trust anyone who isn't a Vonstone. Except you, of course."

An hour, one game of Kalchen, and an entire bottle of wine later, we left Jacob II's office for the advisors' chamber. We wove through a maze of corridors and down two flights of steps to a large, round chamber at the exact centre of the castle. This had been the advisors' council chamber for centuries, mostly because of its complete lack of windows. There wasn't even a single arrow slit, as all the walls bordered other parts of the castle.

Otherwise, it was an ordinary enough room. An ebony table with rounded edges dominated the space. The only decorations were a series of finely crafted weapons along the back wall. A single Vonstone banner displayed their coat of arms, a dark blue shield with a silver mountain cat on one side and a snake on the other.

The two men seated at the table, however, were entirely unlike other men. They were starkly pale, even in contrast to the living Vonstones, and neither appeared to be over the age of fifty, though I suspected both were at least a century old. They were new to me, but they bore familiar Vonstone features: sharp, angular faces with prominent cheekbones, black hair that insisted on being straight as a pin, and piercing blue eyes.

"I am Jacob Vonstone the Fifth," said the older man, inclining his head. By the streaks of grey in his hair, I suspected he was in his forties when he died. "You may call me Kenneth. It's a pleasure to meet you."

"And I am Andre Vonstone," the younger one added.

This one couldn't have been more than thirty when he passed. A long, ugly scar across the base of his throat must have been the cause. I bit my lip to stop myself from gaping at the wound. Who would dare do that to a Vonstone?

"My brother," Andre continued, "Jacob VIII, will be here in a moment, along with beverages more to your liking." He took a swig of something in a dark glass bottle, leaving dark red residue all over his lips.

Perhaps the most interesting thing about Moonshadow was that many members of its royal family became vampires upon death.

Chapter Six

Jacob VIII arrived moments after Jacob II and I took our seats, followed by two young maids with a wheeled cart. The cart had several more bottles like Andre's, a pitcher of wine, and platters of bread, cheese, and sliced meats. The latter were strategically placed between myself and Jacob VIII, who sat directly across from me.

"I hope you found your quarters in suitable condition," Jacob VIII said. "We were given strict instructions not to touch them." He glanced at Jacob II.

"They are well kept." I forced myself to flash him a smile, but really, I was watching the servants scamper out of the room. They seemed even more afraid of the Vonstones than the maids I remembered, and instinct told me it wasn't because of their youth.

"I am pleased to hear it." Jacob VIII piled several slices of cheese onto a piece of bread.

The maids' footsteps faded down the corridor and I straightened, clearing my throat. "Let's get straight to the point. Why am I here?"

"I appreciate your promptness," he said. "Court formalities do tire me so." He laid his bread on the plate. "Four months ago, a new disease came to Moonshadow. It first appeared in a hamlet near Betham. It infects people seemingly at random. Quarantines have not slowed its progress across the kingdom, and there is no cure. The diseased bear red hand marks, which wrap around the neck as if the victims have been strangled."

"What do you expect me to do about it?" I asked. For all my magic, I couldn't end a plague. Like most other demons, I could only heal myself. My stomach churned. Had Loki sent me in knowing I would fail?

I should have known.

"I'm a warrior. An assassin, sometimes. Not a healer."

"Let me finish." Jacob VIII stood and began to pace. "My wife and son suffer from this plague. My son believes he's discovered the source. He is a telar—"

“You want to let a telar become king of Moonshadow?” Now I understood why Marcus wasn’t scared of Rolf’s mindvoice, but why was he here at all? If there was anything I remembered clearly about Moonshadow, it was their fear of telars.

Jacob VIII’s regal face twisted into an expression of pain, but he looked me in the eyes. “He is my only son. Isabella was in an accident during her second pregnancy. Her carriage horse panicked and drove them into a nobleman’s house. She is unlikely to have another child. I cannot send Marcus away and risk leaving the throne without an heir.”

“An untrained telar king could be even more dangerous than no heir at all,” I said. Telars could read people’s minds. Well-trained, they could control those minds. Poorly trained, they were overwhelmed by the noise of other people’s thoughts and descended into madness. The most dangerous of all could do both—

Eternia’s eyes glittered as her guests lifted their weapons, a mix of ceremonial swords and hidden knives, to their own throats. Their hands trembled, their eyes glazed as they tried to fight her grasp—

I forced my thoughts back to the present, to the problem of prince Marcus. “Does he even have proper training?”

“Enough to control it.” Jacob VIII spoke quietly, but his voice didn’t waver. “I am no fool.”

“Good.” Telars *had* created the first true human civilization, and it had prospered for many centuries under their rule. They weren’t all like Eternia.

If word of his gift ever got out, though, there would be riots in the streets. Maybe even civil war. Or worse, an invasion force from Estefar, eager to get rid of a new telar threat like they destroyed Shalinor.

Focus. Loki wanted me to deal with the immediate threat, not every potential problem down the line. “So, where does this plague come from?”

“It’s not where but who,” Jacob VIII said. “A telar created the plague. They’re deliberately targeting Moonshadow. Targeting *my son.*”

How is that even possible? The strongest telars in known history had been the women of the Shalinoran royal family, with magic as powerful as any demon’s. They were able to reach minds across the continent and control large groups of people within their city walls. They had always been the exception, though. Most telars needed to be within a hundred paces of their targets to exert any power of them. Even those who were able to communicate over larger distances needed to know the face of the person they wanted to reach.

“Nobody has that kind of power anymore,” I said.

"The telars of Shalinor used relics to amplify their power." Jacob II folded his hands on the table.

I shook my head. "I lived in Shalinor. Even the relics in Queen Corinthia's workshops lacked the power to do something on this scale."

"It may also be multiple telars," Kenneth said. "Each using their slice of power to spread the plague in a specific area."

"So you want me to find, and stop, these relic-wielding telars." The whole thing sounded impossible.

"Exactly," Jacob II said.

"My son says the voice is strong but distant, perhaps even from beyond the swamp," Jacob VIII added, unrolling a map along the table. "Most likely near the western border."

The Shalinoran border. *Impossible.* Nothing had lived in Shalinor since the Great War. The sun didn't even shine properly there, according to the legends.

"You think they're hiding in the Wastelands?"

"We're not sure. We think it might be an attempt to throw us off the trail," Jacob VIII said. "Someone powerful enough to create a spell like this can disguise their presence. A telar in the swamp, perhaps. You know how they despise us."

I know why they do, too. The swamp where Moonshadow's telars were required to live wasn't exactly a nice place.

"General Alexis has gathered the Slayers' recent records on the telar towns," Jacob VIII went on. "She expects you at dawn."

The puzzle finally clicked together and I cursed under my breath. "Your problem doesn't start in the swamp," I said. "Somebody in Moon Spire, probably the castle itself, gave them Marcus's name and face. Probably the tutor who helped him train the gift."

Jacob VIII narrowed his eyes. "His curse, you mean. And I trust my people with my life."

I raised my eyebrows. "Even the telar?"

"He's dead," Jacob VIII said. "Murdered in an alley three months ago."

Letting someone with such sensitive knowledge walk around by himself in alleys was a foolish decision all on its own, but I wasn't here to criticize the king's actions. "Likely to stop him from identifying the plague's cause."

Jacob VIII's eyes widened minutely, but he nodded as if he had known this all along.

"Whoever killed him is involved," Jacob II said. "His spirit should still be within my reach, especially since tomorrow is the full moon. I will find out if he saw his killer."

Andre and Jacob VIII tensed and exchanged nervous looks. Vonstones who feared communication with the spirits? Time had left its mark on this kingdom after all. Or at least on its royal family.

"Someone this good probably wasn't seen." I ran a hand through my hair. "And they might not have killed directly. Telars can kill through other people. How much mental defence training do regular citizens get now?"

This time the entire room tensed. Jacob II and Andre glared at Jacob VIII. Kenneth chugged the remainder of his blood bottle, not looking at anyone.

I, too, turned to Jacob VIII, my eyebrows climbing so far up my forehead that it hurt. What had he done?

"The king removed mental defence from the standard mandatory schooling fifteen years ago." Kenneth spoke with a practiced tone, one drained of all emotion. "He cut it from standard Slayer training two years later. Only border soldiers and the Royal Guard get that training now."

Cold dread settled into my bones. Every temple class, every merchant school, and every roster of private lessons in Omicaer had included mental defence instruction since time immemorial. Every military I had ever heard of gave its members additional mental defence training. Even the islanders of Eidos, who once worshiped telars, had always acknowledged the telars' potential danger and learned to protect themselves from it.

"You realize your own military can be used against you now, right?" I shook my head. "I've heard enough. I'll need to speak with whoever found the tutor's body, along with anyone who came into contact with him that day."

Jacob VIII drained his wine and began pouring more. "Captain Raldon of the castle guard can help you."

"Good. I'll visit him after General Alexis."

"Her," Jacob VIII said.

"Even better." I glanced at Jacob II. "I'll join you for the ritual tomorrow night."

In the meantime, I needed a drink. Preferably something stronger than wine.

I commandeered a bottle of the king's finest brandy from his personal cellar and headed to the main courtyard. Rolf had curled himself up into a ball in the farthest corner of the courtyard which allowed people to pass him easily. A handful of servants were gathered around him now, whispering to each other.

"Where do you think he came from?"

"Maybe the dragons all live in the demon realm now."

"Good thing they can't *all* come here. Can you imagine, an army of dragon-riding demons?"

I cleared my throat and the servants whirled to face me. They scattered, running back to their various duties.

One maid stayed completely still, her cheeks flushed. "I—I didn't mean anything by it, ma'am."

"Don't let me catch you bothering him again. And before you give yourself nightmares, let me reassure you. Other demons don't have dragons. I'm the only one."

She opened and closed her mouth three times before managing to push more words out. "Right, ma'am; thank you, ma'am." She bolted into the castle, hiking her skirts up to avoid tripping.

Rolf opened one eye and pulled his lips back. *I was thinking about snarling at them, but I thought it would be mean.*

I grinned in spite of myself and sat beside Rolf's open eye. *Definitely mean. And you probably shouldn't do that around them, either. Humans scare easy.* I opened the brandy and tipped the bottle to my lips, momentarily losing myself as it trailed fire down my throat and into my belly.

What? I'm smiling.

I laughed and choked on a mouthful of brandy. Liquor seared my nostrils and I wiped furiously at my nose with my sleeve. *That's your idea of smiling? You're going to scare somebody to death.*

I hope not. A wave of sadness emanated from him, sinking all the way into my core. *I flew low over the city today to see more of it. Everyone screamed and ran away. Are all humans so scared of dragons?*

Dragons used to rule these lands. I leaned forward to stroke his snout and tried to fill my thoughts with warmth, comfort. *Not nicely, either. People don't realize you're different from those dragons.*

I hope they'll realize soon.

The genuine hopefulness in his voice made my heart ache for him. Loki had built torture into his very existence. A kind soul who would only ever be perceived as a monster. Like the children who became demons, only we grew out of it. We became the monsters people expected us to be, losing ourselves, piece by damning piece.

Are you all right?

No, I wasn't, and I never had been, but Rolf didn't need any more burdens than the ones Loki cursed him with. I was here for a different conversation.

We need to talk about Marcus.

He's not afraid of me at all. Rolf's eye narrowed. *But I stopped talking to him after you got angry.*

That made my heart twist even more painfully in my chest, but I tried to ignore it. *Talk to him as much as you want. As much as you can.*

You sound worried.

I took a swig of brandy. *I need you to comfort him, listen to him. Listen especially for anything that doesn't make sense—any hints of madness.* Rolf might be childlike, but any creation of Loki's understood madness.

Madness? Rolf wrinkled his snout. *What's wrong with him?*

Humans with mindvoices, sometimes, if they aren't taught properly—

They get overwhelmed? Rolf snorted, two clouds of smoke bursting from his nostrils. *Father said dragons used to, too, when we lived among humans. He taught me how to stop it before I came.*

I tapped the side of my brandy bottle with my fingernail, thinking. If dragons went through the same thing, then maybe— *Could you teach Marcus?*

I'd love to. Rolf pulled his lips back into that awful grin.

And for gods' sake, please stop doing that.

Chapter Seven

Kahri: Riminira

The walls I had seen every day for the last five centuries were grey. The window looking out over the plains revealed only more grey. The sun's rays were almost forgotten to me, a brief glimpse now and again through an endless series of clouds. I looked around the room and my gaze stopped at the black orb, the greatest achievement of my family. It sparkled with their power, the power of generations—all at my disposal.

Blood magic. To anyone else's senses, the stench of blood in this room was unbearable, a mixture of human and demon blood that would churn even the strongest stomach. The orb always stank of it, and after the war, the stench permeated the entire city. I had grown accustomed to it, but every so often I still woke feeling ill. This was one of those days. Hours passed before I was able to force myself out of bed and climb the tower's many flights of stairs. I had spent centuries waiting for this moment. Nothing would deter me from my task.

Tomorrow, I would not be alone.

Several months after the city of Riminira's death, a half-starved boy from the southernmost reaches of Shalinor stumbled into my city. He was covered in filth from weeks on the road, his clothes torn almost to nothing.

Still, when I saw him collapse by the river, my heart soared. His was the first life I had seen in months, perhaps the only life left in Shalinor other than my own. I went to his side and forced water down his swollen throat. I carried him back to the palace. He weighed little, much less than a boy his age should.

I put him in the bedchamber closest to my own and nursed him back to health.

He woke three days after I found him and told me his story, his sentences punctuated with whimpers as I ran a wet cloth along his still feverish forehead. He was Galvan, the only surviving member of his family. He had walked all the way to Riminira to see if the rumours were true, if the city still stood. He told me he wanted to die on our land—telar land—rather than follow the others into hostile kingdoms.

"I've seen it," he wheezed. "It's as beautiful as they said. I... I can die happy now."

"You will not die yet," I said.

"But I am already dead."

I never knew if he meant on the outside or inside, as he slipped back into unconsciousness. I healed him anyway, helped him regain his strength, taught him everything I knew. Each day with him was a joy, even if the world was grey and gloomy around us. He was the son I never got to raise.

Galvan soon grew into a man, and with the aid of my magic, he lived to be an old man. But I could not keep him forever. Over time he grew old and weak, and one day he asked me to take him outside. I did, carrying him as I had when I first found him. He was bony again, almost weightless. I took him to the river, that was now only a creek, and there we sat on the grass, enjoying each other's silent company.

"You know," he said, "I came here to die, all those years ago."

"Yes," I said, refusing to look at him. I couldn't stand his gaunt face, the red blotches on his skin—marks of the disease my spells could not defeat.

"You saved me. I wanted to thank you."

"Don't thank me," I said, "I've been grateful to have you. And selfish."

"Selfish? You gave me everything."

I shook my head. "You've never known a lover, a family, a community. Only this dead city and my sad old soul."

A hand touched mine and I met his gaze, my soul aching as I saw the warmth in his deep brown eyes, the mark of how much he loved me.

"That is more than I dreamed of finding when I came here. All I wanted was to see the great city before I died." He shifted, grimacing as if the movement hurt him. Of course it did. They all did, the movements of those old bones. "Now, my only hope is that you won't spend the rest of eternity alone."

I squeezed his hand. "I chose my path. But if there is a way to bring my people home, I will find it."

A shudder ran through him, sending a tremor along my arm. "You will stop the death, then."

"I will," I said. "Our kingdom will someday rise again."

I didn't believe the words then, but Galvan did. He smiled and lay back in the grass, staring into the endless expanse of clouds.

"I wish I could see it." He sighed. "The Queendom of Shalinor, raised from the ashes by its greatest hero, Kahri."

"Perhaps you will, in another life." I didn't know if I believed in reincarnation then, but I wanted to. To believe Galvan, and all my people, would someday know a better life.

"Tell me," he whispered. "What our new kingdom will look like."

"First of all," I began, picking at a clump of grey dirt, "it will be green. Plants will grow in every free space. They'll even grow in the cracks between cobblestones. Keeping the plants at bay will be a constant struggle, but the city will be covered in colours all year round." I took a deep breath and closed my eyes, imagining the streets of Riminira once again flooded with life, their sounds and smells filling the air.

"The sun will shine on it often, but not enough to create drought. And people from all over Omicaer will come to see it, and when they are here, they will be kind to our people."

"It sounds perfect."

I smiled. "It does, doesn't it?"

And so a dream was born.

A whisper on the wind caught my attention. The orb, calling my name. It was time. An ancient voice, one more familiar than my own after all these years alone, curled outward from the orb, filling my mind.

Hello my child. I know what you are here for.

Then let us create it together.

The words were ancient words, words of power. They tore my throat on the way out, but I didn't care. It would heal in the morning.

With my hands, I shaped a person in the air. On the other side of the orb, a shadow appeared. First it was a blob, then it became half a man, growing arms and hands, then a full man with legs and feet. I closed my eyes and focused my power, filling the shadow with life, the soul of a real, living man.

A human sound from the bottom of the tower—crying, perhaps screaming—broke my concentration.

I barrelled down the stairs, not even letting myself breathe. For the first time in centuries, prayers ran through my head, prayers for life and abundance and success.

I reached the bottom of the stairwell, where the sound was coming from, and threw open the tower door.

There, sitting against a wall with his head in his hands, was a naked brown boy, perhaps four years old, his head covered with thick, curly hair and his body wracked with sobs.

He met my eyes and fell quiet.

I stared at him in wonder. I had created life. The gods still smiled upon me, despite my curse.

I fell to my knees and wept. The boy jumped into my arms and I wrapped them slowly around him, half expecting my hands to go through him. Expecting him to be an illusion manifested by my hope.

His skin was soft like silk, and his hair smelled like straw. He was entirely real, and I had created him. My womb had been barren for centuries, but it didn't matter now. I had not only created life, I had also done what everyone who has ever lost someone dreams about. I had brought back somebody I loved.

The boy tightened his arms around me, and we wept together.

Chapter Eight

The arena stretched out before me, a familiar oval of hard red dirt surrounded by benches of gleaming black stone. An iron-wrought spider stretched across the roof, suspended on eight monstrous legs. The spider's eye, made entirely of red glass, amplified the scarlet glow emanating from the demon realm's "sky," forming a circle of brilliant light at the arena's centre.

My opponent waited in the circle, one blue finger tapping impatiently on the shaft of his trident. Malthis had outdone himself today, adding spiked shoulders and shiny scales to his already intimidating reptilian form. The crowd loved it. They roared his name as he walked around the circle of light, raising his weapons to each section of the arena.

Temric's lips curved, the closest thing to a smile he could manage. "They're expecting you to fail. That's why he's showing off." His lips pulled back, revealing his fangs, the only marker of his demonic nature. "Don't."

I forced my thoughts away from the threat behind his words and smiled. "I won't fail you."

"No fight matters but this fight," I whispered, shifting my concentration to my form. If Malthis wanted to put on a show, we would put on a show.

With each step forward, I focused on contorting a different part of my body. My nails became claws. My hair fell to the ground around me and thick, sharp horns emerged from my head. My skin solidified, forming my own set of scales. These turned the same shade of red as the dirt I walked on. My feet grew thicker, the toes turning into talons.

By the time I reached the circle of light, every trace of my humanity had been erased. I was the monster, and I was ready to fight.

I leapt out of bed, grabbed my sword, and brandished it about the room for several moments before I realized I was alone. Alone, and an entire realm away from the arena.

Too bad I couldn't get an entire realm away from my memories. Or leave them in the past, where they belonged.

I pulled my blanket back onto the bed, but there was no sleeping now. I dressed and headed out to do the one thing I knew could calm my mind—train.

At this time of night, the castle was blissfully quiet. Even Moon Spire slept eventually, though I could probably still find Jacob II in his office. I didn't want to see anyone right now. Especially not him. I needed distance from my memories.

The practice hall was an enormous building made of black stone with ancient golden runes carved into it. Runes for hope, fortune, wellness, good health, good crops, good hunts. This was where the clans had united under Jacob 1 to fight the undead, forming the kingdom of Moonshadow. A mural along the left wall showed when hundreds lived here, pushing the undead back one mile at a time, while they struggled to rebuild their civilization.

Now it was empty and dark. I approached a white, circular symbol painted near the door and pressed my hand to its centre.

The symbol flared to life. A row of runes carved into the ceiling followed suit, bathing the room in white light and revealing several racks of dull-edged training weapons. Daggers, swords, axes, even a few lances. All beautifully crafted centuries earlier, some as old as Moonshadow itself.

Four painted circles dominated the floor: a green circle for children taking their first lessons, a yellow one for apprentices, a red one for fully-trained warriors, and a golden one for masters. I went to the farthest circle, more out of habit than because it actually mattered. Anyone who came here this late at night would know better than to interrupt my practice.

I took a deep breath as I reached the centre of the expert's circle, drawing my sword as I exhaled. I lowered myself into a fighting stance and began my dance of death, letting instinct guide me through one of my old practice routines. *Slash, stab, roll.* A little slower than normal, with my new blood, but still faster than most humans. With each step, I grew more confident, moved a little faster. Soon I would be back to my usual self, moving faster than most humans could even see. I closed my eyes, losing myself in the familiar motions, letting my thoughts fade behind the sensations of my movements, the wind I created as I slashed through the air.

The clang of blade-on-blade shook me almost as much as the impact. I stared at the silver blade caught on mine, my gaze moving along its edge until I caught sight of its owner. Andre Vonstone, wearing a mischievous grin that reminded me of Loki's.

Anything that reminded me of Loki spelled trouble. Even if that look was more charming on Andre's face.

I met his grin with a scowl and withdrew my sword. "What in the five realms are you thinking, interrupting a practicing demon?"

His smile faded, but the mischievous sparkle in his eyes remained as he shrugged. "It's been ages since I sparred with a worthy opponent."

The words were insufferably arrogant, but his tone sounded honest. And he had caught my sword mid-practice. Perhaps this interruption might become an entertaining one.

"Is Kenneth not a worthy opponent? He's had centuries of practice."

"He's too busy helping my brother run the kingdom." A grimace flickered across his face, immediately replaced by a regally calm expression. "Besides, you're a new opponent. I've always loved a challenge."

This time it was my turn to grin. "If it's a challenge you want, you simply needed to ask." Practice with a real opponent would do me good anyway. "First blood, or first one disarmed, wins. I don't want to hurt you—much."

He pouted. "You're not planning to go easy on me, are you?"

I sized him up with a long, slow glance. He wore sturdy leather boots, canvas trousers, and a sleeveless leather tunic. Not a helmet or hint of metal in sight. "You aren't dressed for a real fight."

"But I could be." He gestured at the nearest row of practice weapons. "Or we could fight with *those*."

"Now, where would the fun be in that?" I raised my sword, clutching it with both hands. "It's no fun without a little bit of danger."

"I couldn't agree more." He shifted into an unusually wide fighting stance and raised his weapon toward mine. "Shall we begin?"

"Are you offering me first swing?"

"If you think you can land it."

Smug bastard.

I darted forward at top speed and feinted left, circling behind him even as he turned to meet my blow. He spun again, faster this time, striking out in my direction. I jumped backward. Warm energy surged through my veins and my mind cleared, the space between me and my opponent thrown into sharp relief.

Andre pursued me to the edge of the circle, his stride fast, sure, and steady. I glanced at his feet, my eyes tracing the path between us, calculating the length of his reach.

He swung and I caught his blow with my sword, this time using all my strength. He stumbled backward, his arms shaking with the effort of keeping his weapon upright. I lunged toward him, aiming my pommel at his wrist.

He righted himself and retreated, taking several steps in the blink of an eye. Beads of sweat formed at my hairline, dripping down my face.

"You're well-trained," I said.

"I was trained not to speak to my opponents. It's a distraction."

I tilted my head to the side. "A distraction can work in your favour."

He charged at me again. I raced forward to meet him, gaining speed with each step. This time when our swords met, I'd make sure he couldn't keep his grip.

Andre stopped and ducked at the last moment. I ran past him, only catching myself at the edge of the circle. I whirled around and caught his next blow with my blade, but without my momentum I barely managed to push him away. I darted backward.

His gaze still followed my every move like a predator stalking its prey, but he was slowing now. Perhaps the way to win this was patience. Even a vampire couldn't keep up with me forever.

I shifted into a narrower fighting stance and let him come at me, dodging each swing at the last moment. The wind from his blows tickled my face, but his sword never connected.

He chased me around the circle twice, growing more frustrated with every miss. Any human would already be too exhausted to hold their sword, but Andre just kept going. Until he stopped and retreated, still in a fighting stance but panting.

"You're not even fighting anymore."

I chuckled. "There are many ways to fight."

I leapt forward, feinted right, and darted behind him. I aimed my pommel at his shoulder and swung with all my force.

Andre moved to block, but not fast enough. My pommel caught him square in the chest and knocked him backward. His skull hit the ground with a crack. I winced, and when I opened my eyes again, there was already a small pool of blood forming around his head. Somehow, he still had both hands on his sword. His smugness appeared to be matched only by his stubbornness.

"You're bleeding."

He set his sword down and checked the back of his head. "Not for much longer."

I sheathed my sword and offered him a hand up. "I hope you'll think twice next time you want to challenge a demon."

"Are you kidding? That was the most excitement I've had in years." He waved my hand away and used his sword to prop himself up, though he only stood halfway. "And it's not like you're going to kill me."

"Anything's possible."

"Don't act like you didn't have any fun, I saw that grin."

"I like teaching smug bastards a lesson."

I turned to walk away, and something round smashed into my knee. Pain jolted up and down my leg and I stumbled, tripped over an uneven floor stone, and fell face first. I barely threw my hands out in time to shield my nose from the worst of the damage, my wrists *crunching* as they caught me.

I rolled onto my back, propped myself on my elbows, and took stock of the injuries. My wrists were swollen and throbbing, my knee twice its usual size and already turning blackish-gray.

Andre straightened, sheathed his sword, and offered to help me up. "Sorry, but I also have a thing about smug bastards."

I glanced at my knee, glanced at him, and burst into laughter.

Andre's brow furrowed, but a moment later he cackled. Our laughter echoed throughout the empty practice hall. It was still bouncing off the walls when we left.

We walked back to the castle in companionable silence, separating at the entrance to the royal wing.

"I'll report to your office tomorrow at dusk," he said. "That gives you plenty of time to get those files from Alexis." He practically spat the last word.

"You say people's names like curse words. Do you like anyone around here?"

"You." He winked. "Oh, and Jacobs the second and fifth, and most of the servants. Even General Cornelius. Just not my brother or—her."

I crossed my arms over my chest. This bad blood ran deep, maybe deep enough—"What about Moonshadow itself?"

He scowled. "If you're looking for the person who helped the telars, you're better off looking at Alexis herself. Or that blasted priest, Cameron. Hell, maybe even my own brother."

"You mean—"

But he was already gone, headed toward his chambers at top vampire speed. I tilted my head to the side and watched him disappear around a corner. General Alexis, Jacob VIII, high priest Cameron—what had they done to make Andre hate them so much?

What did he know that I didn't?

Chapter Nine

Jacob II set his book on the desk and gave me a pointed look. "Two visits in one night? To what do I owe the honour?"

"You're probably the only one who will answer my questions." I placed my half-full bottle of brandy between us.

He grabbed two glasses from the cupboard behind him. "Questions about what?"

"More like about whom." I poured each of us a generous helping. "What does Andre have against General Alexis and the high priest?"

He frowned, tapping his index finger against the edge of his glass. "May I ask what brought this on?"

"He basically accused them of collaborating with the telars." I left out my own suspicions about Andre.

"I can't see Alexis collaborating with Cameron on much of anything. They hardly speak to each other."

"Then why the suspicion?"

He downed his drink and poured himself another. "Andre belonged to the Midnight Order."

I raised an eyebrow. How had a Vonstone ended up in Loki's league of assassins? "And they caught him in the act?"

"Well, Alexis caught him. Attempting to assassinate Cameron."

After twenty-seven hundred years of life, few things surprised me. But a hit ordered on the high priest of Ashe? Unheard of.

"Did you find out why the Order was hired? Have they tried again?" The Midnight Order didn't typically let somebody live after a contract was signed, even if killing them took a few tries.

"Andre's oath prevented him from telling us anything before his death. And after, well, he's hardly spoken to any of us."

"What about Cameron? The Midnight Order must still have him on a list."

Jacob II shrugged. "The temple's taken extra precautions. If there have been attempts, nobody's gotten through, and only Jacob VIII would know about them. I stay out of these things."

"I'm sure Cameron knows." People didn't call the Midnight Order for petty things. Their price was too steep. "I'll ask him in tomorrow."

"Be careful how you do it. Jacob VIII is devout to a fault, and quite close to Cameron. He won't like you sniffing around without substantial evidence."

I nodded. The kings of Moonshadow had always been devout, and, unlike other religious mortals, they had a reason. Ashe had given them the power to fight the undead and survive Magdalene's curse.

"Can you tell me anything else about Cameron?"

"He's an unusual choice for a High Priest. Not yet fifty, and not from a wealthy family. His parents owned a tiny pub in the north. Both dead now, along with his single older brother."

"Convenient, having no living relatives." If he was a telar, he needed a false identity. No living relatives meant nobody to deny his story. Or confirm it.

"Not so uncommon though, especially in the north. The curse is still strongest there."

In other words, the perfect cover story for a telar infiltrator. "I hope that's the real story."

At dawn, I headed for General Alexis's office. The halls were already flooded with activity, mostly uniformed Slayers going for their morning meal. The Slayers all wore lilandium helmets, poorly disguised with thin steel plates. I suspected this was a precaution to avoid panic in the streets. A plague caused enough terror without the added threat of telars.

I slowed on my way past the courtroom. Its giant mahogany doors would remain closed for another two hours, but over twenty nobles were already lined up outside. Most wore grey mourning clothes, several with high-necked collars. Judging by their waxy complexions, these were designed to hide the plague's marks.

No wonder the Vonstones summoned me. So many nobles dying at once could lead to chaos, even if Marcus survived.

Alexis's office lay around the corner from the courtroom, at the far end of the first empty hallway I had passed this morning. She responded to my knock with a string of curses, followed by a terse, "Come in."

I entered with a slight bow, taking the General in as I rose. She wore a modified Slayer uniform with gold trim and a silver G embroidered at her collar to show her rank, but those were the least interesting things about her.

General Alexis was a Classless One. At the age of thirteen, she had traded her face, or at least the option of showing it in public, for the ability to rise in Moonshadow's society unhindered by social status. A thin silver mask obscured her features, secured to her head by a hairnet dotted with white stones that appeared to be lilandium. A wide mouth hole allowed her to eat and drink in public, but her mouth remained essentially invisible from the outside. Only her bright green eyes were visible, thanks to a pair of artfully crafted eyeholes. Thin gold eyebrows pointed permanently downwards gave the mask an air of intimidation.

Her office was designed to be similarly intimidating. The desk and chairs were cherrywood, without a single embellishment. The only decorations in the entire room were two ornate swords hanging on the far wall. A large silver medal on a green ribbon hung between them, proclaiming her a Defender of Moonshadow. The highest military honour in the kingdom.

"Riana, I presume?" Alexis grabbed a box of black notebooks and set it on the desk between us. "These are all the commanders' logs from squads in the telar lands for the past ten years." She lifted another, smaller box of grey notebooks from somewhere near her feet. "These are supposedly all the priests' logs from the Temple of Ashe."

"Supposedly?"

"Look at it. There are maybe fifteen books. I don't know how many priests were stationed there—"

"Then find out," I snapped. "This is supposed to be your job, isn't it?"

"My job is to regulate the Slayers and the city militias, not the temple, as Cameron so kindly reminded me. Only the king himself can order the high priest to divulge their records."

This high priest might not be a telar, but he was definitely hiding something. "Then I will inform the king himself that I need those records."

She snorted. "Good luck with that. He believes Ashe's temple is an impenetrable paragon of perfection."

"You don't sound so convinced."

She stared into my eyes with an intensity that would have unnerved anyone else. "A person who believes in perfection is a person who will never strive to be better."

I couldn't help but smile. I never liked the Classless Ones—too hard to read their feelings behind those masks—but this one, perhaps, I could. "One more question. Do you know why the Midnight Order wanted him dead?"

She shook her head. "All I know is that they haven't tried again. Or if they have, Cameron's hidden it well."

No surprise there, but I had to try. I picked up the boxes of books and inclined my head in her direction. "The Midnight Order doesn't abandon contracts."

"Unless somebody pays even more to cancel it."

"That's only a theory." As far as anyone knew, it had never actually happened. Although what anyone outside the Midnight Order knew about its history was negligible. "You have guards at the temple?"

"Of course."

"Good. Let me know right away if anything strange happens there. Anything at all." I turned to leave, eager to deposit the logs in my room and see this priest for myself.

"Wait," Alexis said as I reached the door.

I paused and raised an eyebrow at her, holding the door open with one elbow.

"You don't really believe Cameron has something to do with this, do you? A high priest of Ashe?"

"Anyone can become a traitor."

Especially when telars were involved.

The centre of the Vonstones' royal dungeon was occupied by a single massive cell with nearly thirty occupants, men and women alike, covered in dirt and stinking of sweat and fear. Dirty straw pallets were laid out around the edges of the cell, forcing prisoners to take turns sleeping. Most looked too afraid to sleep anyway, alert and wary despite the bruise-coloured circles under their eyes.

Several single-person cells were built into the surrounding walls. The worst criminals were kept in these cells, those who couldn't be trusted among the general population. The doors were made of thick, heavy wood. Narrow slots near the bottom of each allowed food to be pushed through, but they had no windows. They also didn't have regular locks and were instead held shut by magic.

I approached the last door and pressed the stone Jacob III had given me into the wood. It glowed bright green for a moment, then swung open, revealing the tiniest room I had ever seen.

A bald man sat in the farthest corner, his knees drawn up to his chest and his arms wrapped tightly around them. His silver cloak had been taken, but he still wore his royal guard uniform, filthy now after so many hours locked away.

The man tried to back even farther into the corner as I entered, scrambling at the wall as if it might give way, perhaps reveal some other way to escape.

"I'm not here to hurt you," I said, pausing just inside the doorway. "Jacob III tells me you're the victim here."

He burst into tears, coughed and finally collected himself. He glanced my way and smiled. "You mean they—they believe me? I won't be executed?"

"Not if you convince me." I didn't even really need convincing. But I needed to hear it for myself.

His face fell. "How do I convince you? They were in my head, then they were gone. After that, I was being dragged away from the king, my hand broken and my weapons taken."

I frowned. He didn't seem to be lying, but I didn't want to believe it. Eternia killed so many people, but the other telars showed me great kindness. Even Eternia had showed me great generosity before madness took her.

"Can you tell me anything else?"

He frowned and stared into the middle distance. "My body—it wasn't my own anymore. It wouldn't listen."

His words made my blood run cold. I knew those words, had spoken them once myself, after my first failure. The arena battle that changed everything, put me under Temric's control and—

Focus, damn it.

"Did you get any sense of who it was? A gender, maybe?"

"He had a shrill voice, almost like a woman's but not. Maybe an old man." He shuddered. "It was agonizing, hearing him in my head. Not being able to do anything but watch as he went for my king's throat." He wiped his tears away with a sleeve, covering his face in more dirt. "You believe me, don't you?"

I knelt beside him and squeezed one of his hands. "I believe you."

His face lit up. "Thank you! Thank you!"

Chapter Ten

After a quick breakfast, I went to see high priest Cameron at the High Temple of Ashe. The temple was a three-storey building of gleaming black stone that dominated Moon Spire's main square, its bulk supported by several grey marble pillars. The top of its arched roof sported a single, massive gargoyle, a guardian believed to protect the walls between realms. A dozen wide steps made of the same grey marble led to the main entrance, which stood open at all hours. The overall effect was an odd combination of welcoming and foreboding, much like Moonshadow itself.

Inside, the temple had a friendlier atmosphere, with twenty rows of well-cushioned pews facing the pulpit and altar. A mural of Ashe's realm, grey and lifeless, yet eerily beautiful, covered the far wall. Between the altar and the mural stood a statue of Ashe herself, one almost-skeletal hand reaching out toward the altar, as if offering whoever knelt before it a hand up.

A group of sickly-looking women in simple black and grey dresses knelt there, being ministered to by a young priest. From the grim expressions I caught on my way past, I suspected they were praying for their lives—or perhaps for quick deaths.

I pushed through a door in the back wall and entered a wide, windowless corridor with a narrow staircase at the end. I skipped the staircase and went to the last door on the left, walking in without bothering to knock.

Sure enough, Cameron had stuck with tradition and kept his office here. Portraits of the temple's founders and the original Vonstones still lined the back wall, but otherwise the room was completely different. It was more inviting, with plush red carpet and matching armchairs instead of spare wood furniture. A small, simple desk had replaced the behemoth Jacob III's high priest had favoured. Framed quotes from the Book of Life hung on the walls instead of quotes from its counterpart, the Book of Death.

The high priest himself was different too, younger and rounder, with a good-natured face. Even now, he smiled and rose to greet me with open palms, as if I hadn't rudely barged into his office a moment earlier.

"To whom do I speak?" he asked in a rich, warm tone. The kind of voice that could earn almost anyone's trust with ease.

"I am Riana, Guardian of Moonshadow."

He raised his eyebrows. "And I should believe you, why?"

I held up my left hand and sent a wave of magical energy through it, pushing my nails to grow into long black claws. "Jacob III summoned me to put down the telar rebellion." Which had truly been Elizabeth Vonstone's rebellion, but only I remembered it that way. Recorded history had other ideas. "Jacob VIII has summoned me now to investigate suspicious activity in the telar lands."

He stared at my claws, wide-eyed but not gaping. "But our trouble isn't in the swamp, or anything caused by telars. It's a plague, and it's right here."

"Don't play ignorant with me. I know Jacob VIII tells you everything."

Cameron sighed and sat, folding his fingers together. "Anything worshipers share with me is spoken in confidence. I cannot confirm anything the king has or has not told me. Besides, I gave Alexis our records of the telar lands."

I rolled my eyes. "Fifteen logbooks? You expect me to believe that's everything?"

"Each temple in the swamp only has one priest. Acolytes aren't required to keep logs."

"That's still a dozen priests. Do you expect me to believe that between them, there are only fifteen logbooks covering ten whole years?"

He opened one of his desk drawers, pulling out a pipe and a bag of reddish-brown leaves. "Ten priests, and yes, I do expect you to believe they only produced fifteen logbooks."

"There are twelve temples in the swamp." The last was finished months before Jacob III's death. Its opening ceremonies were his final public appearance.

"The telars in Giren and Diseus chased our people out of town and burnt their temples, claiming independence from both Moonshadow and the other telars."

"And you let them?" I didn't even try to keep the shock out of my voice. Of all the idiocy I had heard since arriving in Moonshadow, this was the worst. "The *King* let them?"

Cameron struck a match and used it to light the herbs in his pipe, taking a deep draw before he responded. "The king believed they would die off without our help."

"It never occurred to you that their brethren might help them survive?" Either this priest worked for the telars, or he was a damn fool.

"I assumed the Slayers would regulate any passage between those towns and the rest of the telar lands." He took another draw from his pipe, exhaling a thick cloud of smoke directly into my face.

My fingers twitched toward my blade, currently moulded into the form of a hunting dagger that hung from my belt, but I forced my expression to remain neutral. Cameron needed to try harder if he wanted to get a rise out of me.

"At first, they did," he went on. "But three years ago, the king decided to let the telar lands rot, and he pulled most of the Slayers—and all aid—out of the swamp. He's even let them form something like their own government, although, of course, they lack any real power."

"No real power?" I laughed. "They all have power. Terrifying power, if they learn the old ways of controlling it. That's why we put them in the swamp in the first place."

Well, it was why Jacob III sent them to the swamp. I did it because he ordered me to, and our contract made it impossible for me to disobey him. I had begged him not to. Pleaded with him to send them to Shalinor, or give them land to make a new nation. *Oppression always ends in rebellion*, I told him.

"I hate being right," I muttered.

Cameron raised his eyebrows. "Pardon?"

"Never mind. I need a full list of all the priests and acolytes stationed in the telar lands throughout the last ten years."

"A list will be drafted and delivered to your office this evening." He stood and gestured toward the door. "Now, if you'll excuse me, I have work to do."

"We'll speak again, I'm sure." Next time, I would find a way to get some real answers.

Back in my office, I went straight for my bottle of the king's brandy. Only a third of the liquid remained. I drank it all in a few large gulps. It warmed my chest and stomach, and for a moment the world spun. Then it sank deeper into my body, and sobriety returned.

I cursed and set the now-empty bottle down with enough force that it cracked, the sound piercing my head. My temple throbbed. I groaned and rested my face in my hands. Between the unfolding telar conspiracy and my heightened senses, I was developing a permanent headache.

Marcus wants to see you.

Rolf's mindvoice startled me so badly that I almost jumped out of my chair. *Bloody hell. Now?*

Did I do something wrong?

A warm wave of concern came behind these thoughts, washing over me and soothing my soul.

I'm not angry at you. I couldn't even imagine being angry at Rolf.

Then who are you angry at?

I scratched absently at the back of my neck. *Myself, mostly.* And Jacob III, for setting this whole damn thing into motion.

The curse isn't your fault.

Curse? Of course I had nothing to do with Magdalene's curse. I hadn't even been in the mortal realm when she cast it.

Marcus says the plague is a curse.

I frowned, wishing I had more brandy. *I suppose it is, in a way.*

A curse that has nothing to do with you. Rolf's mindvoice carried all the certainty of a child who believes they know everything.

I wouldn't be so sure. I caused the telars' suffering as surely as any Vonstone.

Their suffering?

Most telars live in isolation and poverty. I searched the cupboards mounted on my back wall. One held two glasses, each caked in a thick layer of dust, but there wasn't a single drop of alcohol to be found. I'd have to stop by the king's cellar again after visiting Marcus. *I put a lot of those families there.*

I found Jacob III in his aboveground office, poring over a long scroll, his eyes sunken and bloodshot from too many days without sleep.

"The danger's gone," I said. "You can rest."

"The immediate danger is gone." He ran a hand through his hair. Stress had turned most of it grey in recent months. "But there's still danger, so long as telars remain in Moonshadow. We can't afford a second civil war. I can't rest until I've decided what to do with them."

I sat across from him and grabbed his bottle of wine, filling one of the nearby glasses. "Shalinor has offered to give any telars not directly involved sanctuary in their queendom."

"Shalinor has too much power as it is. I don't want to increase the size of their army."

I glared at him. "Queen Tarla may be insane, but she listens to her generals. They know how important our alliance is, to both nations."

"Still. What happens when Tarla dies?" He shook his head. "They say princess Kahri is more stable, but what does that actually mean? And what if it's a lie? We can't risk giving them more weapons."

I ground my teeth together. "Telars are people, not tools."

"People are the most dangerous weapons of all." He signed the scroll on his desk and held it up for me to see. "I've purchased the swamp from the Temmells. All telars will be required to register with the crown and relocate there. Our Slayers will keep a careful eye on them, as will Ashe's temple."

The irritation building in my chest flared. The Temmells' swamp stretched along the southernmost edge of Moonshadow, and it was the deadliest, most miserable part of the entire kingdom. Only a few thousand people lived in the entire swamp, spread across half a dozen villages and a single real town. They barely managed daily survival.

"So you're going to round them up, take them from their homes, and condemn them to generations of poverty because a few rogue telars made terrible decisions. Aren't you supposed to be a fair king?"

"This is fair," he said. "The telars grew angry because they were hated and abused by regular people. We'll help them build their own insular communities in the swamp. They'll be able to live without fear."

Irritation transformed into hot, burning rage. Why couldn't he see the mistake he was making?

"They'll be trading fear of being killed by angry mobs for fear of dying from starvation and disease." I balled my hands into fists, pressing my nails into my palms, trying to keep my tone even. "Or Slayers who don't consider them human."

He pulled a flask out of his pocket and took a long swig. "You will personally select the Slayers who will escort the telars to their new homes, and ensure that the last problem is not a concern. And the Temple of Ashe has pledged funding for two healing houses."

I laughed. "Two healing houses? Do you really believe that's enough?" There were almost twelve thousand known telars, and likely another three or four thousand more in hiding. Including the telar children, despite my pleas to let them live with other families. "You've already executed two of the oldest telar families in Moonshadow. Now, you're planning to displace the rest? This is how you make people hate you. This is how rebellions are born."

"They'll be too busy trying to survive on that accursed land to even consider rebellion."

"Humans have short lives, but stories live forever. They won't soon forget that it was your family who put them on that accursed land."

Jacob III rolled up the scroll and stamped it carefully with his seal. "You may be right, but at this moment there's no better option."

"Yes, there is." I balled my hands into fists, resisting the urge to reach across the desk and shake him. "Let this rest. The people who did it are dead. Let the others keep their homes, their lives. Make them—"

"I have made my decision."

You don't sound responsible. You tried to stop him.

I couldn't help but smile at the unwavering confidence in Rolf's mindvoice. *But I relented. I let him buy that land and helped him choose the Slayers to move the telars. I even rounded up some of the telars myself.*

You're bound by blood to obey whoever summoned you, right?

Yes. I stared at my hands. They had committed so many terrible crimes on behalf of the humans I served. Even the love of my life demanded awful things from me. *Demons who directly disobey their summoners...well, their blood literally boils.*

Then it's not your fault. You did what you needed to do to survive. Anyone else would have done the same.

Would they have, though?

Chapter Eleven

Marcus's bedchamber was one of the only rooms in the castle with windows. Seven of them, tall narrow strips that projected ribbons of sunlight across the prince's four-poster bed. Marcus might as well have been drowning in the silver-and-green blankets and cushions piled around him. A wet green cloth pouch lay across his forehead. Trails of water dripped down his face. An elderly male healer stood over him, bouncing nervously from one foot to the other.

Marcus smiled and pushed himself into sitting position when he saw me, wincing as he did so.

"Leave us," he told the healer, his scratchy voice little more than a whisper.

"But, Your Majesty—"

"Wait by the door." Marcus took a deep, rattling breath. "If anything happens, Riana will call you."

The healer frowned, but bowed and hurried out of the room, shooting me a nasty look as he went. If anything did happen, he would certainly find a way to blame me for it.

Speaking like this is easier for me. Marcus's mindvoice, at least, remained strong, albeit childish. *You don't mind?*

I shook my head. *Anything to help.*

He smiled. *Do you have a plan to catch her yet?*

Her?

Marcus dabbed at his sweaty face with his left sleeve. *The woman who's doing this.*

Your father didn't say it was a woman. I sat on the edge of his bed, wishing I could heal him. But my kind were only able to heal our own bodies. *Can you tell me anything else about her?*

He frowned. Several moments passed before his next words. *She's old, very old.*

It was my turn to frown. Most telars lost control of their gift over time. Few made it past their seventieth birthdays with their sanity intact, even in Shalinor's golden age.

Then again, Marcus was a child. *How old is very old?*

I'm not sure. She's put some kind of wall between us. But there's a sadness behind her presence, an old one. It reminds me of Jacob II.

As old as Jacob II? That was impossible. Close to it, though... There was the Old Family, a vampiric offshoot of the Vonstones with little love for those who sat on the throne. The plague had also spread throughout their lands. I doubted they would poison their own food supply.

There were legends of others who had lived to similar ages. Like the legend of the last queen of Shalinor, Kahri, said to still watch over the magically preserved city of Riminira, centuries after the rest of her queendom had fallen into ruin.

That was only a legend, though. In reality, the vampires of Moonshadow were the closest humans had ever come to immortality. Even the most powerful mages in Estefar rarely lived past their hundredth birthday.

Maybe it *was* an Estefaran mage. One who was also a telar, their sorrow the consequence of living in hiding for their entire lives. One who wanted normals to suffer as the telars had suffered for centuries. There were no reports of plague in Estefar, but the empire always went to great lengths to hide anything its enemies might perceive as a weakness.

I sat on the edge of Marcus's bed. *Your father said the voice comes from far away. Do you know anything more specific?*

He shook his head. *She hides well.*

I reached out and squeezed one of his bony hands, trying not to think too much about the weakness of his grip. *Not well enough to escape me. Promise.*

He smiled, then burst into a violent coughing fit, hacking worrying amounts of bloody phlegm up onto his blanket.

I called for the healer and backed away. *"This will be over soon. I'll find her."*

"Will you take me flying after?"

The healer rushed past me, his hands busy uncorking a blue bottle. He held Marcus down with one arm and pressed the bottle to the prince's lips. I turned away, my heart twisting in my chest. No child deserved such suffering.

I glanced back at Marcus when the coughing stopped. The healer leaned against the bed frame, empty potion bottle in one hand. He wiped sweat away from his brow with the other and his collar slipped, revealing the edge of a red finger mark on his neck.

I forced myself to smile at the prince. *When you're better. I promise.*

I grabbed another bottle of the king's brandy and returned to my office.

Rolf?

Yes? His mindvoice sounded distant, as if he had gone hunting.

Marcus says the woman who cursed him put up a wall between them. Can you teach him to break it down?

Rolf hesitated. *I can, but we shouldn't.*

I cracked open my new bottle. *If we break through the wall—even a tiny hole—he might be able to learn more about her. Where she is. Who she is.*

The wall keeps him alive. It limits how much her power can hurt him.

Then make him build better walls of his own first.

He's too sick. Controlling his gift at all drains most of his energy.

I rubbed my temples. *So Marcus won't be able to help us.* That left me with the logbooks from General Alexis.

Sorry. I can't connect to her directly either. She's strong.

Maybe she was too strong to beat, but I had to try. For my freedom, and for Marcus. *Just keep an eye on him, then. If she tries to influence him—*

I'll let you know.

Thanks. I grabbed the nearest logbook and opened it.

Unfortunately it, and most of the other notebooks, told me little. All the personality had been carefully drained out of the reports. Only numbers remained: how many telars came to the settlements or were born there, how many supplies were used, and what city-expanding tasks were completed.

These numbers painted a terrible picture of overcrowding and desperation, but they didn't give me what I really needed—a thread of rebellion.

I scanned through almost a dozen of these empty-souled entries before stumbling upon one with personal notes from a Slayer stationed in Diseus—one of the towns that claimed independence.

Here, at last, I found the thread.

> *Day 10*
>
> *I've arrived back in Diseus, this time to stay. The telars here are calmer than*

I remember, saner. The priests tell me they've developed new ways to train their gift, so they can enjoy more of their adult years. They say it's a good thing.

But I see how they look at me when they think I'm not watching. Like predators. Something is shifting here, and not for the better.

The telars in Diseus must have regained some of Shalinor's old training methods. They were the closest town to the ancient queendom's ruins. They must have sneaked an expedition into one of the smaller towns and stolen old books. From the sound of it, they might even have gained control of the local priests.

I took a long pull on the brandy, letting the burn in my throat clear my mind. When it faded, I returned to the book, flipping ahead a few pages.

Day 15

Two of my men got into a brawl at the local drinking hole. One died. The other is severely injured. It will take the healers a fortnight to fix him up.

Two telars died, as well, but there were five in the brawl, and more cheering them on. This might only be the start of our troubles.

This time I moved farther ahead, skipping a full ten pages:

Day 23

The inn erupted in another fight last night. That makes three in less than three weeks. Seven men dead in total. Four Slayers and three telars. I've ordered my men to stay away. We're already outnumbered. I can't afford to lose any more bodies.

And another ten pages:

Day 33

They set fire to everything last night. The barracks, Ashe's temple, even Jaldan's shrine. They burned the people inside alive and chased me and my patrol out of town.

Only three of us survived. Going to Conall to send for reinforcements.

Somebody knocked on my door and I cursed. Of course, I had to be interrupted right when I was finally getting somewhere. Maybe if I kept reading they would assume I was elsewhere.

I skipped ahead another three pages. I didn't quite know what I was looking for, but I knew it would be in this part of the book.

Day 36
Arrived in Conall today. Four Slayers from Giren are already here. No other towns have rebelled. Negotiations with General Blackthorn for reinforcements are ongoing.

My would-be guest knocked again. I glared at the door. Whoever it was, they clearly knew I was here.

"Who is it?" I shouted.

"Andre, remember? I'm supposed to help you."

Right. Him. The vampire with the cocky grin that reminded me of Loki.

"Come in."

He burst through the door and bowed with a flourish, offering me a bottle of blueberry wine.

"I figure we're in for some pretty dry reading, so drinks are in order." He practically fell into the chair on the other side of my desk, with a lazy gracefulness reminiscent of a cat.

I raised an eyebrow. "Can you even drink that?" Mature vampires could drink and eat all the same things as humans, but the maturing process usually took a decade or two.

He laughed and pulled a silver flask out of a pocket on his belt. "I've got something else."

"So do I." I held up my bottle of brandy. "I'll have to enjoy your gift another time."

"Took that from my brother's personal stock, didn't you?" He shook his head. "No, I don't want to know. That'd ruin it." He took a swig from his flask and grabbed a random logbook from the temple's box. "I guess I'd better get started."

I had always preferred working alone, but I had to admit that this would go faster with two of us, provided he stuck around after my questions.

"Why did you try to assassinate Cameron?"

Andre's head snapped up so fast his neck cracked audibly. "Who told you that?"

I shrugged. "Someone who gives up her sources doesn't keep those sources long."

“Alexis, I’ll bet. She always did like spoiling things for me.”

“I’m not here to judge you. I don’t give a damn about the high priest or any of the temples or even the gods themselves. All I need to know is why you think Cameron’s working with the enemy.”

He leaned back, tapping one finger idly on the edge of his flask. “The Midnight Order’s entire purpose is to kill without asking questions. They don’t tell us why we’ve been hired, though I can usually guess.”

I tilted my head to the side. “And your guess for Cameron involves the telars?”

“I never did have a guess for Cameron. Everything about his past sparkles. I don’t trust anything that clean, but I can’t prove anything either.” He opened the logbook he had grabbed.

“Do you think it’s a false identity?”

“I try not to think about Cameron. His smug, living face makes my blood boil.”

I opened my mouth to say something more, then closed it. I wasn’t going to get anything more useful from Andre. “Then let’s get to work.”

“I’ve got it!” Andre shouted, jumping out of his chair.

I flinched, my hands flying to cover my ears. “Keep it down, damn it. What did you find?”

“The perfect opportunity to get answers.” He set a logbook on the table and began reading, tracing the words with his index finger. “‘Despite our presence, these telars don’t follow Moonshadow’s government. They follow Elders, three in each town. These Elders preach their religion and teach the Shalinoran language, but encourage their people to learn about ours, and to live at peace with us. For now.’”

I raised an eyebrow. “How does that help us?”

He scowled at me. “I’m not done. ‘These elders meet with the mayors of the other towns every summer solstice. We are not privy to these meetings. The others refuse to force the issue. I fear what they are doing behind those walls.’”

For the first time since my arrival, a spark of hope sprang into my chest. “Summer solstice is only two weeks away.”

“Twelve days. That gives us two more days to find the spy here.”

“Or it gives me eleven days to look before I fly there alone.” I was growing fond of his company, but an entire week alone with him on the road—and another week to get back—sounded like a waste of time. “I have a dragon, remember?”

"My brother has ordered me to accompany you to the telar swamp. He's not known for changing his mind. And I've got some reservations about traveling by dragon."

"It's perfectly safe with the riding apparatus." At least, for one person. I didn't know how well it would handle two. "Anyway, you should stay to investigate the—"

He let out a cynical laugh. "Nobody's going to tell me anything. I'm the family's worst failure since the Mad King. At least on paper."

I raised my eyebrows. "On paper?" He could be talking about Jacob VIII pulling his soldiers out of the swamp, but I got the feeling that a different wound lay behind his words. Something older, closer to home.

His expression darkened. "Never mind that. I'm coming with you, and we leave in two days. If you want to find out who's working with the telars, you'd better do it quickly."

I met Jacob II shortly before midnight in one of the ritual rooms at the back of the castle. This room was designed to harvest the power of the moon with the circular glass skylight at the exact centre of the ceiling. A series of miniature runes carved into the floor formed a circle of protection, ideal for the journey into death. Jacob II was pouring sea salt in a circle around these runes.

He nodded in my direction and continued his circle, leaning heavily on his silver-topped ebony cane.

"It's been many years since I entered Death," he said. "It's strange, going there again."

"Not even to speak with your family?"

"The only ones I loved enough to enter Death for have been beyond my reach for centuries." He finished the circle of salt and stepped inside it. The moon was entering the skylight's range now. "And it's more dangerous now."

"I suppose the Lady Ashe is eager to claim your soul, after all these years." Her realm had a way of drawing people in, especially those who had lived past their time. The longer one cheated Death, the harder it became to resist the grey realm's call. "Are you sure you want to do this?"

"I'm the only one who can, unless we involve the Old Family."

I shook my head. The leaders of the Old Family, Elizabeth II and her daughter Theraia, had funded the telar rebellion of Jacob III's era. They might interpret our need for help as an opportunity for another war. One the crown was in no position to fight.

The moon reached the centre of the skylight. Jacob II glowed in the beam of its light, amplified by the enchanted glass. He pulled a flute from a pocket on his belt and sat cross-legged, folding his hands together around the pipe.

"I'll be back soon." He closed his eyes and dropped his voice to a whisper. "*Methras Entalm Mordoth.*"

The light around him intensified and his body stiffened. His breathing ceased. Cold energy emanated outwards from him in waves, trying to push past the salt circle barrier.

Several moments passed in silence. I paced around the edge of the room, trying to fill the silence with the sound of my footsteps.

The moon shifted away from the centre of the skylight and the glow lessened, but Jacob II didn't return. My chest constricted, and I rested a hand on my sword. If Jacob II's soul got pulled into death, his body would be vulnerable to possession. The invading spirit wouldn't be able to escape the salt circle, but a possessed body needed to be destroyed.

Frost formed around Jacob II's body, thickest around his hands. I moved closer as the frost thickened, drawing my sword. The protection of the moon was gone, and Jacob II was on his own in the realm of Death.

"Dammit Jacob," I muttered. "Come back."

His body remained motionless, without even a twitch of the eyelids. I paced around the circle, trying to ignore the growing tightness in my chest. Jacob II was an experienced necromancer. He knew Death. He knew his way back.

What if Ashe didn't let him return? What if she kept him? I couldn't stop her. I couldn't even enter Death. All I could do was kill whatever came back in Jacob II's place—while it wore my oldest friend's face.

I should have known Loki's job would be something like this, an impossible—

The frost on Jacob II's body crackled. I inched toward the circle's edge, lowering myself into a fighting stance as the frost fell away from his hands.

His eyes opened, and he gasped for air. More frost came loose, falling away from his body in thick chunks. I stood at the circle's edge, sword ready to strike.

"Who speaks?" I asked, trying to sound commanding rather than nervous.

"Jacob Vonstone the Second." He returned the flute to its pouch.

There was no change in his posture, his tone, or his eyes. Not even in his energies.

But spirits of other necromancers knew how to control these things. I tightened my grip on the sword. "Tell me something only Jacob II would know."

Jacob II's expression grew distant. "My son always wished he could marry you."

My hands relaxed, but my heart ached. Jacob III, my Morgan. "He always said that."

"You don't sound like you believed him."

"If a king really wants to do something, he will, rules be damned."

Jacob II grabbed his cane from the circle's outer edge. "Things were different after the rebellion."

"The rebellion I stopped." I shook my head. "What did the tutor say?"

He raised an eyebrow but didn't push it. "Nothing useful. All he saw was a brown hood and a pair of leather-gloved fists. Did you learn anything from the guards who found him?"

I groaned. I had forgotten about them entirely, too busy chasing answers about Cameron. "I'll pay them a visit tomorrow."

Chapter Twelve

The captain of the guard worked and lived in a stone house jutting out from the castle's outer wall, about twenty paces from the main gate.

I found the captain outside this building, conferring with one of the green-cloaked city guards. Her rank was marked with a black C embroidered on the collar of her Royal Guard uniform, a silver version of the Slayers' uniform, but that wasn't what caught my eye.

Captain Raldon was the tallest human woman I had ever seen, towering over the officer she addressed. Her tawny-beige skin seemed even darker when contrasted against her lilandium helmet. A narrow scar above her left eye suggested a history in battle.

She dismissed the guard she was speaking to and waved me over. "Lady Riana, correct?"

I snorted. "I am Riana, but the last thing I'd call myself is a lady."

She chuckled, only partially looking at me, as her gaze surveyed the yard. "That makes two of us. How can I help you?"

"One of the prince's tutors was murdered a few months ago. I need to speak with the gate guards on duty that day and the person who discovered the body."

She shifted her weight, her left hand settling on the hilt of her sword. "Petyr Teldim. Mutilated, not just murdered."

"Mutilated?"

She grimaced. "Torn to pieces. We barely managed to identify him. Whoever killed him wanted to make sure the body couldn't rise."

"And to make sure you found him." Most people murdered in Moonshadow simply disappeared, destroyed outright to prevent them from rising. "How much of him did they find?"

Her mouth tilted downward and her eyes grew distant, as if she was staring back through time at the body itself. "All of him, strewn across an alleyway. Limbs hacked apart at the joints. Even his—" She paused, and when she spoke again her voice was thick with disgust. "His member was removed. I've never seen a body so thoroughly mangled."

I frowned. Sending a recognizable body part, often a torn-off piece of flesh with a birth mark, was a common technique used by killers to send a message. But leaving an entire body, torn to shreds, in an alley? If the person sending this message wasn't part of the telar conspiracy, Jacob VIII had much bigger problems than any of us imagined.

"You told the King of Teldim's condition?"

"The moment his body came through the gate. I assumed that was why you were here. It's beyond suspicious, especially with—" She cut herself off and turned to the gate. "I should find those guards for you."

I moved to block her view, or more realistically to stay in it, since I barely reached her shoulders. "Especially with what?"

For the first time since we started talking she looked at me with both eyes, running her gaze up and down my body as if looking for some obvious sign of trustworthiness.

She leaned closer to me and lowered her voice. "Teldim wasn't an ordinary tutor."

I tilted my head to the side. "You think they want him dead because of his gift?"

"Yes, but also—" She hesitated. "The Vonstones aren't as loved as they once were."

"Captain?" A deep, baritone voice with a thick Estefaran accent interrupted us.

I stiffened. Of all the human kingdoms, Estefar was the worst. Built by evil sorcerers on the backs of slaves, its history was bathed in blood, most of it telar blood. Some of it—

My body exploded outward, tearing through Ma, her guts smacking against the wall behind her—

No. I wouldn't relive those memories. I forced my attention back to Captain Raldon, who now addressed a dark-skinned royal guard with curly black hair sticking out from under his helmet. He was from the southern reaches of Estefar, then. Nowhere near my own birthplace. His collar was embroidered with an L, signalling the rank of Lieutenant.

"Yes, Lieutenant?"

"Vargus wants to know why the court won't see him."

Raldon rolled her eyes. "Tell him the king's court is no place for drunken rages."

"I did. He demands to speak with you directly."

She sighed. "I'll be right there."

"I take it this Vargus is a regular nuisance?"

"He runs one of the bigger pubs in town. The brawls have been particularly bad lately, and he thinks it's the city guard's job to maintain security inside his establishment."

"They stand in for pub security—"

"Twice a year, on festival days. If he asked nicely, they might agree to help. But he arrived drunk, and he was anything but nice. We carried him out and told him to petition the Knights of Jaldan if he doesn't want to hire a bouncer."

I raised my eyebrows. "I suspect that didn't go so well for him." The Knights of Jaldan only maintained order within their own temples, and were renowned for staying neutral during any conflict, in any nation. They certainly wouldn't condescend to mitigating bar fights.

Raldon smiled. "The guards you're looking for are officers Yarrow and Alren. They worked the day Teldim disappeared."

"What about the person who found the body?"

She shook her head. "They were off-duty Slayers. I don't remember their names, you'll have to speak with General Cornelius."

The guards who let Teldim leave couldn't tell me much more than Captain Raldon—only that he insisted on entering the city alone—so I went to General Cornelius next. He managed the Slayers' day-to-day affairs, so his office was in the corner of the keep nearest to the barracks.

General Cornelius wasn't a big man, but he was big enough, able to look me in the eyes when he rose to greet me. His seat was simple hardwood, his desk's only embellishment a set of clawed feet. Bookshelves packed with hundreds of books lined the walls. A house shield hung on the wall behind him, an ox with a sword between its teeth emblazoned on it. The Temmell crest. Their family had a long, proud tradition of military service.

Their family had also been the ones who sold Jacob II the swamp and helped force the telars into it, but that was another matter. I couldn't hold this man personally responsible for the actions of his ancestors.

"May I offer you something to drink?" General Cornelius held up a bottle of wine.

I resisted the urge to wrinkle my nose. I never did like wine much, certainly not compared to the brandy still sitting on my desk. "I need to speak with the Slayers who found Petyr Teldim's body."

He frowned. "That might be difficult."

Everything in this damn place was difficult. "What do you mean?"

"They've been reassigned to Therault. Left last week."

So, they would be halfway to the northernmost corner of the kingdom by now. Exactly what I needed.

"Call them back." With some luck, I would already know who caused the plague by the time they arrived. Without that luck, those Slayers might be my final lead.

General Cornelius opened his top drawer and grabbed a black mirror. "I'll send a message to the Therault fortress, but it will be three days before they see it."

"I don't care. I need to speak to those Slayers, and not through a mirror." Spying on black mirror conversations wasn't easy, but it was possible, and I couldn't afford the risk.

"I'll get them back. Do you need anything else from me?"

"Actually, yes. How many lilandium helmets do we have?" The Slayers and the royal guard wore them, but I hadn't seen a single servant wearing one.

"Three hundred in Moon Spire. The rest are dispersed throughout the border fortresses. We only had seven hundred to begin with."

"How many are at the Estefaran border?"

His eyes went glassy for a moment and he absently tallied something off on his fingers. "Three hundred, split evenly across the main fortresses."

"Get them back. Everyone in this castle needs one. Including temporary ones for guests." I gestured at his bare, bald head.

"Anyone who wants to work in the castle needs three years of mental defence training."

"Even the best mental defence practitioner can be overcome by a powerful telar." And the one infecting Moonshadow had an incredible amount of power. "Unless my investigation proves otherwise, we must assume that the king is in serious danger, and we must assume telar involvement."

"What if Estefar invades while our defences are weakened?"

"That won't matter if Moonshadow descends into civil war first. Besides, Estefar isn't interested in Moonshadow." At least, not while the land remained cursed. "Get those damn helmets back. I want to see every single servant wearing one by the end of the month."

"I'll have to speak with the king. He ordered the helmets—"

I held up my hand, disgusted with his lack of preparation. When had the generals of Moonshadow become so soft? "I'll speak with him myself."

Shouts from the king's office brought me to an abrupt halt as I rounded the nearest corner. I held the wall to steady myself and focused on the voice, letting the sound grow until it filled my head.

"You cannot ask me to do this. The laws we developed after the Mad King's defeat strictly forbid my kind from making legal rulings." Kenneth sounded insulted, as if Jacob VIII had attacked his honour.

"These might be my wife's final days. Or my son's. Or both."

"You are a King, a Vonstone of Moonshadow. You must behave like one." Kenneth lowered his voice, but his tone was still laced with venom. "My great-grandfather will say the same thing."

Jacob VIII lowered his voice in return, speaking with the quiet calm of the worst type of madman. "I'll remember you saying that when they die, and I miss it because I'm in court."

"See to it that you do, and that you continue acting like a king while you mourn."

Kenneth stormed out of the king's office. I flattened myself against the wall as he passed, his eyes narrowing briefly in recognition.

I waited for several moments before knocking on Jacob VIII's door.

"Enter," he shouted.

I cringed, schooled my face into a mask of calm, and walked in. "Your Majesty, I—"

"Andre's already been here," the king said, crossing his arms over his chest. The dark circles under his eyes had grown, and his head drooped as if he might nod off at any moment. "The supplies for your journey are being prepared. Do you need something else?"

That pesky Andre. "Your Majesty, I wish to continue investigating Petyr Teldim's death. If I take the dragon and go alone, I'll get there in less than half a day. That gives me almost two weeks to find out what happened to Teldim."

"You're here to find out who's behind this plague. It's obviously not Teldim, because he's dead. I order you to forget about him."

"But—" I could already feel the compulsion building, not in my mind, but deeper, in my blood. My whole body warmed with it, the desire to obey my summoner. I had forgotten how overpowering the compulsion was, and how intoxicating. "Teldim—" The warmth became boiling heat and I bit my lip to stifle a yelp.

Jacob VIII waved his hand dismissively. "Doesn't matter now. I order you to leave for Diseus at sunset tomorrow, with Andre, on horseback. You will find the person responsible for the plague and end their life."

The new compulsions washed over me, making my veins buzz with energy, but they weren't as hot as the first one. I could think through them. "What if—"

"I order you to leave my office immediately."

Instant fire filled my veins. My skin began to stretch, as if my blood was trying to escape it. I gritted my teeth and forced words out anyway. "You can't ignore the threat in your own city."

Bubbles formed on my skin, pockets of white hot agony. Tears streamed down my face, but I didn't move, didn't even let myself blink.

We sat in silence for several moments, Jacob VIII watching the bubbles on my skin begin to pop with morbid fascination.

When he finally spoke again his voice was little more than a whisper. "I said, get out."

I wanted to call him a fool, but my tongue was bubbling now, too, and my vision was going dark. I stumbled out of the room, knocking my chair over. The heat receded the moment I got through the door. I collapsed against the far wall of the hallway, gasping for air while my tongue slowly returned to normal.

I clung to the walls as I made my way back to my bedchamber, exhausted from the effort of healing myself. A new, warm strength blossomed in my chest—a commitment. I wouldn't live like this anymore. I couldn't. When this ended, I would flee to the farthest island in the mortal realm and live out my life alone. No human would control me again.

Chapter Thirteen

The crowd roared and I answered in kind, raising my short sword. I bolted across the arena, my stretched-out legs carrying me halfway across its length in two strides. Malthis rushed forward to meet me. I feinted left with my sword. He took the bait and I punched him in the stomach with my free hand.

He spat on my face, only his saliva was acid and my skin burned. Bits of flesh melted and fell off my bones, sizzling as they hit the ground. Panic welled up in my chest. What kind of talent was this? Why didn't Temric warn me?

I staggered backward and he spat again, this time hitting my sword hand. I screeched and brought my hand close to my chest, dropping the weapon.

Malthis pounced, knocking me to the ground. He sat on my chest, pinning my arms to my body with his knees and sending a fresh wave of agony through my searing hand. I froze, my heart slowing to a crawl. I was trapped. Pinned like this, I couldn't make the signal for surrender.

"You have to free my hands," I whispered.

He traced my jawline with a single claw. "I don't have to do anything except keep you alive. If you beg, I might let you surrender before I've completely mutilated you." He paused halfway up my face, his claw coming dangerously close to my right eye.

I wanted to run my own claws through his eyes, but I couldn't move my hands. I couldn't even feel the one he'd spat on.

"Please let me go."

He leaned in, his foul breath filling my nostrils. Acid dripped from his teeth onto my eyes and I tried to scream, but he slammed his hand into my throat and took my air. I was going to die here—

I jumped so far that I fell out of bed, my sweat-soaked blanket tangled around my legs. I kicked it off and dragged myself to the nearest blank patch of wall, leaning against the cold stone. I shivered, but the cold felt good, distracting.

After what seemed like hours my heartbeat returned to a normal pace, but my mind raced.

Malthis was dead. I had put centuries between myself and those memories, cast out every thought of him and the arena.

Damn it, I was doing it again. I needed to do something. Get my body moving, and my mind back into my body.

I dressed as quickly as I could with my shaking hands and went for a walk. Instinct guided me through the castle's many twisting corridors. I tried to focus on my footsteps, my breathing, my body in the present moment, but my mind kept going back—

Malthis yanked his thumbs out of my eyes and snarled.

"Please?" The voice was several octaves too high to be mine, but the way the word tore at my throat meant it had to be mine. Me, begging for my life. Wasn't somebody supposed to help? Weren't there rules? I gave the signal, didn't I?

I didn't know anymore. All I knew was that I wanted to live. "Please?"

Malthis laughed. "Did you say something?"

He drove his fist into, no, through my shoulder, tearing a hole in my—

The memory vanished abruptly, leaving me at the end of an old, musty hallway. Once this corridor had continued for another fifty feet or so, but the area had been walled off to stop the spread of plague.

A portrait hung on the wall, its image obscured by several decades of dust. When was the last time someone came down here? Why did they leave this portrait here, alone?

I pulled my sleeve down to cover my hand and wiped away the dust, starting in the far corner. It came away in a cloud and filled my nostrils, making them itch. I sneezed, and sent the rest of the dust flying. The cloud settled over me, coating my clothes, but I barely noticed. I was too busy staring at the portrait.

Jacob III, my Morgan, sat on his throne. He wore his favourite crown, a simple silver circlet with tiny points made of sapphires. This portrait must have been painted when he first became king, for there were no hints of grey in his hair and only the vaguest hint of sadness in his eyes. He hadn't lost his wife, then. Hadn't even met her.

And he certainly hadn't fallen in love with me yet. Our love came many years later, after—

I rapped on Jacob III's door. "It's Riana, Your Majesty."

He didn't hesitate. "Come in."

I clamped my jaw to keep myself from gaping as I entered. His regal demeanour had fallen to tatters. He slouched over a large glass of amber liquid. Tear streaks covered his cheeks. More tears shone in his eyes, but he suppressed these with a gulp of liquor, then slammed the cup against the table hard enough to send liquor sloshing over its edge.

He cursed. "I'm sorry."

I shook my head. "Don't be. You're grieving." I sat across from him, putting my hands over his so he wouldn't take another drink.

"I'm not grieving, I'm angry." His hands tightened so much on the glass that I half expected it to break. "None of those bastards visited Elaina when she was ill, but they're all happy to feast on my food and drink my wine in her name."

I gently rubbed his hands with my thumbs in a vain attempt to soothe him. He pulled away, almost knocking his glass over, and buried his head in his hands.

"You should be out there, celebrating her life with them," I said. "Saying your farewells, making toasts."

"You know how long she was really dead," Jacob III's voice trailed off into a whisper. "How long her soul spent in limbo, tied to a ruined body. I've already said my farewells."

I touched his wrist, the only piece of bare skin I could reach. "She is at peace now."

"And so is our kingdom. But me—" He cut himself off and downed the rest of his drink.

"The war inside our minds is the hardest of all." I was fighting my own internal war even now, resisting the urge to pull him into my arms and comfort him with kisses.

He said nothing for a long time, staring at the bottom of his empty glass. I watched him for a while, but eventually had to look away, unable to bear his pain. I had grown too attached to Jacob III, a mortal king who would never be mine. Even if he did become mine, he would die in a decade or two. He would go on to the afterlife while I returned to the demon realm.

He slowly lifted his gaze to my face. The intensity in his eyes made me shift uncomfortably in my seat. Was he finally going to tell me why he brought me here?

"Will you sleep with me?" he asked, in a tone that was almost desperate.

I blinked several times, leaning as far back in my chair as I could. "You're drunk, and still in mourning, and—"

"Not like that." He wiped at his remaining tears with his left sleeve. "I—I want someone to hold me. It's been so long."

Of course. Elaina hadn't slept in his bed in almost three years. Many other men would have started affairs long ago, but Jacob III was incredibly devoted to his wife. Three years had passed so quickly for me that I thought nothing of it, but judging by the pleading expression on his face, it must have been an eternity for him.

"Why don't you ask one of the servants?" Most would have leapt at the chance to warm his bed, and not only because he was a king.

"They don't care about me. You do."

I took a sharp breath, wondering what he meant by that. Did he know how I felt? What this would do to me, holding him while he mourned his wife?

"They blocked off the tunnels in Kenneth's time."

I jumped and glared at Andre. Did he have to turn up everywhere I went?

"The Red Death, right?" The disease had wiped out a third of Moonshadow's people and continued its path of destruction through Torvaille and Estefar, decimating the world's human population.

He nodded. "It spread like wildfire down here. The servants simply couldn't keep the vermin out." He moved closer to me and glanced up at the portrait of Jacob III. "Was he as great a king as the stories say?"

I opened my mouth to respond, but nothing came out. *Was he?* I thought so, once. Even after he forced the telars into the swamp, I admired him. He acted without hesitation, never doubting himself. He acted always in the best interests of the kingdom, or at least what he thought was Moonshadow's best interests. All the things that, on paper, a good king should do.

"Riana?" Andre's voice was gentler than I would have imagined possible. He moved closer again, almost close enough to touch. "Are you all right?"

"I—he was a great king, even if he wasn't as great as the stories say. Nobody ever really is, you know."

"Is what?"

"As great as the stories say." I certainly wasn't.

Chapter Fourteen

Kahri

I made breakfast with summoned goods from a special storehouse my people kept for me to call upon. I sat at the table with my new companion, the boy I had created. The first person to eat with me here in almost five centuries.

"I lived here before," he said. "I dreamt of it. I almost died by the river. You saved me."

I grinned. *I've done it!* I had not just created life, I'd given one of my people a new life. He was not merely a boy. He was Galvan. My boy.

"Why did you rescue me?" he asked, his face scrunched up tight, as if he was trying to focus on the memory, but couldn't.

"You were the first Shalinoran I'd seen in years." Seeing him had been one of the happiest moments in my long life. It was the moment I knew more of my people must have survived, that my legacy lived on somewhere.

"Shalinoran?"

"From Shalinor. Our queendom." My queendom.

He nodded, eyes lighting up with recognition.

On that first day, I took him around the palace, telling him about the cleaning duties he performed in his first life. I spent the next three days showing him the city, so he could explore while I worked, and never be lost. Each day he recalled more of his old life. He remembered studying under me, and bit by bit regained the techniques I'd taught him. The techniques our people in the swamp had lost when they fled Shalinor.

On the fourth day, we went for a walk along the creek. He paused beside a large rock a few hundred feet away from the palace and bent down to examine it. For a long time, the only sound was the slow movement of the water.

"I died here," he said, looking up at me. "You were with me. I was old. Very old."

"Yes," I said.

"How am I young now?"

I sighed and told him to sit with me. I explained everything—the centuries I spent studying, the decades of failed experiments, and the day I realized I'd been taking the wrong approach all along. Nobody had done what I wanted to do before. Even the Vonstones, who invented necromancy, needed a body to bind a soul to. Studying their work wouldn't help me. I had to create my spells from scratch.

"So I did." I spent a hundred years perfecting the plague spell. The telars in Moonshadow helped me pick targets. I couldn't infect someone I knew nothing about, but with their help it was easy. They sent me an image or a name, and I found the person's aura. "Some of the telars acted as conduits, allowing me to claim souls all across Moonshadow."

Still, the plague had been the easy part. Restoring life, creating flesh and blood out of thin air, had proven much more difficult. I started working on that spell only days after Galvan's death, and when I restored him, I still wasn't certain it would work.

"And now, here you are," I said. "I meant to make you older, a man instead of a boy. But this, I think, is even better." I had forgotten what it was like to have a child around, to experience life through their innocent eyes.

He stared at his hands in wonder, then he smiled at me.

"Thank you."

The next day, I went back to work. I reached out to my network of telars and collected new targets. Now that I'd afflicted so many, infecting more was easy. I could reach minds farther away than ever before, using each diseased person as a beacon to increase my range. My mind breached Estefar for the first time, plaguing three mages. I relished in their suffering. They had destroyed my home, my people. Now I would tear them apart, from the inside out.

The day passed quickly, and soon Galvan appeared, opening the tower door.

"Dinner's ready," he said.

"There's one last thing I have to do," I said. "I'll be down soon. And knock next time."

He blushed, staring at his feet. "O-of course. I'm sorry."

He hurried away, careful to shut the door gently behind him. I smiled. He had always been like that, gentle with even the toughest things.

I took a deep breath and reached out with my mind, seeking a familiar soul—a friend in the swamp.

Yes, mistress?

I grinned at the familiar sound of Fiona's mindvoice. For generations I hadn't been able to contact my people, but finally her voice had broken through the silence, screaming with the pain of a sensitive mind. I soothed her, trained her, and helped her protect herself and her family. She became a leader to her people, bringing them her limited understanding of my ways.

She had never liked my plague, but she was determined to bring our people out of suffering, no matter the cost. She had been waiting for *this* particular order for years.

It is time. Send your six finest and all the supplies you can spare.

Of course, milady. I could hear the smile in her voice.

I smiled back, as if she could hear it in my silence.

Chapter Fifteen

When the first hints of dawn came I grabbed another bottle of the king's brandy and headed to the walkway atop the castle wall to watch the sun rise over the city. I chose a point halfway between two guard towers and climbed onto the waist-high stone ledge intended to keep guards from falling and sat cross-legged, carefully placing my bottle beside me.

My gaze roamed over the city, my brow furrowing as I took in the neighbourhoods closer to the wall. The castle and temple might remain essentially the same as they were in my time, but the city itself had changed enormously. Hundreds of magical street lights had been replaced with flickering oil lanterns. Buildings were falling into disrepair in all but the wealthiest areas. Almost every green patch of land during Jacob III's era had been covered with small stone houses, and even some of these were starting to fall apart.

In Jacob III's time, Moon Spire was the thriving centre of humanity's youngest civilization. Now it felt sick, like a city on the brink of death.

I took a swig of brandy and stared at the city's outer wall. What did the neighbourhoods beyond it look like? A collection of wooden hovels?

The first edge of the sun appeared on the horizon and I leaned forward, breathing deeply as the air around me changed, filled with new life. Moonshadow might be falling apart, but the mortal realm was still a wonderful place.

"I've always loved it up here."

I jumped off the ledge, drawing my sword with my free hand as I turned to face the tower stairs. Captain Raldon raised her hands above her head and backed away.

"Do you love interrupting people's meditations?" I asked, with more venom in my voice than I intended. I was angry at myself, not her. Why didn't I hear her coming? Or Andre? Why did I find myself lost in memories now? What was the point of all those years I spent locking them away?

Raldon gestured at my brandy. "I didn't think that was what you were doing."

"I came here to watch the sunrise. And meditate. Alone." I sheathed my sword.

"These towers are patrolled every hour at night, and three guards are stationed at each tower during daylight hours. It's not the best place to seek solitude."

There was no good place to seek solitude around here.

"But I'm glad I found you here," Raldon said, completely oblivious to my scowl. "Some things aren't safe to say on the ground."

I tilted my head to the side. "About Teldim's death?" The words burned my tongue, a reminder of Jacob VIII's order.

"No. The unrest in this city didn't start with him or the plague. And that's what you're really here for, right? To save Moon Spire?"

I crossed my arms over my chest. "Something along those lines."

She knelt by the hatch leading down to the main wall and used her forefinger to draw a rune at its centre. The symbol glowed bright purple and sent a wave of energy through the wood, making it shine.

"Nobody will interrupt us now." She moved to the other side of the tower and leaned against the ledge. "People don't trust the Vonstones anymore. Haven't since the original Marcus Vonstone."

"The man who defeated the Mad King."

"Yes. He ruled well, brought the city—the kingdom—into a new era of prosperity." She absently scratched at the back of her neck. "His son, King Jacob VII, changed things. Enacted curfews in all major cities. Brought unreasonable taxes down on the people. Raised the punishments for the most minor of crimes."

"Made them hate him." The same pattern had repeated itself countless times, and humanity seemed destined to repeat it many more.

"He did worse, too. Kidnapped a dozen women, made them concubines, and killed them when he grew bored. Maybe even killed his own wife, according to some of the rumours."

Andre's words filled my mind—worst failure on paper. This must have been what he was talking about it. Whether it was true or not, Andre believed it. There had to be a good reason.

"King Jacob VIII loosened most of the laws when he took over," Raldon said. "He's a better man than his father. But he's not a kind man. He often chooses the cruelest punishments allowed for a given crime, and he favours people based on his own whims." She bit her bottom lip. "People are afraid he will turn into his father."

A solid, cold lump of fear formed in my chest. I glared at my arms, remembering the way they blistered, the way Jacob VIII's words seared through my body until I obeyed his commands.

"It's already started," I murmured.

"Did you say something?"

I shook my head, turning back to the horizon. The entire sun was visible now, except one streak covered by purplish-red clouds. Several small groups of Slayers moved toward the castle, returning from their nightly patrols outside the city walls. They paused to extinguish the oil-based street lanterns as they passed.

"If they find out his heir is a telar, too—"

"There might be another rebellion," said Raldon. "Led by the people this time, not one of the Vonstone cousins. They would slaughter all the nobles they could get their hands on, starting with the entire Vonstone family."

She didn't have to say the rest. The kingdom would be left in shambles, forcing the few remaining mages to work themselves into early graves to repair everything. Moonshadow would essentially have to start over, this time without magic. Not enough to make a difference, anyway.

She came to stand beside me. "And somebody—Teldim's killer—already knows."

I spent the rest of the day wandering the city, disguised in a servant's clothes and the face of an old woman, my blade now shaped like a butcher's cleaver. I moved slowly, focused on the people around me rather than any specific destination. Filtering through dozens of conversations, I searched for some hint of conspiracy.

All I heard were sounds of death and fear: announcements of the dead, questions about who would be next, inquiry about when—or if—the healers would find a cure. There were a few rumours that they already had, but the royal family wanted to cull the city's population before they released it. Other rumours circulated claiming the entire royal family was sick. One feverish voice even suggested that the vampiric members of the family were ill too. This plague was magic, after all, why shouldn't they be afflicted?

This plague is magic. I closed my eyes and focused on that voice, a weak sound coming from the edge of the city. An elderly man, or perhaps just one who had been sick too long. Either way, I didn't have much time.

I burst into a run, pushing people out of my way as I raced down the street and around one corner, then another, following the voice.

"Never felt anything like this sickness before. Can't be—" The man lapsed into a ragged coughing fit that quickly became retching.

He's dying. I sped up, forcing my legs to grow slightly so I could move faster as I entered a network of alleys leading to Moon Spire's oldest slum, Mordell.

I burst into the Circle of Shrines, a large square that boasted shrines to all four of Moonshadow's deities. Several people lay on the ground around Ashe's shrine, a small building made of glowing grey stone and dominated by a person-sized altar. All the penitents looked ready to die, their faces soaked in sweat and tinged green. Angry red hand marks covered their necks.

"Can't be natural," whispered the man closest to the shrine. Long white hair obscured the marks on his neck, but I saw the telltale fingertips all the same.

I hurried over and knelt beside him. He stank, like he had already begun to rot. I wrinkled my nose and leaned forward, resting a hand on his forehead. Heat surged through my body and I flinched backward, gaping at him. How could a human body hold so much heat?

He squinted at me and smiled, revealing a mouth almost completely devoid of teeth. "S'all right. I've seen too many moons anyway."

I leaned as close to him as I could stomach. "Do you know what's happening to you?"

He giggled. "'The curse is lifting,' they said. But I knew better. Magdalene's curses don't fail, they change. Needs more corpses to raise, you see? We killed too many."

"You think Magdalene is doing this?" I gestured at the other dying people gathered around the shrine, trying to ignore the cold dread filling my body. This couldn't be another aspect of her curse, could it? Or an entirely different curse, for something else Moonshadow had done? For shunning the telars, Magdalene's chosen people?

The old man grabbed at my skirt, nodding frantically. "You have to believe me. Warn the Vonstones. If they want her to stop, they must let her keep the bodies. She needs more—"

He erupted into another coughing fit, spasms wracking his body. I backed away, yanking my skirt out of his hands. My body, my mind—everything went numb and cold.

Did Loki expect me to go up against the most vengeful goddess who ever lived? Or was this man just crazy?

"Please be wrong," I murmured, edging my way out of the square. "Please, please be wrong."

Chapter Sixteen

One change of clothes, a transformation back to my old self, and half a bottle of brandy later, I sat at my desk and stared at a tall black mirror I had dug out of storage. A red cloth was draped over it. My head throbbed with the storm of emotions battling in my mind. Was the old man crazy or a visionary? Should I ask Loki? Would he tell me the truth?

"Only one way to find out." I took a deep breath and yanked the cloth away from the mirror. I pressed two fingers against the glass, letting my energies flow into it—a signature of sorts. "Call Loki."

The darkness inside the mirror began to spin, moving so rapidly that a human wouldn't have been able to see it. Colours swirled back out from the centre, forming an image of Loki. Today in the guise of a bald man with a bright red beard, the same form he had worn during our first meeting.

He grinned. "How lovely to see you."

I ground my teeth together. Nothing would be more satisfying than to smack that grin off of his face. "What kind of mad quest have you sent me on? Is this plague some twisted part of Magdalene's curse?"

He sighed dramatically. "Oh, Riana. Always jumping to the most exciting conclusion, even when it makes no sense."

Rage exploded from my heart and I didn't bother trying to keep it out of my voice. "It makes perfect sense. Magdalene's a vengeful, vicious wretch, and you're hardly better. This world would be better off without any damn gods, and so would I."

"I'm sorry you feel that way," he said, not batting an eye. "But I assure you, Magdalene has no part in this plague."

Loki sounded genuine. At least, as genuine as he had ever been.

"Then who? Who is powerful enough to do something like this?"

"You're on your own for this one," he said. "I've interfered in mortal affairs enough."

I raised an eyebrow. "Interfering in mortal affairs is your favourite way to pass the time."

"Even gods change."

He vanished, replaced by the dark swirl in the mirror.

An hour later I made my way to the stables, spurred on by the compulsion of Jacob VIII's order. I would leave tonight, whether I wanted to or not.

Andre was already there, checking the straps on his horse's tack. Moonshadow's royal horses were impressive beasts—twice the size of a regular horse and three times as calm. They needed to be to endure carrying the undead, a burden that would spook most animals.

An elderly groom brought me a stallion, outfitted for traveling with heavy tack, including a headpiece with four small glowing stones along its side. Malarite, a stone found in abundance throughout the caverns of Moonshadow's northern mountains. Numerous small stones placed at careful increments along a horse's tack made it possible for them to travel safely at night. The Vonstones, and the Slayers, had used these saddles for centuries.

"Saddlebags are packed with twenty days' worth of supplies," the stable hand said. "He's ready when you are."

"Thank you." I grabbed the reins and waved the servant away.

I stayed still beside the horse for several moments, letting him examine me and understand my scent. His eyes widened a bit at the taint of demon magic, but he showed no other signs of distress. I rubbed his muzzle and moved closer.

"I will not be your burden long," I said.

He sighed and lowered his head, accepting me as his rider.

Marcus said you're going somewhere. Shouldn't I come with you?

I started at Rolf's mindvoice, and the stallion narrowed his eyes. I stroked his muzzle again, whispering soothing sounds as I mentally cursed myself. *This isn't a good time. Stay and train Marcus. I'll call you when I need you.*

But I'm supposed to help you. This thought rode a wave of frustration and impatience that reminded me of a child whose privileges have been revoked.

You are. I need you to keep an eye on Marcus until I get back.

You said you would call me—

I'm hoping it won't come to that. I doubted words alone would get anywhere with these people, but I had to try. I didn't want more blood on my hands than absolutely necessary. *Besides, it'll only take you a couple of hours to reach me from here.*

What if that's too long?

Then burn everything down around my corpse. I stroked the horse's mane and searched the saddlebags, making a mental inventory of the contents: spoon, bowl, dried jerky, two waterskins, feed for the horse, leather bedroll with wool lining.

You're serious about that last part? Rolf asked.

Yes. If I don't find them, the only way to end the plague—the curse—is to kill everyone in the swamp. And hope the person behind the plague actually lived there.

I don't want to kill all of those people.

Neither do I. But there are a lot more people dying now. At least, there would be, if this plague expanded much more. Or if Marcus died. A second civil war in less than a century might destroy Moonshadow entirely. *I'll check in with you before I go to bed, promise.*

All right. Be safe.

I chuckled. *Always am.*

"Ma'am? The king is waiting for you at the main gate."

I stifled a groan and clasped the saddlebags shut. "I'll be out in a moment."

I mounted my horse and rode out into the night. Everyone else was already gathered around the portcullis, before the drawbridge. Andre wore an uncharacteristic scowl. Jacob VIII looked even more exhausted than the last time I saw him. Jacob II leaned heavily on his ebony cane to compensate for his twisted foot.

Jacob II spotted me first, greeting me with a wave and a grin.

Jacob VIII followed his ancestor's gaze and smiled at me, but his smile contained no warmth, only a grim satisfaction.

"You'll find scrying ink and a silver bowl in your saddlebags," Jacob VIII said. "I expect updates every three days."

"We won't even be in Diseus for seven," I said.

He narrowed his eyes. "Every three days. That's an order."

The compulsion wouldn't work over three days, but there was no point arguing. "It will be as you wish, Your Majesty."

I bowed and spurred my horse on, riding past him to Jacob II. "I'm glad you came."

"You are one of my oldest friends." He reached into his pocket. "I brought you something."

"Really? I'm honoured," I said, and for once, I actually meant it.

“I believe this was yours. A mutual friend gave it to you for good luck. You left it here.” He handed me a brooch, a silver rose resting on an emerald green circle.

My heart slowed as I stared at the familiar flower. The stem’s bottom bent to form a small V. I ran my fingers along the cold metal edge, remembering.

Jacob III—Morgan, I was meant to call him now—was beautiful as he entered my room and shrugged off his cloak. I moved to embrace him, but he shook his head. I held back, suddenly afraid. Was this the end?

He took a step toward me, reached out and ran one hand along the side of my face.

“You are so beautiful,” he said, “but your blood—we can never marry.”

I held completely still, bracing myself for pain. He probably wanted a woman he could marry, a second chance at a real family. Something we could never have, no matter how much his son adored me.

Tears welled up in my eyes and my chest constricted. These past few months had been magical, but they couldn’t last. He was a human, a king. If the people discovered our transgressions, he would pay for them in blood.

Was anything worth that kind of risk? Even love?

Morgan wiped my tears away with two soft fingers.

“Do not be afraid. We may never marry, but I brought you this, because you will always be part of my family.”

He held the brooch out in his open palm and I let the tears stream down my face, only now they were tears of happiness, not fear.

“Don’t scare me like that,” I said.

“Riana?” Jacob II’s deep voice brought me back to the present.

“Thank you,” I whispered and closed my fingers around the brooch. “I’ll need the luck.”

Chapter Seventeen

The first two nights of our journey proved rainy, but otherwise uneventful. Andre talked about anything and everything for the first few hours. Thankfully, he gave up starting a conversation by midnight. I spent the time wrapped up in my own mind, hunting through the past few days' memories for some clue I might have missed. Something that would tell me who created the plague, or at least who killed Teldim.

Nothing came to me.

At the end of the third night, we reached Elgin, a small town guarded by a ten-foot stone wall and an unusually large contingent of Slayers. They recognized our crests and insisted on rolling out the royal welcome and directing us to the mayor's house.

The mayor was an elderly man with a white beard that extended all the way to the top of his round belly. He greeted us at the door and showed us our rooms, then invited us to breakfast.

"I'm not that type of guest." To prove it, Andre bared his fangs.

The mayor blanched. "O-Of course, my lord. I suppose—"

"I brought my own supplies, don't worry."

"And I'm not hungry," I said, trying to keep my amusement out of my voice.

"Right. If you need anything at all, please do let the servants know." The mayor bowed and strode away stiffly.

"Travelling is much more fun now." Andre grinned from ear to ear.

I rolled my eyes. "Rest up. We reach the swamp tomorrow night."

I entered my room before he could respond, but I couldn't follow my own advice. Every time I closed my eyes a different terrible image appeared in the darkness of my mind. Jacob VIII, ordering me to ignore a royal tutor's murder, the glint of madness in his eyes. Marcus, dead, his little body grey-green and emaciated by sickness. Me, returned to the demon realm and chained to a wall, subjected to the inner family's penchant for cruel 'experiments.' Claws and teeth yanked out with all manner of devices. Patches of skin stripped off with a blade, always growing back so the torture could begin again. *This* was the true curse of demonic blood—the ability to survive any suffering.

No. I would never go back to living at their whim, and I would never be enslaved by another human. If I failed now, it would be the end of me. Even if I had to make it so.

The thought of my own death was the first comforting one I'd had in days, and I fell asleep at last, with a smile on my face.

I met Andre in the mayor's entrance hall at nightfall. The mayor had come to bid us farewell and was hurriedly telling Andre about how Elgin could benefit from a royal donation.

"We could improve our roads, make it friendlier for merchants—"

Andre snorted. "What merchants want to come here? It's the last stop on the way to the poorest county in the whole damn kingdom."

The mayor flushed, opened his mouth, and then snapped it shut.

"Still, good roads are essential," I said. "We'll mention it to the king."

The mayor jumped to his feet and bowed as low to the ground as his belly allowed. "Thank you, milady. Your horses have been groomed, saddled, and resupplied, as best we could."

"I'm sure it will be more than sufficient," I said, before Andre could say anything else to upset the man.

The mayor thanked me several more times as he led us out of the house. A pair of stable hands had our horses waiting by the gates. Both servants trembled with fear. The younger one's eyes darted in every direction, as if looking for an escape route.

I frowned, scratching my nose to hide my displeasure. The people's respect for the Vonstones had always been tinted with fear, but this? This was terror. And terror never ruled a people for long.

Captain Raldon was right. No matter what I did, war loomed on the horizon for Moonshadow.

By the end of the night, we were deep in the swamp. The road's condition grew worse with every hour, slowing our pace almost to a crawl as our horses picked their way around the ever-increasing number of muddy holes in the path.

The land around us—and calling it land was generous—went through an even more dramatic transformation. The trees grew thinner, more crooked, with branches that drooped like vines. Muddy ground gave way to algae-filled pools. Hordes of insects buzzed above these pools. They stayed well away from us, deterred by the poisonous stench of magic in our blood.

We started our search for a safe campground well before dawn, but the swamp had little to offer. In the end, we settled for a narrow strip of slightly muddy land big enough for our horses, one tent, and one carefully placed bedroll.

Andre's foot squelched into a deep pool of muddy green water and he cursed, stumbling back. "Bloody hell. This place is even more miserable than I expected."

"That's why your ancestors chose it." Jacob III had known exactly what he was doing.

This spot was less than ideal, but if we held off any longer, Andre would be exposed to sunlight. He wore the thick black gloves and hoods the Old Family used to walk safely during the day, but new vampires found it nearly impossible to stay conscious once the sun came out, and exposure to even a sliver of sunlight could be catastrophic.

No, we couldn't afford to keep looking. The sky was already beginning to change from inky black to the deep grey of a cloudy day.

At least they weren't storm clouds.

"We could share the tent," Andre said as he hobbled our stallions together.

My eyebrows shot so far into my forehead that it hurt. "That's rather forward of you."

"I meant to stay out of the rain. There's enough room for two bedrolls." He straightened and winked at me. "But I don't mind if we share one."

If he'd been any less obnoxious, I wouldn't have minded either. He had everything I liked in a lover. Confidence, intelligence, flexibility, and a certain demeanour that suggested plenty of past experience. But he was grinning again, with that damn mischievous sparkle in his eyes that reminded me too much of Loki.

"I'll sleep in the damn rain."

He sighed. "Look, I was joking—well, partially—but you don't have to sleep in the rain and you definitely don't have to sleep with me."

I glanced at the sky again. Heavier, darker clouds were gathering at the southern horizon, carried northward by a steady wind.

"We'll share the tent, but I'll keep to my own bedroll."

Chapter Eighteen

The courtroom where the inner family conducted their persecutions—trials being too kind a word—was equal parts magnificent and imposing. A tiled mosaic of darkness spiralled out from the centre of the room, one massive tendril forming the path to the door. The walls were made of the same red glowing substance as the demon realm's "sky". The vaulted ceiling had many demons painted on it, all in their true forms, undergoing various forms of torture.

At the centre of this room stood the Master, one of the original five demons and head of the inner family. Most of our kin used their natural forms because maintaining human form exhausted them, but the Master actually enjoyed his. Probably because his twisted features and six rows of sharp teeth scared even the most fearless among us.

Temric threw me at the Master's feet with enough force that the flesh tore away from my knees. I inhaled sharply but forced my expression to remain calm. The inner family enjoyed nothing more than watching others suffer. The Master enjoyed it more than the rest.

"This one broke the sanctity of the arena and murdered Malthis," Temric said.

The Master ran his long, green tongue over his teeth. "Remind me, what was the punishment for murder in the arena?"

"Five years of torture, I believe," Temric said, without a hint of emotion in his voice. "Repeated amputation of the limb used for the murder was a favourite."

This time I couldn't suppress my reaction; a violent shudder tore open the wounds still healing in my stomach. Everyone knew the stories, but I always assumed they were like the folk tales mortal mothers created to scare their children into obedience.

I never expected to find out they were true the hard way.

A terrible, throaty sound that must have been laughter erupted from the Master's throat. "How delightful. And which limb would that be?"

"She used her right hand, Master."

A tentacle shot out of the Master's back and wrapped around my wrist, yanking me forward. I fell. My arm popped out of my shoulder as I hit the ground. I screamed, pain searing my thoughts away.

"This one, then?" the Master asked. "I suppose it was your dominant hand when you were human."

"It was the hand closest to my blade." The words fell out of my mouth, followed by an internal string of curses. Why couldn't my mouth wait for my mind?

"Shame you didn't use both hands," the Master continued, as if I hadn't spoken at all. "That would have been twice as much fun." His eyes narrowed at the end of this sentence, and he ran his tongue over his teeth again.

The tentacle tightened around my wrist, crushing skin and muscle and bone—

A scream woke me, and I tried to scramble out of my bedroll, but someone held me in place, pinning my arms to my chest. Hot panic surged from my chest into my throat and I pushed outward with all my strength, opening my eyes—

Andre stumbled away from me, his hands raised above his head to show surrender. "You were thrashing about in your sleep, I thought—"

"It's dangerous to interrupt. I reach for my weapons first, without thinking."

"But you'd rather be awake, right?"

The tent was rather cramped, and I dreaded tonight's journey, but it was still better than the demon realm. Certainly better than my memories of the Master. "Yes."

Andre relaxed and lowered his hands. "Then it's worth the risk. I had nightmares every night for a long time. I wish somebody had stopped them more often."

"The difference is that mine aren't nightmares," I said. "They're memories."

"So are mine." Andre grimaced. "The sun will set soon. We should get our boots on."

"Don't you need breakfast or something?" Andre asked, rummaging through his saddlebags.

I sighed. Andre's obnoxiously casual nature had returned moments after he confessed to his nightmares, and I had even less patience for it now.

"Technically, you aren't eating breakfast either."

He wrinkled his nose. "Technicalities always seemed rather cumbersome to me."

"I bet," I rolled my eyes. He sounded more like Loki with every word.

"What's that supposed to mean? And really, don't you need food?"

"If you must know, my kind only needs to eat once a week, unless we're healing." Our bodies had the ability to recover from anything short of decapitation, but we became ravenous during the healing process, eating several large meals a day.

Andre triumphantly grabbed a black stone bottle, one of the magical cold bottles the Vonstones' earliest mages created, designed to keep blood fresh for three months. "Let's hope that doesn't become necessary."

"I thought you came for the fight." I adjusted my sword so the blade hung diagonally across my back.

"I came to get away from my brother. Fighting's fun, but—" Andre took a gulp of blood, wiping the remnants off his lips with one sleeve as he continued. "Only when it's a challenge."

I couldn't help but smile. My thoughts exactly, even in the arena where a challenge meant excruciating pain and weeks or even months of healing.

My smile turned to a frown as I considered the first part of his statement. "Why do you hate your brother so much?"

He gaped. "You're joking, right? He banished me, executed me, turned me into a vampire, and made me swear a magical oath to serve him."

"That all happened a few months ago. Your hatred seems older." The kind of hate a person nurtured from childhood.

Andre folded his arms over his chest. "You still think I have something to do with this conspiracy."

"Not you."

I yanked his bedroll out of the tent and rolled it up, giving him time to digest my words. He remained silent for an agonizingly long time, and stared at the ceiling as he finished his bottle.

"You think my brother's under their control? Is that even possible? He hasn't even taken the helmet off to wash his hair in months."

"This plan didn't start a few months ago." I dismantled the tent as I spoke, eager to get on the road. "And not complete control. Manipulation. Altered thought patterns and memories, created over an extended period of time."

He tapped the lid of his blood bottle with two fingers, frowning into the space above my head. "There must be a reason you believe this. Something specific."

I explained the circumstances around Teldim's murder and how Jacob VIII ordered me to ignore the case and that I downed an entire wineskin to compensate for how the lingering compulsion burned my tongue. I reminded him of the orders to stop sending Slayers to the swamp and the removal of mental defence training for Moonshadow's children. "These aren't the actions of a rational king, haven't been for a long time. Him being manipulated is the best we can hope for."

"What's that supposed to mean?"

I tied a rope around the folded tent. "If he's not being manipulated, he's losing his mind. Manipulation, he can recover from. Madness—" I stared at the cloth in my hands, unable to finish my sentence. There had to be a way to cure madness, or at least to live well in spite of it, but humans hadn't found that solution, yet.

When Andre spoke again his voice had lost all tone, all hint of emotion. "If he is being manipulated, who do you think is responsible?"

I glanced at his face, my heart slowing as I met his eyes. I recognized that expression, that resolve. The cold-hearted desire for revenge, which could burn in a human heart for a lifetime, or within a demonic heart for centuries.

"It could be anyone who's had consistent access to him for the past fifteen years."

He raised an eyebrow. "But there's someone you suspect most."

I suspected Cameron most, but the last thing I needed was Andre acting on my unproven suspicions. "Not yet. I need more time in Moon Spire."

"Then we'd better get moving."

The rain started not long after we set out, a steady pour that soaked through my clothes within the first mile. Our pace slowed further as the entire road became a muddy pit and the algae-filled pools around us overflowed. If this kept up, we wouldn't reach Diseus in time to catch the elders' meeting. Or maybe we needed to abandon the horses and fly. But I didn't want to bring Rolf into this until absolutely necessary.

An eerie creaking sound from the road behind me drew my attention—the sound of bones rubbing against each other where skin and muscle had worn out.

"Undead," I half-shouted, drawing my sword and bringing my horse around to face the oncoming fiends.

Andre jumped off his horse and drew his sword as three deformed skeletons, held together by a handful of rotting muscles, stumbled toward us. The furthest one dragged its left leg. It was cracked in several places, but the thing never stopped moving as if it was determined to snuff out our lives. The other skeletons seemed more intact, but they moved almost as slowly, struggling to get through the rain and muck.

All three of them sizzled, the heavy rain boring holes through their bones. If we let them follow us for another half mile they would disintegrate.

But they would also attract more of their friends.

Andre sprang into action, placing himself between me and the skeletons as he charged. A series of runic blessings flared into life on his sword, bathing everything in a bright silver light.

"Arrogant bastard," I muttered, although I enjoyed watching the way he moved, his assassin's grace combined with his vampiric power.

He dove low, catching the first skeleton in the kneecap. It shattered, and the skeleton fell backward into the muck. The second figure lunged for him, swinging one bony fist. Andre spun and caught it in the ribs with his sword. The bones exploded, this time shattering the entire skeleton.

Yes, I loved watching him fight. He made quick work of the third skeleton, driving his blade through its skull, then returned to the first as it struggled to stand on its remaining foot. He stabbed downward.

A bony hand yanked his leg out from under him. Andre's blade flew out of his grasp, sinking into an algae-filled pool several paces away. The half-formed skeleton crawled over him, trying to push him farther into the muck, to drown him.

I willed my sword to become a knife, closing my eyes and forcing the metal to redistribute its weight. It protested at the dramatic change, but it contorted into the perfect throwing knife within moments.

My eyes snapped open to discover the skeleton straddling Andre, shoving him down.

I hurled my knife at the skeleton, my heart leaping into my ears as it spun through the air. The arc was too high, I wasn't going to make it, my knife would be lost in the muck, that was my worst throw in two millennia—

Andre punched the skeleton in the sternum. The bone cracked, and the skeleton stumbled backward.

My knife landed squarely in the centre of its skull. The skeleton glowed silver, then exploded into thousands of pieces. My knife fell onto Andre's chest, landing flat.

He grabbed the knife and scrambled to his feet. His entire body was covered in greenish-black muck, his clothes likely soaked through with more than rain. I couldn't help but wrinkle my nose at the thought.

"Where did my sword fall?" he asked, returning my knife.

"In that pool." I pointed to an algae-filled pond, now overflowing onto the road.

He grimaced. "Oh well, I suppose I'm already covered in shit."

He waded into the pond, cursing with every step. He bent over to feel around the bottom, the greenish-black muck spreading all the way up to his neck. Thoughts of Magdalene's curse crashed into my brain. The spell that brought the northern tribes together, that created and defined Moonshadow.

Those were undead, all right, but nothing like the spirited fighting corpses of Jacob III's era. Not a serious threat to even the most poorly trained Slayer.

If the curse disappeared entirely, could the Vonstones still hold Moonshadow together?

I didn't want to be around to find out.

Chapter Nineteen

Despite the darkness and the overflow, Andre found his sword quickly, and we set out again. The rain ended an hour or so later, but it didn't matter. Our clothes would be wet for days, and Andre stank like a sewer.

"Honestly, I don't know why anyone worships the gods," he ranted. "Other than Ashe, they've done nothing for us. And even she hasn't given a damn about us in at least a hundred years."

"Magdalene gave your people life." She gave all humans life, and once upon a time, she loved them all, too. At least, that was how the story went. I knew Magdalene's wrath firsthand, and I couldn't believe she had ever been benevolent.

"You fought those corpses too, right? You know who cursed our land to make them rise?"

"I watched the whole thing."

The inner family gave us special permission to watch the mortal world with them that day. Hundreds of demons had crowded into their viewing room. Magdalene went from tribe to tribe, cursing the humans who refused to stop worshiping Kalum, her treacherous and banished husband. The other demons cheered.

My heart twisted. Nobody deserved to live in terror their whole life.

But I was the only one who saw it, because I was the only one who knew another life. My life with Ma, full of warmth and gentleness.

"You watched?" Andre spat. "Then how can you talk about Magdalene like she *helped* my people?"

I shrugged. "Your people fought each other for thousands of years. Gruesome, bloody wars. The curse united them. Moonshadow wouldn't exist without it."

"That happened in spite of Magdalene, not because of her. She wanted our ancestors dead. But she wasn't allowed to outright kill them, so she cursed our land instead."

I rubbed my temples. He was making my head ache. "You're right. She wanted to slaughter your ancestors, bathe the land in their blood. Is that what you want to hear?"

He glowered at me. "It's the truth."

"And there's nothing we can do about it, so you're wasting your breath ranting about it." I glanced at the now-clear sky. The moon hung low, almost finished with its nightly journey. "We need to focus on finding a place to camp."

We found a large slanted rock jutting out from the road, high enough to rise above the surrounding river of muck. I hobbled our horses while Andre stripped down to his underwear, and then stretched his clothes out across the stone so they wouldn't grow mould.

"Can't you just dry these off or something?"

"The curse in my blood binds my abilities," I said. "I am magic, but I can't use most forms of magic. Each demon is proficient in a single form. Mine certainly isn't drying clothes."

"Another thing we can thank Magdalene for."

"You should thank her for that one." I gingerly removed my horse's saddle and laid it on the driest patch of stone I could find. "The inner family, what we call the first demons, is more depraved than any group of humans I've encountered. I hate to imagine what would happen if their powers were unleashed on the mortal realm."

"They're really that bad?"

"They are now. Who knows what they'd be like if they never had to live with the curse." I liked to believe that when they still walked the mortal realm, they were good people. That being cursed, or perhaps living in the demon realm too long, made them awful. These thoughts made it easier to believe I could be a good person, too, if I could escape the curse.

If I were free.

"I've been thinking." Andre unfolded the tent. We had agreed to share again, because two tents would never fit on this rock. "About my brother."

I stiffened, one hand holding my horse's brush in midair. "And?"

"You remember when I told you to question Cameron?"

"Yes." I forced myself to focus on brushing my horse, trying not to think too hard about where this was going.

"I said it out of spite, then. But it makes sense, that my brother's being manipulated, and Cameron, well, if anyone could manipulate my brother—it's him."

"Because he's so devout?"

"It's more than that. Cameron won my brother over with Isabelle, not religion."

I swallowed hard. Did that mean—

"Temrius, that's his middle name and what I still call him in my head, didn't want to marry, but a king needs an heir. There was so much pressure on him. So many noble women trying to win his hand. He couldn't stand any of them." Andre took a deep breath. "When he met Isabelle everything changed. Suddenly all he could talk about was getting married."

"You think she's behind all of this?" I never suspected her because she had the plague too, but what better cover than giving herself, and her son, the plague? They had already survived longer than most of the victims. I assumed it was because of the royal healers, but what if it was part of her plan?

"Not behind, but involved. Her and Cameron both." Andre scratched the back of his neck absently. "Temrius stopped the mandatory mental defence lessons around the same time."

I grimaced. How could I have missed that? The centuries between summonings had clearly dulled my instincts. "I hope you're wrong."

"What are we going to do if I'm right?"

"We'll worry about that after we speak with the telar elders."

I waited until dawn plunged Andre into unconsciousness, then peeled off my own soaked clothes and laid them beside his to dry. The summer sun was amazing on my naked skin, and I stretched out next to the clothes, basking in its warmth. I closed my eyes and cleared my mind, letting the sensations of light and heat and air caressing my body fill my being.

Andre's voice broke the peace, his words sinking into my mind and restoring the headache I had developed upon entering the mortal realm.

Isabelle, the match Cameron found for Jacob VIII, participated in a telar conspiracy either with Cameron's help, or, perhaps, because of his manipulation.

Good thing I still had eyes and ears on the ground. I took a deep breath and amplified my thoughts, trying to push them across the kingdom.

Rolf, can you hear me?

We hadn't spoken in two days, and I worried that I exceeded his mindvoice's range, despite his assurances to the contrary.

You sound unhappy.

There isn't much to be happy about. I ran a hand through my hair, pulling apart a series of knots as I explained the situation to him. *What has Marcus said about his mother?*

Rolf paused, and his next thoughts were accompanied by an image of him with his eyes downcast. *Not much. She's really sick. He doesn't like talking about it.*

My fingers caught on a snag and I yanked them through, hissing through my teeth. *Ask about her before she got sick.*

I'll try. What do you want to know?

I glared at the thick, damp and incurably tangled hair now in my hand. I loved my natural hair, but keeping it knot-free had become an impossible task.

Riana?

I'm thinking. I threw the clump of hair into a nearby pond and returned to finger-combing the remaining knots. *Anything, really. How does she get along with the king? His family? How does she behave on her own? How religious is she? Is she friends with the High Priest?*

That's a lot of questions. This thought came with an image of Rolf's face, his bottom lip curled downward to reveal the base of his fangs.

Start with one. Or start with something else. Maybe ask about how they play together. Ease into it, but find out soon. If the queen worked for the telars we needed a new plan.

I'll try my best, promise.

Thank you. I rubbed my temples. *I'm sorry to ask so much of you.*

I'm here to help. This time the image was of Rolf smiling, revealing the full extent of his tall, sharp teeth.

I chuckled. *Didn't I tell you to stop doing that?*

Chapter Twenty

The last three nights of our journey passed as uneventfully as the first three. We didn't encounter a single person on the road, living or otherwise. Rolf shared all kinds of trivial details about Marcus's mother, but nothing to confirm either innocence or guilt. Marcus was too inexperienced to notice the right things.

We reached Diseus an hour after sunset on the eighth night of our journey. The town was protected by a seven-foot wall of partially rotted wood. Enough to keep out wild animals and the dimwitted undead, but not much more.

The town's main gate, made out of slightly healthier wood, stood closed. Two men in mismatched armour guarded it, or perhaps it was more accurate to say one. The other leaned on the wall and dozed, punctuating the quiet night with the occasional loud snore.

The alert guard caught sight of us and shook his companion awake, frantically whispering something I didn't bother to hear. The newly-awakened guard's expression made it clear enough. A Vonstone was visiting their backwater town, and they were terrified.

Both men drew their swords as we approached. The anti-undead runes on the blades flared into life, emitting a brilliant blue light. The guards exchanged looks of open-mouthed horror, but to their credit, they remained at the gate with swords ready.

"No-Nobody's allowed into town after dark," the newly awakened guard said, his eyes darting between me and Andre.

"I am Andre Vonstone, the king's brother and most trusted emissary." Andre spoke in a deep, commanding voice free of his usual mockery. "We have business with your elders."

The "most trusted emissary" was the most blatant lie I had heard this century, but Andre's transformation from his usual self into a proper member of the royal family was rather impressive.

The guards exchanged glances. This time it was the other guard who answered. "Please, Your Majesty. They'll kill us if we disobey."

Andre's eyes narrowed. "What do you think I'll do if you disobey me?"

"If you could only come back in the morning, Your Majesty, I'm sure they'd see you."

Andre snarled, displaying his fangs. "Do I look like someone who can return in the morning?"

Both guards spoke at once, their words growing louder and more frantic as each one tried to be heard over the other.

"Enough," I shouted. "This is simple. If you let us in, you have a chance to leave Diseus and live. If you don't, we will kill you where you stand."

I drew my sword for emphasis, pushing it into a longer shape than normal. The younger guard dropped his sword and cowered against the wall. The other man held his ground, but his jaw went slack.

"What are you?" he asked. "A demon?"

I cackled. "Excellent intuition, this one. Would you like to see the extent of my powers?"

"N-No. We'll leave. You can talk to the elders. Just—" He fell silent, staring at his feet. He shook so badly that I half expected him to drop his sword.

"Just let us go," the other one said, sheathing his sword. "Please."

"You can go anywhere you want after you open this gate," Andre said.

"Anywhere?" The guard's face lit up.

"Within the swamp, of course."

The guard's face fell, but he nodded. "Of course."

"I'll do it." His friend sheathed his sword. "They were still meeting in the temple when I picked up the gear for tonight's shift." He threw his whole weight into the gate and shoved it open with his shoulder. "Might be in their chambers now."

"And where, exactly, can we find those chambers?" Andre asked.

"Also within the temple. Don't know exactly where." He stepped out of our way and bowed. "Honoured to meet you, Your Majesty. And"—he glanced at me—"you, I suppose."

I inclined my head. "You've been most accommodating." I tossed him a gold coin from one of my saddlebags. "This should help you... relocate."

The guard thanked me profusely. I rode into town without another word. Andre followed, a few steps behind.

Despite its outward appearance, Diseus was clearly a town climbing out of poverty. The road was better here than it had been since we entered the swamp. The houses were well maintained. Oil-filled street lamps stood on every corner.

Magdalene's temple towered over it all, a surprisingly elegant mansion at the far edge of town. The structure was made of stone, except for its great wooden door. Decades must have passed before enough materials, even with contributions from every town in the swamp, were gathered.

Magdalene's temple was also the only building with guards. Four men stood vigil this time, all as poorly armed as the first two. They drew their weapons as we approached. More blades blessed to kill the undead.

I drew my weapon in response. I didn't want to kill them, but I was tired of people getting in my way.

Three guards charged us, shouting as they ran, probably to scare the horses. Moonshadow's royal horses weren't the type to scare, though. They got angry instead. I barely needed to encourage my stallion to charge forward, kicking the first guard in the head as I swung my sword at one of his companions. The second guard dove out of the way and narrowly avoided the blow.

I cursed and brought my horse around, only to watch the man collapse, a knife sticking out of his chest. The third guard who charged us lay twitching on the ground beside him.

Andre dismounted to retrieve his knife and I returned my attention to the temple, searching for the final guard. He was nowhere in sight. The temple's entrance remained closed.

"Bet they've barred it now, too," Andre said.

I shook my head. "I would have heard the bar falling." Not to mention the door closing. The guard who had abandoned his post had gone somewhere else altogether.

Andre passed me his reins and approached the door. He grunted as he pushed it, leaning into it with his whole upper body. The door creaked open, its movement slow but steady.

"Damn, this thing is heavy," Andre muttered. "Aren't you going to help?"

"You seem to be doing well enough on your own." I dismounted and hobbled our horses.

A gasp caught my attention and I swivelled on my heel to face a thin, dirty child no older than twelve. He had one hand clamped over his mouth, and his eyes were wide with terror.

I raised my hands, palms open and empty. "We're not here to hurt you. In fact, I have a job for you."

The boy's eyes narrowed, but he didn't move. I offered what I hoped was a gentle smile and reached into my pocket, retrieving a single gold coin.

"You watch our horses," I said, tossing him the coin. "Take them into the temple stables and stay with them until we return."

He caught the money with both hands and stared at it, then at me. "What's to stop me from taking the horses, too?"

"You'll get another coin when we leave. Besides, you don't want to steal royal mounts. What was the punishment again?"

"Execution," Andre said. "By bloodletting."

All the colour drained from the boy's face. "R-right. Of course."

He hurried away, leading the horses. Andre crossed his arms over his chest and shook his head.

"Actual gold? He'll be lucky if he's not robbed by the first person he encounters."

"Maybe. Or maybe he'll be able to help his people." I strolled past Andre to enter the temple.

The main hall was filled with large statues of magical beasts—harpies, griffins, dragons, all creatures that used to roam the land—strategically placed to watch worshipers enter. A twenty-foot-tall statue of Magdalene stood behind the altar, her hands outstretched toward the rows of statues, as if she was giving life to them.

"Where do you think they are?" Andre eyed the statues as if they might actually spring to life at any moment.

"In there." I pointed at a stone door behind the altar. A green symbol consisting of several loops knotted together was painted on its centre.

"Are you sure?"

"The symbol represents Magdalene's holy order."

Andre grimaced but followed me across the room. Several trap runes along its length came to life as we approached the door, warning off anyone without the right blood—impressive spells, ones I imagined were beyond these telars. Few possessed both the telar gift and magic at the same time. Those who did were rarely skilled with either.

Or perhaps they weren't so impressive. I pressed one hand against the door, palm open.

It opened easily at my touch, without even a stinging sensation. Illusions, then. Still, strong enough to trick my eyes. Whoever cast them could prove dangerous.

I raised my sword and entered a small dining room. Eight men and one woman sat talking around a long table. Magical energy weighed on my shoulders the moment I entered, the blood-like stench of mortal magic tickling at my nose. The person it belonged to had diffused it with the room's air, making it impossible to tell who they were.

Eight guards, all wearing similarly mismatched armour and sporting more Slayer swords, rushed to meet us, swords raised. I lowered myself into a fighting stance.

Someone whistled, stopping the soldiers in their tracks.

A short man with shaggy auburn hair rose to face us, his eyes filled with naked rage. "What is the meaning of this?"

I blinked three times before I responded, surprised by the calm in his voice. He looked ready to burst a blood vessel. *Perhaps he's being controlled by someone else in the room.* Which meant somebody in this room was powerful enough, and well enough trained, to keep their hold on him despite our surprise entrance.

I sheathed my sword. We needed to proceed with caution.

"I am Riana," I said, "Guardian of Moonshadow. This is Andre Vonstone, the king's brother and most trusted emissary." The last part was still a lie, but it rolled off the tongue nicely.

"I don't care who you are," he said. "What do you want?"

"To speak with your council," I said.

"You kill our guards, deface our sacred space, and expect us to speak with you peacefully?"

"You will speak with us," Andre said. "The peaceful part is optional. But I'd like to remind you that we've already killed three of your guards. We won't hesitate to kill the rest."

The auburn-haired man opened his mouth to speak, but a young man with stark white hair raised a hand to silence him.

"Please, there is no need for further bloodshed. You are welcome to speak with us, and to share in our meal." The white-haired man gestured to a platter at the centre of the table, still laden with slices of meat. "Somebody grab chairs for our guests."

Everyone in the room scowled at his invitation, but nobody objected. The guards around us sheathed their swords. Two disappeared through a side door, likely for the chairs.

"Excellent," the white-haired man said. "Now, where are my manners? I am Aldaen, representative of Diseus."

"Thank you, Aldaen," I said. "We'll try to keep this short. I understand you have other matters to attend to."

"We appreciate the gesture," he said, leaning back in his chair. "Now, what is your business with us?"

"You know why we're here," Andre said. "There's a plague killing thousands of our people and someone in this swamp is responsible. If you know what's good for you, you'll tell us who it is."

So much for the diplomatic approach. I should have made him promise to let me do the talking. Not that I really trusted him to keep such a promise.

The auburn-haired man barked a laugh. "You came here to accuse us of starting a plague? What do you think we are, gods?"

Aldaen's eyes narrowed. "Or monsters?"

"Let's be clear." I leaned forward and let my face revert to its natural crimson form. "The only monster in this room is me. Even the plague's creator is human. If you help me, you will be rewarded. If you don't, you and anyone with even the slightest connection to this plague will be slaughtered."

We've learned to distrust rewards from the Vonstones. The woman's dispassionate mindvoice filled my head. From the way everyone turned to face her, she must have been projecting it into everyone's minds. *Why should we trust you?*

"Because if you don't help us," Andre said. "We'll start killing telars. And we'll keep killing them until we get the right one. Who knows? Maybe we won't stop then. Maybe we'll kill every damn—"

"None of that will be necessary," Aldaen said. "Our people have suffered enough. We don't know who did this, but we will help you."

The rest of the council glared at him, but no one challenged him. The woman nodded, though her glare was the deadliest of all.

"It's been a long day," the auburn-haired man said. "Perhaps you could return to discuss the details of our search tomorrow?"

"My companion's condition disagrees with sunlight. We will have our discussion now, or your village will be burnt to the ground by morning."

What little colour there was drained from his face. "You can't."

"Don't underestimate me." Something told me they were involved, but I didn't want to hurt anyone until I was certain. "How do you propose to help?"

He shifted the collar of his tunic to reveal a leather string holding a round, bluish-black pendant with sparkling silver runes carved into it. He lifted it off his neck and set it on the table. The dark material rippled, as if it was made of liquid rather than stone.

I sniffed twice, focusing on the spell. The enchantment was indeed powerful, the source of the magical energy in the air. It was also inactive, energy dispersed around it rather than concentrated.

"This pendant is one of the few Shalinoran relics remaining to my people," Aldaen said. "It's drawn to telars. The more powerful they are, the more powerfully it is drawn."

Many such pendants existed once, but the telars themselves never owned any. They didn't need help sensing each other. *So how did this one get here?*

"Won't it be confused by the other telars surrounding it?" Andre asked. "We're surrounded by you people."

Aldaen shook his head. "If there's a telar powerful enough to plague an entire kingdom, this necklace will be drawn to them above all others. Power like that is—well, frankly, unimaginable. Even the Shalinoran queens did not possess such power."

Some of the Shalinoran queens had, in fact, possessed such power, but mentioning that would expose my suspicions.

"If this relic is from the Shalinoran era, it should have no trouble locating her," I said instead.

Aldaen smiled and bowed. "None at all, my lady. But it does come with certain limitations. It can only be used at dawn."

Andre grimaced. "What did we say about the sun?"

I waved dismissively. "It's fine. I'll have an easier time with the relic anyway."

"Then we are agreed?" Aldaen asked.

"We are agreed." I held my hand out, palm open. "But I keep the relic tonight. Consider it a gesture of good will."

What do you offer in return? The woman's mindvoice filled my head again, powered by a surge of anger that filled my chest with searing heat.

I looked her over, considering her more carefully this time. She held herself like a noblewoman, keeping her back straight and meeting my eyes without hesitation. Her grey eyes were backed by a deep sadness, but her face looked like no emotion had ever touched it.

Could she be the plague's creator? A woman this young?

I pushed my magical energy toward her, testing, but nothing responded. She was a powerful telar, but she wasn't the mage.

I couldn't help being a bit relieved.

"We offer nothing," Andre said, "because you are in a position to demand nothing. And you will speak to me with your regular voice, not that cursed mindvoice."

The woman's mouth twitched. *I have only this voice.*

Andre scowled. "Then you will not speak to me at all."

Aldaen slid the pendant across the table. "Keep this with you tonight. The guards will see to it that you have comfortable accommodations."

Chapter Twenty-One

Comfortable accommodations in the telar swamp consisted of two identical narrow stone rooms in the basement, lit by oil lanterns rather than magic. The stiff beds and complete lack of decoration made them feel more like prison cells, but I didn't mind. Centuries spent in dungeons made it possible to sleep on anything, and I only planned to stay long enough to convince the servant hovering at the end of the hall that I was asleep. Hopefully, he would then go away.

Andre knocked—punched, really—my door twice in quick succession and entered without waiting for my response.

"What in the five realms are you doing?" he demanded. "We're here to interrogate them, not to negotiate. You don't really think that thing's a Shalinoran relic, do you?"

"It's powerful enough." The air around it crackled, and it stank like a pool of congealing blood. I hadn't seen a relic this powerful in centuries. "They're trying to help." I jerked my head to the left, trying to let him know about the servant eavesdropping around the corner.

He followed my gaze, wrinkling his nose as he did so. "I hope you're right."

"Trust me and get some rest."

"Rest? It's not even midnight. I've got enough energy to run a dozen laps around town."

"Then do it. It'll get you out of my face so I can sleep." I leaned forward and whispered the next words into his ear. "Or make them believe I'm asleep."

Realization dawned on his face, followed by a sheepish expression. "All right, I'll let you rest."

After he went back into his room, I returned my attention to the pendant, lifting it to the light.

I found the mark I was looking for almost immediately. A small, dark line near the top of the pendant that a regular person might mistake for a crack in the material.

I touched this mark and it transformed into a white symbol. An infinity loop with a crescent moon carved into one side.

The vanity of mages never failed. They marked every artifact they made with a signature. And I recognized this one.

Queen Corinthia's workshop was my favourite part of the castle, despite the heavy stench of mortal magic in the air. It buzzed with activity at any time of day or night, her many assistants toiling away at inventions. I loved learning about their projects, and they delighted in teaching me the details. They weren't allowed to discuss them with others, not even Princess Eternia.

Tonight, I wanted to learn more about the communication mirrors. Similar devices had existed for centuries, but only mages could use them. These mirrors would allow instant communication over almost any distance, regardless of a person's innate magic.

I made it two steps into the room before I spotted Queen Corinthia, poring over a sparkly black jewel. My mind told me to flee, but my body froze. The queen rarely came here anymore. What could she be doing here now, at this hour?

She placed the jewel on a nearby table and rubbed her eyes, then glanced around the room. She stopped when our eyes met.

I didn't know what that look meant, but it couldn't be good.

Her lips tightened into a thin line and she waved me over. I shuffled forward, eyes downcast.

"You're supposed to be protecting my daughter," she said, in the tone she usually reserved for nobles who misbehaved in court.

"Princess Eternia is asleep in her room, guarded by two of your best soldiers and several magical locks."

Queen Corinthia rose to her full height and grabbed my chin, forcing me to meet her eyes. She stood only slightly taller than me, but her presence filled the room. Her anger unfurled around her in the form of magic. I shrank in response, wishing I could leave. But running now would only infuriate her further, and I couldn't leave until my contract ended.

Or was ended.

"Assassins gained control of my soldiers before. They broke the magical locks. That's why I summoned you, remember? I needed someone completely immune to the telar gift."

"A decade has passed since then," I said. "Things are better now. There's peace—"

"Peace means nothing for people like us." She let go of my jaw and then picked up a crystal pen. Three runes flared to life along the side facing me. She carved a symbol into the black jewel, an infinity loop with a crescent moon tucked deftly into one side. "There will always be somebody who wants our power, and who is willing to kill for it. Like the Kelmans."

"The royal family of Torvaille? Surely you don't feel threatened by a kingdom of nonmagicals? Shalinor could crush them easily."

"It's not war that I'm afraid of." She set the jewel aside and her symbol vanished. "And I don't want to invade Torvaille. Or destroy them."

"Then what are you going to do?"

"Befriend them." She flipped over the jewel to reveal several more runes embedded into the stone with pure silver. "This pendant will help them detect telars in their homeland. Shalinor once gifted similar pendants to Estefar's rulers."

"And they used them to enslave thousands." Estefar's mages rose to power on the backs of telar slaves, and the pendants she spoke of allowed them to find those slaves. Those gifts, given before the Shalinorans understood the Estefaran mages, ruined hundreds of families' lives for generations, and would continue ruining them until Estefar fell.

"What they do with their telars is not our concern. My duty is to the people who live within our borders."

"How can you say that?" The words fell out of my mouth before I could stop them. Since I was already in trouble, I continued. "I've seen the way those telars are forced to live. It's...it's awful." They didn't get the worst of it, either. That was reserved for the nonmagicals who worked under the telar slaves' control.

"War would be worse for all of us," she said. "Get back to my daughter's room. She is only safe when you are by her side."

The jewel I saw then didn't shimmer this way, but if Aldaen told the truth, it was the same kind of pendant. Corinthia must have made more. How many? Who did she give them to?

If only that first job had lasted longer, if only I had found some way to make Corinthia trust me, then I might know.

But I had failed Eternia, and Corinthia had died with her.

I cursed and shoved the pendant into one of the pouches on my belt. I'd figure it out at dawn.

First, I wanted to figure out the people who gave it to me. I closed my eyes and focused on sound, letting my hearing grow to its full potential.

Hundreds of noises filled my head, the farthest ones layered on top of the closest ones. My head throbbed with the weight of them. I dug my fingers into my thigh, the sharp pain a welcome distraction. I forced myself to breathe slowly, deeply. I sorted through the sounds, one layer at a time, pushing each sound out of my mind as soon as I acknowledged it.

Andre pacing in the room beside me. The servant still waiting in the hall, drifting off toward sleep. Forty-five people sleeping, most in underground chambers. Twelve servants sleeping in a single, long room at the far end of the basement. Two men walking upstairs, in the main hall, speaking in hushed tones.

"I still think this is a bad idea. What if she wins? What if she comes after us?"

"She's not omniscient," Aldaen said. "She'll never believe we sold her out. If she does, we'll say they tortured us."

I stiffened. *She* could only be the plague's creator. But, their plan was to sell her out? Why?

They went through a door, entering the stables, and I returned my focus to listening, straining to hear them above the horses' excitement.

"I hope you're right."

"When have I ever led you astray?" Aldaen asked.

"There's a first time for everything. Farewell, Aldaen. We'll keep in touch."

"Always," Aldaen said.

A horse left the stables, breaking into a trot when it cleared the door. Aldaen strode back into the temple, heading to a room directly above my own. From the sounds of things hitting the floor as he walked across it, this was most likely his bedchamber.

I opened my eyes and shut out the sounds of the temple. I didn't need to hear anymore. Aldaen was vulnerable now, and he was going to tell me everything.

I strapped my sword to my back and went to Andre's room. I, at least, waited for him to respond to my knock before entering.

Andre had his shirt off, his sword across his lap, and a polishing cloth in his hand. He welcomed me with his usual grin, but it disappeared when he saw my expression.

"I take it you're not here for company."

"If I wanted company, I'd seek it somewhere else." I gestured at his naked chest, which I liked more than I cared to admit. "Get dressed. We might be leaving before dawn."

He sheathed his sword and tucked the polishing cloth into his belt. "Care to tell me what's going on?"

"I'm on my way to find out."

A sound at the end of the hall caught my attention. The servant that had been watching us was now running upstairs, toward Aldaen's room.

"Shit. I've got to go."

I ran after the servant, hurtling around the corner. He disappeared onto the second landing as I reached the bottom of the stairs. I took them two at a time, pushing my nails into claws as I did so. I wouldn't have time for the sword.

He was at Aldaen's door when I cleared the stairs. I growled and leapt at him, my claws grazing his face as he fell backward into Aldaen's chamber.

"What is the meaning of this?" Aldaen asked, his voice an octave higher than normal.

The servant blubbered something unintelligible as he scrambled away from me. I drew my sword and entered the room.

The temple itself was ostentatious, but Aldaen's chamber was exactly what I would have imagined for a priest in the telar swamp. Only slightly bigger than my guest room and filled with some of the shabbiest furniture I had ever seen.

Aldaen, too, looked shabby now, in a grey cotton nightshirt. He had an axe, but his arms shook so violently I doubted he would be able to swing it.

"What are you doing here?" His voice shook almost as badly as his arms. "Why are you trying to kill my servant?"

"I only wanted to knock him out so we could speak in private." I took three steps forward. Now his servant lay at my feet, curled into a ball and crying.

"Let him go, and we will speak alone."

I moved sideways, giving the servant a clear path to the door. "I'm happy to."

The servant didn't notice, too busy crying into the collar of his tunic. Aldaen grimaced and kicked the man.

"Get out of here," he said.

The servant's eyes widened, and he jumped to his feet. "Th-thank you sir." He bowed and darted out of the room.

I advanced toward Aldaen. "You already know who is behind the plague."

To his credit, his expression didn't change at all. He must have spent years training for this moment.

I would think about the meaning of that later.

"I don't know who it is."

"You don't get it, do you?" I sneered. "I heard you walking your friend to the stables. You're going to tell me tomorrow, anyway. Why delay the inevitable?"

"I think you misunderstood what I said."

"Really? I believe your exact words were, 'she won't believe we sold her out.'"

Aldaen lowered his axe. "You heard correctly." This time he lowered his voice, too. "But you misunderstand. I know nothing about the plague's creator. Only the woman who speaks for her. Fiona, the woman on our council."

I grimaced. I should have known. The way she carried herself, like the most important person in any room she entered. The way everyone in the room reacted to her mindvoice. She was different, stronger than the others. The perfect representative for an even more powerful telar who wished to remain hidden.

"What do you mean, speaks for its creator?"

He sat on his bed, laying his axe down beside him. "She's always been vocal at meetings. This year, she admitted that she's been speaking on behalf of another woman—one who created the plague as vengeance against the Vonstones."

My blood ran cold. I advanced farther into the room, my sword still raised and ready to slice through his neck at a single false move. "Vengeance for your people or vengeance for herself?"

He shrugged. "She says it's vengeance for us, and maybe it is for some, but my people don't want the Vonstones dead. We want them to leave us alone. For the past ten years, they have." He offered me a bitter smile. "Though I suppose that's over now."

"It can start again if you tell me everything Fiona said."

"She wants us to accept her as our new ruler." His hands balled into fists. "Not Fiona, the plague's creator. A woman who's never set foot in this swamp."

I tilted my head to the side, a terrible idea dawning on me for the first time. What if this plague was created by one of Estefar's slaves, working with their masters? What if Estefar wanted to conquer Moonshadow, and the one safe—if miserable—place telars had to live? "She's never been in the swamp? Do you know where she comes from?"

"Not a clue. That's what bothers me so much. We don't know anything about her, except that Fiona expects us to trust her."

"But you don't."

He chuckled. "I don't even trust Fiona. So, I'll tell you that she and her brother left."

"Her brother?"

"The man with auburn hair. Allister. He speaks for the telars in Conall and the surrounding towns."

This situation continued to get worse. Conall was the biggest city, really the only city, in the swamp. If Fiona's brother controlled it, then she effectively controlled it, or, more accurately, the woman behind her did. "And he's already pledged their allegiance to the plague's creator, I assume?"

"I don't know. We barely had time to discuss it before someone interrupted our meeting."

I didn't quite believe him, but I didn't have time to press the issue. Every moment we talked, Fiona got farther away. "Where did they go?"

"To the south gate," Aldaen said. "From there, who knows?"

I raised an eyebrow. "I would imagine you do."

"You imagine wrong. Their lack of trust is why I'm telling you anything at all."

I narrowed my eyes. "If I find out you're lying, I'll be back for your head."

One side of his mouth curved upward. "I would expect nothing less."

I shot him a final, scathing look and ran out of the room. I pushed my thoughts outwards as I ran, mentally calling out to Rolf and hoping against hope that he was still awake to hear me.

What's wrong? Rolf's thoughts came slowly, heavy with grogginess.

I need help finding someone. I sent an image of Fiona and her brother with the words. *They left together, but might have separated. I want the woman.*

Is she the one who cursed Moonshadow?

No. She works for them.

So you need to question her.

Exactly. They went south, from where I am. I almost collided with Andre at the bottom of the stairs, running headfirst into a wall instead. *Tell me when you find them.*

"Sorry," Andre said, "I heard shouting—"

"Let's go." I grabbed Andre's arm and dragged him toward the stables. "We've got to find the woman."

Andre's brow furrowed. "The woman from the council?"

"I'll explain on the way."

Chapter Twenty-Two

Kahri

The thought hit me on the way to my observatory—a message laced with so much fear that it almost knocked me over. I steadied myself with the wall and lowered myself onto the stairs, the message bouncing around in my head.

They know it's you.

A single, simple sentence, but it was the beginning of the end.

I didn't have to ask who "they" were. I'd made a mistake. Driven by fantasies of revenge and intoxicated by my own power, I infected Moonshadow's prince. It was my crowning achievement, throwing them into chaos. Destroying the Vonstones, my sworn allies, who abandoned me in my darkest hour.

I only noticed his gift when he asked me a question: *Why are you hurting me?*

The smart thing to do would have been to kill him instantly. To overwhelm his little body before he told anyone about me, and make sure nobody else discovered the true nature of my plague.

But I couldn't bring myself to do it. The boy was too sweet. The innocent way he asked, the sweetness of his mindvoice almost broke me. I offered to buy his silence by ending his sickness instead.

He refused, with a righteous tone that made me smile. It sounded so much like myself when I was young.

I liked him. I let him live.

Now I walked to the edge of my tower, grabbed the wall and leaned out the window as far as I dared, letting the wind whip my hair around. A thousand years earlier, I watched my sister jump from this tower while our people died around us. I prevented the Estefaran soldiers from looting and pillaging the city, ensured the preservation of its buildings, but I had already lost the one thing that mattered. My family.

It took me three days to realize what I had done. Three days of wandering around my perfect city, wondering why I felt so empty.

No matter what I did, I would never fill that void. Restoring Galvan and even Caerwyn, my dearest servant, could only fill tiny sections of the massive hole in my heart.

When I let Marcus live, I accepted that it would eventually mean my undoing. Welcomed it, even.

I had only hoped it wouldn't come so soon.

My orb helped me press into the boy's mind, searching for hints of what I was up against.

The images came at once, bold and vibrant. A demon summoned to hunt me down, the prince's vampiric uncle, and—a dragon. Nothing like the great winged beasts my ancestors once controlled, but a dragon nonetheless. A snake of the sky, with silver fur that shimmered when light hit it.

The dragon pulled its lips back, revealing fangs taller than a human. I cursed and expelled the image from my mind.

I lay on the cold stone floor and stared at the ceiling, all hope drained out of me. With a dragon, they could arrive any day now. My plans would be destroyed, along with the souls I had already restored. The man I restored the day before, Caerwyn's husband Ellial, had drained too much of my energy for me to fight. I didn't know how long it would be before the power came back. The process took longer every time.

No. I couldn't believe they were on their way. I had to believe I had time. Time to make a plan, to protect my city and—

"This is the end, you know," said a familiar male voice.

I straightened and there was Loki, dressed in the black robes my people wore to mourn. His expression showed no hint of his usual mischievousness, only a deep sadness that shook me to my core. Even during the final days of the war, he had never lost his joking nature.

"I said your rule must end, even if your life did not." He stared into my eyes without wavering, without blinking.

We had made love many times, but I had never felt so naked before him. I couldn't look away, either, frozen by fear—or perhaps by his magic. It was impossible to tell.

"You should have listened."

I still couldn't look away, but my voice worked this time. "I did listen. For five centuries, I listened—"

"No, for five centuries you plotted." He smiled, but it didn't reach his eyes. "I always knew, of course. It was one of the things I liked about you."

Memories of us flooded my mind. Lying in bed together, holding each other, kissing each other, laughing with each other.

"Did you?" I asked.

"Did I what?"

I balled my hands into fists. "Did you like me? Or did you want to watch me suffer until I became determined enough to break the rules? Was I just another mortal toy?"

He frowned. "I cared for you deeply. Still do. But even I must do my part to maintain the natural order of things."

"And what is that order?"

"Riana will kill you," he said. "I chose her."

"Y-you..." I shouldn't have been surprised. He knew my weaknesses better than anyone, could select the perfect demon to destroy me.

He held a finger to my lips, then leaned forward and kissed me. I softened, unable to resist his warmth. He pressed me to him and wrapped his arms around me. I buried my face in his neck. I had missed this. He hadn't come to me in so many years, I almost forgot how good his touch felt.

"Make sure your people leave before she gets here," Loki said. "I'd hate to see all those centuries of work go to waste."

"You should do it yourself. It's only fitting," I muttered. He was the one who got me into this mess, after all. He convinced me to make one final stand against Estefar, to agree to his rules.

He kissed my forehead. "I can't."

"What do you—"

He vanished, leaving me cold and alone. I fell to my knees, tears soaking my cheeks. For the first time in centuries, I knew true fear.

Chapter Twenty-Three

I found her! Rolf's thought rode a wave of excitement that brought a reluctant grin to my face. *She's alone, riding southeast. What do you want me to do?*

"Can we go now?" Andre asked, reining his horse in beside mine.

I raised a hand to silence him. *How far southeast?*

Rolf responded with an image of the land below him. He was flying much lower than normal, so this only showed me a small tract of land, but it was enough. Diseus remained visible on the horizon, Magdalene's temple sticking out above the wall.

Keep eyes on her. If she turns onto another road, let me know. Two hostages always proved better than one, especially if they had a close relationship. *We'll be there soon.*

"Yes," I said to Andre. "We'll take the first southwest fork in the road."

He grinned. "Now you're talking."

We maintained a solid canter for the next two hours. I wanted to gallop, but we simply couldn't risk it on this muddy road. Breaking one of our horses' legs would cost more than any time we might gain.

Her horse is slowing down. Rolf still circled overhead, sticking to cloud-covered patches of sky to conceal his form. *You'll catch up soon.*

I drew my sword. *How soon?*

Any moment now.

I heard her now, too, or at least her horse, trying to pick its way past the mud holes.

Think you can scare her off her horse? I asked. "We're almost there," I added, for Andre's sake.

He went to draw his sword, but I shook my head. If my plan worked, we wouldn't need weapons.

A shadow darted across the moon, and Rolf came crashing out of the sky, landing with enough force to shake the ground. He lifted his head and let out a great roar. A stream of fire burst out of his mouth, throwing the flooded road into sharp relief, briefly, before it fizzled out.

Any regular horse would have reared and galloped away, terrified for its life. Even my Vonstone-bred stallion flattened its ears and backed up several paces before I could calm him.

Fiona's mare, however, remained calm and still. The beast turned to face us with a slow, controlled movement that was altogether unlike any horse I had met.

No, those movements were human, passed from Fiona's mind to the mare's. In another lifetime I had watched Eternia train her gift by doing the same thing.

I nudged my horse forward one step, then two. He was reluctant to approach Rolf, but he obeyed my commands. Good. She couldn't control more than one at a time.

I drew my sword. "Fiona of Conall, you are under arrest for treason. If you answer our questions, we might be convinced to let you live."

She made an awful croaking sound that might have been a laugh. *That information is worth far more than my life. Or anything else you're authorized to negotiate with.*

"Get to the point," Andre said, bringing his horse up beside mine.

If your king wants to know who I'm working for, he'll have to ask me himself. And before I answer, I'll need him to agree to some terms.

"My brother would never negotiate with the likes of you," Andre spat out.

Fiona made the croaking sound again. Definitely a laugh. *You'd be surprised what a man becomes willing to do when his family is on the line.*

Are you sure you don't want me to roast her? Rolf asked, rather hopefully.

My lips twitched into a smile. *We need her alive.*

"Why would we let you anywhere near our king?" I asked. "You don't trust the Vonstones. You're more likely to attempt an assassination than a negotiation."

Desperation makes people predictable. If it comforts you, I'll swear a blood oath not to hurt him, now or in the future.

Andre and I exchanged looks. Blood oaths were serious business, fatal to anyone who broke them. A blood oath with a demon did something even worse to a person's body, mutilating it beyond recognition. She would be lucky if she even completed the harmful act before it twisted her insides apart.

Perhaps she really did want to negotiate.

Fiona raised her eyes toward the sky. It was beginning to transition from black to grey. *You really ought to make a decision.*

Andre's face contorted with rage. "There's no—"

"You must swear another oath as well," I broke in.

And what is that?

"To immediately cease communications with the person who created this plague."

The croaking sound came again, filling the air between us. *Consider it done.*

I tied Fiona up and dragged her to the campsite Andre found us, a blissfully large patch of solid, dry ground. Rolf coiled his body in a circle around it, preventing both attack and escape.

We got our tents up without a moment to spare. Andre all but fell into his, overcome by the exhaustion that came with sunrise. I, on the other hand, had no intention of sleeping.

I sat cross-legged in front of Fiona and draped my sword across my knees. Somehow, she appeared even more regal now, despite being covered in muck and tied up. Her back remained straight, her expression neutral, her gaze unwavering as she met my eyes.

"I accepted your deal to get Andre inside before sunrise," I said. "But I need more answers before I'll agree to any blood oath." Breaking a blood oath was fatal, but perhaps dying was part of her plan. "If I don't like your answers, I'll kill you."

Her mouth tightened into a thin line. *I will only speak to your king.*

"I have other questions. About who caused this plague."

I may answer, but it will cost you.

"You aren't in a position to make demands." I patted my sword for emphasis.

She smirked. *You need my information.*

Part of me wanted to run my sword through her smug face, but she was right. I needed her information, and I didn't know another way to get it. "You're wasting my time. What do you really want?"

She rolled her eyes. *Do I have to repeat everything? I want to negotiate on behalf of my people. I want to trade.*

"For what?"

Freedom. To walk anywhere we want, live anywhere we want, and work anywhere we want. To thrive, as our ancestors did.

I tilted my head to the side. This woman seemed far too cold to hold such idealistic goals. "You don't really believe a single piece of information is worth all that, do you?"

Her smirk grew into a wide, sadistic smile. *Oh, but I do. And I'm prepared to die protecting this information if your king disagrees.*

There wasn't even a hint of hesitation, in her thoughts or her expression. "You wanted us to catch you."

I have a reputation to maintain.

I bit back a curse. How did she know we would even be there? What else did she have planned? How much had Andre and I already played into her games?

This woman might not be the plague's creator, but she was to be feared all the same.

Shall we make the oath? My arms are going numb.

"One more question." The one that had really been bothering me this whole time. "Why did you agree to break your alliance with the plague's creator so easily?"

Fiona's smile faded, and she looked away for the first time. *We both want freedom, but she wants to gain it by conquering Moonshadow. I want to gain it by forcing Moonshadow to recognize us as equal citizens.*

"And you think this is your chance to make that happen."

She nodded. *Without starting a war.*

In other circumstances, it might have been an admirable goal. "Is this really better?"

The plague hasn't touched my people.

"So, you don't care how many of Moonshadow's citizens have to die, only how many of them are your kind?"

They care no more about our lives.

I grimaced at the reflection in my blade. She was right. The people of Moonshadow hated telars, feared them. They would shed no tears over a plague devastating the swamp. Nor would they lift a finger to stop it.

I sheathed my sword. Fiona wouldn't die today.

"I will give you the words," I said, reaching under my sleeve to unclip the dagger there. The small blade was much better suited to a job like this. "You must speak them exactly. If you try to give yourself a loophole, I will kill you."

She nodded and held her hands out. I sliced through the rope. After this, it wouldn't be necessary. She would be a willing companion, or she would be dead.

"Your words are 'I will go to Moon Spire to negotiate with King Jacob VIII. I will not harm King Jacob VIII, his family, or his servants so long as I am there. I will not manipulate the King's family, servants, guards, or Slayers into harming any member of the Vonstone family. I will no longer communicate with the creator of the telar plague, or help her spread it.'"

She scowled. *This is quite the oath.*

"I am something of an expert on blood oaths," I said. "And the ways around them." That expertise was what landed me in this situation in the first place. "Do you agree to my terms?"

She huffed but took the dagger. *Your terms are reasonable.*

"Good. The final words are 'I swear all of these things, with an oath from my blood to yours.'"

Fiona put the knife to her palm and slowly pressed the blade in. Blood welled up around the cut and pooled with each word she spoke.

I will go to Moon Spire to negotiate with King Jacob VIII. I will not harm King Jacob VIII, his family, or his servants. I will not manipulate King Jacob VIII's family, servants, guards, or Slayers into harming any member of the Vonstone family. I will no longer communicate with the creator of the telar plague, or help her spread it. I swear all of these things with an oath, from my blood to yours.

She drew the knife down and across her palm, deepening the cut, and handed me the blade. I made a single, long cut, pushing the knife into my hand until it scraped against the bone. Reddish-black blood covered the blade, gleaming in the morning sun.

I grabbed Fiona's hand and pressed her palm against mine, letting the blood mix together. "I accept this oath, from your blood to mine."

Our blood combined, and a surge of terribly hot energy raced through my veins, filling my body. Fiona's hand tightened around my own and her jaw clenched, but she didn't pull away. Her body glowed with a faint reddish-black aura, then shuddered and collapsed, her nails tearing the back of my hand as she fell.

She groaned, or perhaps it was another attempt at laughter. *That hurt more than I expected.*

"Blood magic is supposed to hurt." It was the only magic every human alive could perform, but the cost was high. "Get some rest. We leave at sunset."

I wiped the dagger clean and went to meditate in my tent, hoping some solitude would clear my head.

Did she tell you who created the plague? Rolf's mindvoice was as enthusiastic as ever. Was there anything he didn't get excited about?

No, but she will.

I hope she tells you soon. The Queen doesn't have much longer.

I bit my lip. I had forgotten the queen was sick, too busy thinking about how to save Moonshadow's heir. But if she died, Jacob VIII's spiral into madness would only accelerate.

Saving Moonshadow was starting to look like an impossible task.

Chapter Twenty-Four

We arrived in Moon Spire around midnight on the night of the new moon. Rolf flew ahead to the castle. Heavy rain greeted us, the clouds releasing their burden as we entered the city gates.

At this hour, most cities were asleep, but Moon Spire still pulsed with activity. People spilled out of bars, some celebrating and others instigating belligerent arguments. Sex workers peddled their wares, collecting bar patrons on their way home. City guards patrolled the streets, discouraging brawlers.

But the city was also alive with something else: the sounds and smells of death. The burners, magical pyres designed to dispose of bodies rapidly in times of plague and war, filled the city with a terrible, stinking smoke. Around us, people struggled to squeeze another moment's life out of their wasted bodies, coughing, hacking, and spitting up blood. A man stumbled out of a bar and collapsed in the street, gasping for air.

The faces of the sick multiplied as we approached Ashe's temple. Dozens of sick people surrounded it, crowding a young priest with a cart full of potions. They spilled down the stairs onto the street, blocking our way. The priest handed out tinctures as quickly as he could, but it wasn't fast enough. He didn't have enough for this many people.

We had been gone a little over two weeks, and things were easily ten times worse.

I brought my horse to a halt and raised my hand to signal for Andre to do the same.

He moved his horse to stand beside mine. Fiona's mare stopped behind him, without her so much as touching the reins.

Another young priest emerged with more potions. He noticed us and whispered something to the first priest, then handed over his supplies and disappeared back into the temple.

A man sitting near the bottom of the steps coughed. Blood spurted from his mouth and drained into a sewer grate only a few feet away from me. The man doubled over, the coughing fit wracking his skinny body. A woman standing behind him knelt to hold him. Her neck bore the plague's marks too.

Is there a reason you stopped us? Fiona asked, her mindvoice filled with the self-important impatience of a noble forced to wait in the king's court.

I gave her the darkest look I could muster. I understood the nobles who were waited on hand and foot for their entire lives, but how did one acquire such a petulant, superior attitude in a place as miserable as the telar swamp?

"This is why you're here." I gestured at the nearest group of plague victims. "These people are going to die if you don't help us. Every. Single. One."

She shrugged. *Many of my people have died in plagues. Moonshadow didn't help them.*

"Moonshadow didn't create those plagues either."

Cameron appeared at the temple door. Dark circles had grown under his eyes. He scanned the crowd while some of the sickest grabbed at his robes. He absently said prayers for them, his gaze still searching, but his face lit up when he saw us.

The high priest pushed through the crowd toward us, stopping twice along the way to pray over dying people. He stopped a few feet away from me and bowed low. "The city's deteriorating. The plague strikes more every day. Our healing rooms are full. Now we can only send them home with pain relievers and prayers."

"Marcus?" I asked.

Cameron grimaced. "He rarely goes farther than the bathroom now, and even has to be carried there sometimes. Do you have a cure?"

A sharp pain pierced my chest. "No, but we have what we need to find it."

He looked meaningfully at our new companion. "Then I suppose I should let you return to the castle."

"Yes," I said. "May Ashe's blessings be with you. Take care of the people, Cameron."

"Of course. May her blessings also be with you."

He stepped back and we rode away.

Jacob VIII stood waiting for us on the castle steps, dressed in greyish-white robes of mourning. Dark, greasy strands of hair poked out from under his lilandium helmet. The circles under his eyes were even larger than the ones Cameron now sported.

My heart plummeted like a stone. Had Marcus died *now*, moments before we arrived? I dismounted, and the others followed suit. Three servants came to lead away our horses. Jacob VIII didn't speak until our horses were gone. He was too busy staring at Fiona.

"I told you to kill the plague's creator, not bring her here."

"She's not the plague's creator," I said.

His face darkened. "Then who, in the five realms, is she?"

"She has the information we need to end this plague," I said. "She came to trade for it."

He rounded on Fiona, sizing her up for the third time. "What exactly do you know?"

I know who caused the plague and where to find her. I'll tell you everything, if you agree to my terms. Fiona remained as calm as ever, both in her mindvoice and in her expression.

Jacob VIII's face darkened further. "Who do you think—"

"Who is it?" Andre asked, gesturing to the robes. "Is Marcus..." He trailed off, staring at his feet.

"Isabella. Yesterday." Jacob VIII said, all the fierceness drained out of his voice. He brought himself back up to his full height. "We'll continue this conversation in my office."

Cold dread filled me, making every little hair stand at attention. I followed the king without argument. The last thing I needed was for him to use the compulsion.

Jacob VIII's office was a disaster zone. Paperwork lay scattered across his desk, covering everything but a single corner, where a bottle of brandy and an obsidian tankard sat. A thick cloud of wakara, an incense often used to induce a state of meditative calm, permeated the air.

The king sat heavily and took a long swig of his drink. His hand shook when he held the vessel to his lips. I couldn't tell if it was from weakness or drunkenness.

A servant brought extra chairs and arranged them around the fallen papers. Another servant brought a glass of wine for me and a bottle of blood for Andre.

I took the seat directly across from Jacob VIII, hoping this would encourage him to direct most of his venom at me. Bringing Fiona here had been my decision, after all.

Andre sat on my left. Fiona didn't move. She watched Jacob VIII with a wary expression.

"Sit, woman." Jacob VIII took another swig of his brandy.

Her mouth twitched, but she obeyed, perching on the edge of the third chair. *I am Fiona of Conall. I speak for the telar people and I will be treated as a diplomat, not a prisoner.*

Jacob VIII glared at her. "How dare you address me with your mindvoice, not once, but twice? Speak like a normal woman."

"She's mute," I said quickly.

"You brought me a damn mute? You expect me to talk to her like this?"

I narrowed my eyes. "I expect you to do what is best for your kingdom, Your Majesty. Talking to her is the fastest way to get the answers we need."

"Make it quick. I have funeral arrangements to complete."

I will not simply give you information. Fiona's mindvoice was even colder than normal. *This must be a trade, between your people and mine.*

"You dare to give me terms?" He took another gulp of brandy, slamming his tankard on the desk. Brandy sloshed over the rim, soaking a stack of papers. He paid it no mind. "I am a king. A king with a dragon and a demon. I could have your towns burnt to a crisp with your people inside before the sun rises."

Fiona's solemn expression didn't change. *And you still wouldn't have cured this plague.*

Jacob VIII said nothing, his eyes suddenly distant, as if he was doing mental math. His scowl grew more pronounced as the moments passed, and he came to the only possible conclusion. Fiona was right. She had kept the identity of the plague's creator a secret, even from her own people, to make herself irreplaceable. Without her, it might take years to discover the perpetrator.

Years Marcus didn't have.

Jacob VIII leaned back, now cradling his drink in one shaky hand. "What are your terms?"

You will not retaliate against my people for the actions of an outsider.

His lips curved upwards slightly, almost enough to be a smile. "That's easy enough."

She returned his half smile. *I'm not done. You will recognize my people as full citizens of Moonshadow. We will be allowed to begin new lives outside the swamp. We will be permitted to work anywhere we want, doing anything we are capable of. Our children will go to the same schools as your children.*

All three of us gaped at her. I knew she wanted peace, but this?

It would be a miracle if this worked.

"For a single piece of information?" Jacob VIII spat. "You can't be serious."

"She is nothing if not serious," I said.

Andre nodded. "Our people's lives are at stake here. Marcus's life."

Jacob VIII finished his drink, wrinkling his nose as if the brandy scorched his insides. He set the tankard down and wiped his mouth with his sleeve.

He might even send me home, after all of this. My heart slowed at the thought. I couldn't go back there, I couldn't—

"So be it," Jacob VIII turned back to Fiona. "But if you lie, I will burn Conall to the ground."

Fiona smiled for real this time. *Her mindvoice is the most powerful one I know. She lives far to the east, in an ancient ruin.*

A heavy, stunned silence filled the air between us. Everyone knew the legend of Kahri, the last queen and—according to the stories—the sole survivor of Riminira's final battle. Many people had attempted to rob Riminira's corpse of its treasure. None had returned. Legend said Kahri killed them herself.

Loki's face flashed through my mind. "All stories are rooted somewhere in truth," he had said—about Dragon's Keep. At least, I had thought it was about Dragon's Keep. What if he had been talking about something, some*one*, else entirely?

Her name is Kahri.

This time we stared in horror, not shock. Fiona remained untouched by our expressions, keeping her own icy gaze on the king.

For several agonizing moments, the only sounds were everyone breathing and my own heart slowly beating.

"But—why?" Jacob VIII asked at last.

Moonshadow abandoned their alliance with Shalinor the moment it became risky. She has every reason to strike at you.

"She has reason to strike my family, but the people did nothing to wrong her."

The people of Moonshadow persecuted our kind for generations. They are all guilty, in her eyes. Fiona shifted her weight. *Now, I would like to discuss my return to my people. I intend to leave at dawn.*

The king laughed. "You will return when this plague is over, or not at all. Riana, accompany this woman to one of the lilandium cells."

Fiona's composure vanished at the mention of lilandium, replaced by open-mouthed horror. *Lilandium is torture for my people. I am a diplomat, not a prisoner. I will be treated with respect.*

"You are a prisoner until I've determined the truth of your words," he said. "Riana, get this woman out of my face. We'll meet in the advisors' chamber at sunset tomorrow."

I nodded and grabbed Fiona's elbow. She glared but allowed me to lead her away.

The cold that settled over my body as we walked away was a new kind of dread, one that increased with every step. Queen Kahri, the last survivor of humanity's first civilization. A woman who lost everything doing the thing I had once asked Queen Corinthia to do—stand up for telars in other nations.

I threw Fiona into her cell, told her breakfast would arrive in the morning, and headed for my bedchamber. At least, my body did. My mind was too busy thinking about Kahri, about the war, about—

Demons poured into the inner family's court from every direction—dozens of them, no, hundreds. The room was too crowded to count them all.

A new platform jutted out of the floor at the far end of the long room, its base stood taller than the largest demon in the crowd. The Master appeared on this platform as the final group filtered into the room. He clicked his teeth together with a loud, grating sound.

"Welcome, one and all. Today is a momentous day for our kind. The largest summoning in history. Three hundred demons have been called." He paused to allow for the collective gasp.

"Three hundred?" The crowd felt big enough to be three hundred, but who would summon so many demons at once, sacrifice so many human lives? What kind of monster could even suggest such a thing?

"The mages of Estefar call upon you to end their war with Shalinor," the Master said.

The Master continued to speak, but I didn't hear him, overwhelmed by the images in my head. My childhood in Estefar, an endless series of torments that had grown worse every year. My thirteenth birthday, hiding in Ma's safe house while slavers combed our town for nonmagicals.

My fourteenth birthday. My transformation. Ma's death. Centuries of torment, followed by—

Followed by a decade of Eternia's face, of sunlight and joy, of peace—all in Shalinor. The first glimpse of happiness I knew in centuries. The only glimpse of happiness I knew for many centuries afterwards.

I failed Shalinor then, failed to see Eternia's madness until she ruined everything.

"I can't," I whispered, as the other demons cheered around me. "Shalinor—I can't."

I didn't, either. When we arrived in the mortal realm, I let another demon take my sacrifice. He was too bloodthirsty to even notice. He and two hundred and ninety-eight other demons went to end the war. With my contract only halfway complete, I felt no compulsion to join the war, or return to the demon realm. I stayed behind, cleaning up the hall where they had summoned us, and making it my home for several centuries.

The demons ended the war, but Kahri's final spell killed them all, along with everything else for hundreds of miles. I was presumed dead, and I had no desire to disillusion the inner family. I led a quiet life to avoid divine notice and expected to spend the rest of my days in the mortal realm.

Five-hundred-odd years later, I accidentally killed a descendant of my sacrifice. His blood was the most delicious thing I ever tasted, and it gave me an enormous power. I hadn't realized how much I lost, neglecting my unfulfilled contract, until this blood filled my veins. I was as powerful as the morning I left the demon realm, maybe even more so.

This power served as a beacon, bringing Loki to me. I was grateful, then, that it was only him and not the other gods. Or the inner family.

Now I was in my office, drinking a bottle of the king's best brandy like it was water and thinking that perhaps the inner family's torture would have been preferable after all.

Halfway through the bottle, I uncovered my black mirror and conjured an image of Loki into my mind, with the last face I saw him wearing. This time he appeared instantly. His usual careless grin irritated me even more than normal. I longed to smash my bottle through it and his scheming head, consequences be damned.

"You sent me here to kill Kahri." I had so many questions, but those were the only words that came out.

He shrugged. "You were supposed to end the war. In a way, your punishment is being forced to complete the contract you abandoned."

The shock in my chest ignited into a ball of hot rage. "You bastard, you know why I didn't fight in that war."

"Are you still that attached to Princess Eternia? She's been dead for thousands of years. Shalinor has been dead for centuries."

"Kahri is alive." And probably the last living member of Eternia's family. "You can't ask me to destroy Shalinor's legacy."

Loki's eyes narrowed. "What about Moonshadow's legacy? Didn't you love this kingdom, once, too? Doesn't some part of you still love Jacob III?"

I grimaced. "What do you know about love?"

Loki's expression darkened. "I have lived through endless centuries, since long before your birth. You know nothing of the love I have felt." He vanished.

I stared at the mirror for a long time, drinking slower now and mulling his words over in my head. In all these centuries—Loki brought me to the demon realm when I started changing—I had never seen him so serious. Who could he have loved that much? Gods weren't easily impressed, least of all him.

After a while, I crawled into bed and wrapped myself in the comfort of my blankets, my mind filled with thoughts of Loki and Kahri and Riminira.

Death might prove preferable to freedom after all.

Chapter Twenty-Five

Malthis cackled and drove his claws through my kneecaps. My body was a bloody mass, its edges starting to shift into fog. I had long ago gone numb with shock. Soon, I would lose my form, then my life. Nobody was saving me now. Nobody would gather me back together.

I flailed outward with the little that remained of my right hand, desperately searching for anything, even a loose piece of ground, that I could use to hit Malthis.

My left hand closed on the hilt of his abandoned sword and I coalesced all of my essence in my arm, swinging with every bit of strength I had left. Something heavy and warm and textured hit my face and rolled off. Malthis collapsed on top of me, blood soaking what remained of my face. The magic in his blood mingled with my own as my body put itself back together, filling my mind with a strange, pulsating buzz.

I don't know how many moments passed before I realized the crowd was silent. Too silent.

I didn't need eyes to know why. I had felt it hit my face. Malthis's head.

I had broken the arena's most sacred rule. One of our family was dead.

The Master's grip tightened on my wrist, crushing the bone. I screamed. He laughed and dropped me.

"So easy to torment," he said. "This will be a fun decade."

Temric moved to stand beside me. "Master, Malthis disgraced our family many times. We agreed if he did so again, we would kill him ourselves. This one did us a favour, getting rid of him. Might I suggest a lighter punishment?"

The Master clicked his teeth together. "What did you have in mind?"

"Give her a contract. If she succeeds, we absolve her of all guilt. If she fails, her punishment doubles."

I stared at Temric. Why was he helping me? Why give me a chance to go to the mortal realm? Every demon coveted the privilege to live under the sun again, even for a few days. This was no punishment.

There had to be a catch, something I wasn't seeing. But I had no power to stop it, even if I could see it.

"The Queen of Shalinor is preparing to perform a summoning," Temric went on. "I think Naomi's talents are perfectly suited for the job."

His words echoed in my head. Queen of Shalinor—

The room melted, a seamstresses' shop forming around me in its place. I held a burgundy coat with a golden lining. "What do you think of this one, Princess?" The words seemed strange, but I didn't know why. This was Princess Eternia's favourite seamstress.

Several moments passed without a response. "Princess?" A chill settled over my bones and I whirled to see a wall of dresses, but not a soul in sight.

I dropped the coat and rushed to the front of the room. Nobody was there, either. Only a row of dummies displaying the seamstress's finest creations. "Princess!"

Still no response. Did she leave? How did I not hear her footsteps?

I cursed and ran out of the shop, barrelling down the street, toward the nearest forbidden neighbourhood, hoping against hope that I could rely on her restless nature to lead her there.

The lower market in Vandemor was literally lower, a three-hundred-step climb from Noble Row. The seamstress's shop stood only half a block away from these stairs.

Over time, this staircase fell into disrepair. Most of the steps were cracked. Others had worn away completely, becoming tiny stone slopes instead. Some were pitted with holes created by magical strikes.

None of them bothered me. I took them three at a time, instinctively knowing where to land. Each jump gave me more speed, but less hope. No matter how I strained my ears, I couldn't hear Eternia. Where could she have gone? Had someone taken her right out from under my nose? We shouldn't have come into the city alone, but Eternia had the power of compulsion, and no qualms about using it. She forced me to sneak her out of the castle, and now—

I collided with a woman at the bottom of the steps and we both went flying to the ground. I bunched myself up, rolling as I hit the ground. The force of my landing rattled my teeth, and a sharp throbbing sensation in my side told me there would be bruises.

I staggered to my feet and offered the woman a hand. She raised her head and I froze, horror filling my body like a wave of ice.

A dagger stuck out of her left eye. Blood and green ooze leaked out of the wound around it, soaking her nose and cheek and lips.

Laughter. Child's laughter, from somewhere behind me. I spun again, this time drawing my sword.

Eternia stood at the edge of my sword's reach. An older, even more beautiful Eternia, in a blue dress.

A blue dress soaked in blood.

She changed again, her dark hair turning blonde, her green eyes becoming a sharp blue, as wrinkles formed around her eyes.

"We are the fallen queens of Shalinor." Her face changed more rapidly now, morphing between the two faces. "You destroyed our legacy."

I fell out of bed and crashed to the stone floor, bruising myself the same way I had in the nightmare. My stomach churned. Cold air froze the sweat clinging to my body as I stumbled to my toilet and emptied my stomach. The blackish-green colour of my bile made me hurl again. I hastily flushed it down before I was stricken a third time.

I lay on the floor, enjoying the sudden cold. I stretched my arms out and opened my palms, feeling the energy of the stones. Solid, stable energy. I drew this into myself, trying to soothe my soul, to bring myself into the present moment—

But the floodgates in my mind broke, and an onslaught of images filled my head. Eternia splashing in the lower market's fountain with the poor kids, the day I thought I lost her, laughing at me the whole way back because I couldn't calm down. Finding Eternia sobbing in her room one night when I returned from the Queen's workshops. Listening to her confess that she wept every night. Every other night she had remembered the sound-trapping spell.

I had confronted her brother, promised him death if he ever hurt her again. The next day, he left.

I thought I had protected her.

"Stop it, damn it." I pressed my hands against the sides of my skull, as if to somehow compress my memories back behind the mental walls I had built. As if those walls weren't still crumbling.

A sob erupted from my chest, then another, and another. I curled up into a ball and let the tears come.

Chapter Twenty-Six

Sunset came all too soon. I washed the tear tracks off my face, dressed, and made my way to the advisors' room. One way or another, I had to see this thing through. If I didn't destroy Shalinor's legacy, I would be letting Moonshadow fall. Thousands of people dead, all because of my inability to end a life that, in reality, should have ended centuries earlier.

Besides, I had promised to take my own life rather than return to the demon realm. I wasn't ready to make good on that promise yet.

The advisors' council had gathered by the time I arrived. Jacob II, Andre, and even Kenneth greeted me with smiles, but they were eclipsed by Jacob VIII's scowl.

"The sun set half an hour ago," the king said. "Don't be late again."

I apologized and took the empty seat on Andre's left. "I presume, with all that extra time, that you've filled everyone in?"

"They're aware of the situation."

"Yes, we're all aware of who the enemy is now." Jacob VIII paused to empty his tankard."What we're wondering is how you propose to defeat her."

My mouth dried up. I hadn't really thought about the method I'd use. The idea of going through this at all was too overwhelming. "Rolf and I can fly there by tomorrow morning. She's a powerful mage, but there are limits to how much her power can affect me. And I doubt she's had much weapons practice in the past five hundred years."

"Her magic reaches far," Jacob II said. "She'll strike you down when you enter Shalinor."

"I doubt it. Maintaining this plague must be draining a significant portion of her power." Otherwise, no strategy we attempted stood a chance. "She won't be able to do anything until I'm close enough to hit her back."

"Is there nothing that can be done from here?" Andre asked. "The treasury contains dozens of relics. Maybe one—"

"Most of those only work on the undead," Kenneth interrupted as he absently scratched the base of his neck. "Even if they worked on the living, they wouldn't have the range to reach her."

"Then let me go and end this thing," I said. "If I fail, Rolf will melt Riminira with her inside. She'll die either way." I had no idea if Rolf's fire was hot enough to melt the stone city, but it sounded good.

"Nobody's rushing into this," Jacob II said. "Even you haven't fought this kind of power before, Riana. You might not be able to win this alone."

"The blood of the gods runs through my veins." Well, one god, but that was irrelevant. I ran a hand through my hair. "If I can't defeat her, no amount of human soldiers can."

"There's strength in numbers." Kenneth dug his fingers deeper into his neck, drawing blood. He paused to lick it off. "If, as you say, her magic is spread thin, a war party might be enough to sway things in your favour."

"It would also take extra weeks to get there," I said. "Weeks Prince Marcus might not have."

"I'll go with you," Andre said, leaning forward. "Two are better than one, and Rolf can carry us both, right?"

"Yes, he can carry two."

Andre would make excellent backup, too—better than any human, at least. And I had to admit that part of me had grown rather fond of him.

"I've heard enough," Jacob VIII said. "If you go alone and fail, we'll need to send the soldiers anyway. You will take a contingent of one hundred Slayers and three healers to Riminira, and you will end Kahri's life."

Was he even listening?

"Andre, Rolf, and I can defeat Kahri. Mortal soldiers will only slow us down."

"I've given my orders," Jacob VIII said. "Alexis is selecting her finest as we speak, and will provide a full list of the soldiers accompanying you tomorrow at midday."

"At least let me choose my own soldiers." I wanted to shout, but I kept my voice low and even. Diplomatic, if a bit threatening. "I know what we're up against."

"You don't know her soldiers." Jacob VIII drained his tankard. "Isabella's funeral is in two days. You are expected to attend the proceedings. Three days from now, at sunset, you will take the soldiers Alexis gives you, and put an end to this menace."

I seethed. Why summon me if he didn't trust me enough to choose my own soldiers? But all the decades I spent surrounded by politicians had taught me to pick my battles. "It will take four weeks to reach Riminira with an army—longer if we travel at night to accommodate Andre."

"Sarentin will enable me to travel during the day." Andre glanced at Kenneth. "I assume we have a healthy stockpile?"

Kenneth frowned, but nodded. "An entire cold room. Everything the Mad King left behind."

"Isn't that what drove him mad?" I asked.

"He was already mad," Kenneth said. "Sarentin merely accelerated his decline."

I crossed my arms over my chest and looked at Andre. "And you want to use it?"

"It will allow me to travel—to fight—during the day. We need every advantage we can get."

"I don't like it," Jacob II said. "In five weeks, your body will become addicted. The severity of the withdrawal could kill you permanently."

"I'll travel in a wagon until we reach Shalinor," Andre said. "Once we're over the border, it's only ten days."

"Good," Jacob VIII said. "Take as much as you need."

"You're not hearing me," I said. "Even traveling during the day for most of the journey, it will take a full war party four weeks to get there. Marcus might not survive. You should consider remarrying."

Jacob VIII's face turned a terrible shade of red. Andre shook his head at me and drew his hand across his throat. Even Jacob II looked worried. Still, I pushed on.

"A secondary heir will ensure that your line continues. It will also make the people more confident in you, and the royal family."

Jacob VIII slammed his tankard onto the table and pushed himself to his feet. "I. Will. Not. Marry. Another. Woman."

He stormed out of the room. I gaped at the door as it slammed back into place. Isabella hadn't been dead long, sure, but royalty often made new engagements within a few weeks when the bloodline was threatened.

"He doesn't like women," Kenneth said.

Andre snorted. "My brother doesn't like anyone."

Jacob II gave both his descendants stern looks. "Don't trivialize his preferences." He turned his attention back to me. "He prefers men. Marrying Isabella and conceiving Marcus was the most difficult thing he ever did."

I blinked. "Plenty of noblemen have preferred other men. They still created heirs."

"He will remarry if Marcus dies," Kenneth said. "He understands the importance of an heir."

"It's a shame, really," Jacob II said. "If he was an ordinary man, a blood heir wouldn't matter. He would be able to marry anyone he wanted."

I headed to Alexis's office after the meeting, hoping to catch her at work on my list of soldiers. With a little bit of luck, she would listen to reason where Jacob VIII hadn't, and let me choose my own soldiers. Even if I wouldn't have time to test them all.

"Who is it?" Alexis called.

"Riana," I said.

A rustling sound came from the other side of the door, then a click. Probably the sound of the metal netting covering her hair as she slipped her mask back into place.

"Enter."

Something shiny caught my eye after I crossed the threshold and I stared at an all-too-familiar display weapon. A deeply curved sabre, like the ones popular in Shalinor during Eternia's day, with a jewelled silver hilt. Two initials were scratched into the hilt: K. N.

Could it be? No. More than one person in Shalinor had those initials. The blade wasn't good enough, either. Queen Corinthia employed only the finest smiths, especially when it came to protection for her own son.

"I assume you're not here to examine my weapon collection."

I wasn't, but I needed to know. "This is from Shalinor, isn't it?"

"Yes."

"How did you get it? There can't be many of these lying around."

She stiffened. "You'd be surprised what one can afford on a general's salary."

"This isn't the kind of thing you sell. It's priceless."

"Not to people who are desperate."

"I don't have time for this." I crossed my arms over my chest. "Tell me how you got this sword. Unless you want me to assume that you're working with the telars."

"I am no traitor. I will tell you the truth, if you swear not to tell the king."

I raised an eyebrow. Why keep it secret if she wasn't a traitor? "If it threatens him, or the safety of this kingdom, in any way... "

She shook her head. "I would never endanger my king or Moonshadow."

I was skeptical, but she had proven herself trustworthy so far. Perhaps she had an innocent reason to own this artifact. "Then I swear on my life that Jacob VIII will never know about this conversation."

"Good." Alexis opened a drawer and pulled out a flask. "I inherited the sword from my father. He claimed it had been passed down through our family since Shalinor's glory days. I never really believed him."

"Your father was a telar?" That didn't sound like such an innocent reason to me.

She nodded. "A traveling merchant. He never stayed in one place long."

"Then why did you end up in the orphanage?" Unless she, and her father, planned this to get her close to the king: to spy on them and report back to Fiona and Kahri, helping them spread the plague.

No, Fiona wasn't old enough to have planted Alexis. But Kahri was. *Damn it.*

"Alexis?" This final answer would tell me everything I needed to know.

She looked away. "My mother confessed his secret to a john one night. Father left for the swamp before they could drag him there. Said it was better to volunteer than to get arrested."

"He was right." Slayers didn't treat found telars well. City militias were even worse.

"I begged him to take me with him, but he said the swamp was no place for normal children, like me." She fiddled with the lid of her flask but didn't open it. "Right again, I suppose. But my sister, she had the gift, so he took her. They left me with mother and her clients, and I hated them for it." The bitterness in her voice was palpable now, getting thicker with every word. "I hated him more when mother died. I was alone then, because he left me. Him and my sister both, they abandoned me, and I ended up alone at the orphanage.

"The sword went into the temple vault when I became an orphan. They returned it to me, along with all those terrible feelings, when I took the Classless oath."

I tilted my head to the side. "If it causes you such pain, why keep it?"

"To remind me of why I chose a life without family." She placed her flask on the desk between us, unopened. "Now that those wounds are freshly torn, care to tell me what you want?"

"The king said you were choosing my men."

"Already done," she said. "I sent a runner to slip the list under your door an hour ago."

I seethed. The king must have made his decision before the council meeting. The whole thing had been a show. "I wanted to choose my own soldiers."

"It would take days for you to read all of my files," she said. "But I can give you the ones for the Slayers I've already chosen. I can replace up to ten of them with equally skilled warriors."

"Only ten?"

"I run units all across the kingdom. Several are more than two days' ride away. You will be gone before they could even arrive."

Waiting longer would end in Marcus, and possibly thousands of others, dead. Her choices would have to do. "Give me the files."

"Braiden Cowell's only twenty," I said. "I don't want to take him."

"He slew an entire mob of undead when he was only seventeen," Andre said. "His entire squad fled, but he fought the mob and won. Alone."

"Kahri is nothing like the undead." I shook my head. "She's far cleverer, for starters."

"You make it sound like we're all going to die out there."

"We might." I sipped my blueberry wine, watching him over the rim of my glass.

"We'll stand a better chance if we take someone like Braiden Cowell with us."

"If you really want, we can take him." I didn't have much faith in these men, anyway. To be honest, I had none in myself either. My body might withstand her magic, but I had no idea how to kill her. Or if it was even possible, with the preservation spell on her and Riminira.

The only thing I could do was make sure every Slayer in my platoon mattered.

I had spent so long double- and triple-checking the files of the men we chose that Andre left to feed, muttering about me being paranoid.

"A single detail out of place can be deadly," I said.

"You ought to start trusting people sometime. We're here to help."

The door swung shut behind him. I leaned back in my chair, took a big gulp of wine, and dove back into my work. By all accounts, the men Alexis chose were the best. All men who had defeated large undead creatures with little or no help. Most had patrolled the swamp at some point, and were old enough to have completed the full five years of mental-defence training instead of the two-year training Jacob VIII instituted. If their lilandium helmets were knocked off, they still stood a decent chance of retaining mental control.

But none of those facts gave me confidence.

I sighed, slid the files to one side of my desk, and then started writing notes of summons. I sealed each one with the ancient royal seal, a blood-red V with a skull embedded between its points. I didn't stop until all the notes were written.

Chapter Twenty-Seven

While most royal funerals were enormous affairs, involving all of Moon Spire—and for some, the entire kingdom—flocking to the castle grounds, Isabella's was conducted in private to keep out the plague.

I stood in the entrance hall for hours, watching Jacob VIII and Marcus greet one noble guest after another. The living Vonstones, the Voncruths, and every one of Isabella's seven siblings were in attendance, along with several local nobles. I didn't even try to keep track of their names. If I defeated Kahri, I wouldn't be using my newfound freedom to return to court.

"Is that all of them?" Marcus asked, slumping into his father's side. "I'm exhausted."

"Straighten up," Jacob VIII snapped. "A king never shows his exhaustion."

Or his madness.

Jacob VIII had kept both in check all day, probably thanks to Marcus's presence. Or perhaps it was the work of the calming draught in his flask, from which he took secretive sips at every opportunity.

"That was the final confirmed guest, Your Majesty," the steward said, holding up a scroll. "If there—"

The great wooden door opened again and a giant of a man in polished black brigandine entered the room.

"Announcing Elizabeth Vonstone the Second," he bellowed. "Representative of the Old Family."

My hand flew to my sword. Jacob II told me the Old Family welcomed her back, but to make her their representative? What were they playing at?

Elizabeth sauntered into the room, graceful as ever, and lowered the black canvas hood that protected her from the sun.

I inhaled sharply.

She was one of the most beautiful women I had ever seen. Not a single blemish, wrinkle, or scar marked her face. The grey streaks in her hair only made her more distinguished. Her lips were painted a deep crimson, providing stark contrast against her pale skin and sea-blue eyes.

But it wasn't her beauty that stunned me. No, what got me was something altogether different. Something that, in retrospect, shouldn't have surprised me at all.

In the six centuries since our last meeting, she hadn't aged a day.

The black mirror in the corner of Jacob III's office chimed, a clear, high-pitched sound that brought all the hairs on my body to attention. Jacob III eyed it like it was a venomous snake.

I checked the enchanted sundial on the back wall. High noon. "Elizabeth."

Elizabeth the Second's army, bolstered by several telar contingents, had reached Moon Spire's outer wall the night before. She contacted us with simple terms. Surrender the throne to her and accept permanent exile from Moonshadow, or the siege would begin in earnest.

But this wouldn't be a simple siege. Elizabeth's telar contingents could reach beyond the walls, turn civilians against each other and the guards. Most of the civilians had been evacuated to Relthea, the city farthest from the fighting. Some couldn't make the journey, too many to give them all lilandium helmets, even with the generous gift from Shalinor to solidify our alliance. They were gathered in the castle's great hall, far enough away to avoid manipulation, as long as the army stayed outside the city.

If the telars broke through the wall, however, the castle would descend into chaos.

My job was to keep that from happening.

The bell chimed again. I cursed.

"I'm not ready," Jacob III said, burying his head in his hands.

I squeezed his shoulder. "Yes, we are. The plan is in place." A twinge of pride at the steadiness of my voice streaked through me. I hadn't been this terrified in decades.

"You're sure?"

"Shalinor's forces will reach us tonight, and her castle tomorrow morning. All we need to do is keep them, and her, distracted for a while."

The bell chimed a third time. Jacob III stood, smoothed the fabric of his tunic, and tore the cloth off the mirror.

"King Jacob Vonstone the Third, speaking."

Elizabeth's face emerged from the darkness. "Good to see you, brother. Have you considered my terms?"

Jacob III didn't surrender the throne, and we kept Elizabeth's forces back until Shalinor broke them, but we never caught Elizabeth. She didn't resurface until years after her death, when she reappeared to negotiate for the land the Old Family now lived on. As much as what they did could be called 'living'.

Now she was a half-dozen paces from me, bowing to Jacob VIII and entering the castle like an honoured member of the royal family, not a traitor.

Oh, how I hated humanity's political games.

"It's been a long time, Riana," she said, flashing me a smile that was all fangs. "How are things in the demon realm?"

The castle bell rang, the sound echoing through the entrance hall. I smiled back at her, grateful for the distraction.

"I believe you know your own way to the crypt?"

"Of course." She inclined her head toward Jacob VIII. "But our king should lead the procession."

Jacob VIII's lip twitched upwards, but he didn't return her smile. "Let us go say our farewells."

He didn't wait for us to respond, either, heading straight for the Vonstone crypt at the back of the castle grounds.

Even with only a few families gathered, the funeral procession was an impressive sight. Most wore mourning grey, but they still found ways to make their garments elaborate. Lace and shimmering silver jewels were incorporated into every lady's clothing. Many wore ruby brooches, pendants, or earrings shaped like phoenixes. Even on this gloomy, foggy day, the rubies sparkled.

Elizabeth found her place beside the only other guests in black, the three vampires who needed dark cloth to shield them from daylight. I followed Jacob VIII and Marcus through the crowd, which parted to let us pass.

I joined the front line of guests. Marcus and Jacob VIII went on to stand beside Isabella's body, the king taking his dead wife's hand. She had been dressed in high-collared silver finery for her final ceremony and laid out in a simple wood coffin, her body withered but her expression peaceful. Cameron stood near her head, holding a small bowl of sacred oils. Two servants roamed the crowd, the first one handing each noble a large silver candle and the second servant lighting the candles.

When all the candles had been lit, and the two servants had returned to the coffin with their torches, Cameron spoke.

"May Ashe bless this woman and give her a happy home amongst her ancestors in the world beyond ours." Cameron lowered a diamond phoenix statuette into the coffin. "And may her soul be reborn someday, so her light may continue to shine on this plane."

"May this woman rest among her ancestors and among the gods until such a time as she may be reborn," Jacob VIII said. "May she someday be given a second chance at life."

"Farewell, Isabella Elora Vonstone," Cameron and Jacob VIII said together.

The two servants threw their torches into the coffin as Cameron began the chant to send Isabella to Ashe's realm, the realm between lives. One by one, the nobles joined in, forming an eerie choir. The flames grew quickly, devouring Isabella, leaving only a blackened phoenix and the frame of an hourglass amidst the ashes.

Cameron swept the ashes into a small stone box. He raised a hand and the chant subsided.

"Who will carry Isabella's body to its final resting place?" Cameron asked.

"I will." Jacob VIII held out his hands.

"Carry it with the same love and tenderness shown to a newborn babe," Cameron said, handing him the box.

"Always, for I may find her soul reborn in any child." Jacob VIII pulled the box close to him.

"But only if her old body is safeguarded." Cameron bowed. He took the blackened phoenix, holding it high above him. "Who will carry her heart?"

"I shall." An older woman I presumed to be Isabella's mother stepped out of the crowd.

"Carry it as if it were more fragile than glass." Cameron handed her the phoenix.

"Always, for if it breaks, she will never be reborn." She took the phoenix and stood beside Jacob VIII.

"Yet, if it is whole, she will see many new lives." He took the hourglass and held it out to the crowd. "And who will carry her fate?"

"I will carry her fate." Marcus's voice didn't waver as he stepped forward, even though his whole body trembled with sickness and grief.

"Carry it with care and conviction, as though it were a delicate flower," Cameron said.

"Always, for it may be destroyed at any moment." Marcus took the hourglass and stood next to his grandmother.

"Yet, if protected, it will bring her many glories." Cameron cleared his throat. "Now let us carry Isabella to rest, that her spirit may be freed to begin anew."

Two of Isabella's siblings came forward and led the way into the crypt, holding their candles in front of them. The stairs descended into the ground. Cameron led the rest of the procession into the depths. One by one, they disappeared into the darkness, taking pieces of Isabella with them. I held back. I had been in that crypt before, but today I felt out of place. Several others, those who weren't family, hung back as well.

Someone touched my hand. Jacob II, smiling at me with the sadness only centuries of loneliness could bring.

"You are family to me," he said. "That would be enough for her."

We followed the procession into the crypt. Every twenty steps we came to a landing where the flickering light of a dozen silver candles revealed the grey stone platforms intended for the souls of future Vonstones. We went four landings down. The stairs dug farther into the ground than any other structure in Moonshadow, but little room was left.

The procession remained quiet, as each relative stepped forward to give up their piece of Isabella. Jacob VIII went first, stepping into an alcove and placing Isabella's ashes on a stone altar. He whispered a prayer so quietly even I didn't fully understand it, then pulled away. Isabella's relatives took turns stepping up to her altar, each one whispering prayers of their own.

Marcus came forward last, tears streaking down his face, as he placed the hourglass on Isabella's altar. A sob erupted from his throat as he backed away. Jacob II rushed forward and held him, letting the boy cry into his cloak.

Cameron said a final prayer to close the ceremony and led us back up the stairs. At the top, he stopped to blow out the candles as people exited. Isabella's siblings, the two who led the procession into the crypt, closed the stone door and left their candles sitting by the entrance.

One by one, the nobles who had remained outside came forward, blew their candles out, and left them around the crypt. Soon the entrance was completely surrounded by candles. The nobles turned away, as one group, and travelled solemnly to the castle. It started to rain, but the procession didn't hurry inside. Rain was considered the gods' way of mourning, and running from it was an insult to the dead.

Chapter Twenty-Eight

The funeral feast was simple but abundant, an endless stream of bread and meat and pastries. Jacob VIII scarfed each serving down and ordered the next before anyone else in the room had finished their plates.

Marcus, sitting in Isabella's old seat, hardly touched his food. The boy didn't speak to anyone either. He seemed to be somewhere else altogether, his eyes glassy and his body trembling. Between sickness and grief, he looked ready to give up altogether.

I kept one hand on the hilt of my sword as I watched the proceedings, searching the crowd for any hint of trouble. My gaze was frequently drawn to Cameron and Elizabeth, who had angled their seats toward each other to facilitate what sounded like a hearty debate on the existence of vampire souls. *Or a coded conversation about their treachery.*

If they were doing something illegal, though, they were cautious enough to leave me with nothing more than a growing distrust of this strangely young high priest.

Jacob VIII rose to his feet halfway through the second course, his wine glass lifted toward the ceiling. The room fell silent, guests throughout the hall raising their own glasses in expectation of a toast.

"Thank you all for giving my wife such a beautiful send-off into the next life," he said. "May we unite again soon under happier circumstances."

He toasted the air and downed his wine. Glasses all over the room clinked together as sixty people toasted back to "happier circumstances."

"You are all welcome to continue this celebration of Isabella's life," Jacob VIII said. "I am retiring now, for a king has many duties. I bid you farewell and goodnight."

Some minor noble led a toast to the king. Jacob VIII downed another glass of wine in thanks, then hurried away, anxiously tapping the side of the flask in his pocket.

"I also wish to retire for the night." Marcus pushed himself up from the table. His plate of pastries remained untouched. "Thank you all for the love you gave my mother, in life, and in death."

He toasted the crowd as well, taking care to consume only the tiniest sip of wine before he headed for the exit.

He got three steps away before a violent spasm wracked his body and he collapsed in a heap on the floor, wheezing.

I darted to his side. An elderly woman in a royal healer uniform beat me there, already yanking a small green bottle out of the leather pouch at her waist. I held Marcus down while the healer force-fed him the liquid. Hundreds of voices whispered around us.

"Look at him. He's dying," a woman muttered. "And Jacob VIII won't even think about remarrying."

"The Vonstone blood isn't what it used to be," a man whispered.

"What will they do if he dies?" another woman said.

"Quiet," I shouted. "The healer needs to focus."

Marcus was unconscious now, his body still, except for his rhythmic breathing. He still wheezed, but it sounded much better. He would be alive a little while longer.

"He shouldn't have been out in the rain today," the healer said. "He needs rest."

I scooped him up in my arms. "I'll take him to bed."

I tucked Marcus into his bed and folded the blanket around him to prevent him from moving too much if the spasms returned. His eyes opened halfway, and he groaned. More of a growl, really, his throat was so raspy.

The healer brought a cup of water to his lips and Marcus drank eagerly.

"Good." She squeezed his hand as she took the cup away. "I'll be back with more."

"Thank you." He flinched, as if speaking caused him great pain.

She left the room and he let out a sigh of relief. I tilted my head to the side. Shouldn't he want her around?

"I miss being alone."

I stared at him. Telars couldn't read a demon's mind unless given permission, but he apparently didn't need to.

"Should I go?"

He shook his head. "Whe—when I fell, it was because I sensed her."

The familiar, icy feeling of dread filled my bones. Was Kahri going to claim Marcus now, after all this time? Would she tear Moonshadow to shreds before we even began our journey to save it?

"She—" He coughed into his sleeve, tears welling up in his eyes. *She was searching for information. About you and Rolf.*

I didn't know if that was better or worse. "Do you know what she found out?"

She knows you're leaving with a bunch of Slayers tomorrow night. I don't know anything more.

"Are you sure?"

Promise.

Rolf's coiled body filled most of the outer courtyard, leaving only a narrow path to the stables open. His fur shimmered with pearly opalescence under the magical lights coming to life along the castle walls.

He opened one eye as I approached, revealing his back fangs in a half-smile. *I was starting to think they'd never let you out.*

I'll be out of here for good soon. I didn't know where I would go when I gained my freedom, but it didn't matter. I wanted to get far away from here. Moonshadow looked like the kingdom I remembered, but it was no home to me now. *Do you have enough energy left to fly?*

For a little while. Where do you want to go?

I frowned. I didn't know where I wanted to go, either. *Anywhere you want.*

South, then. I miss the warm winds.

"Dramlech." The leather belt-strap for riding appeared around Rolf's middle. I smiled and climbed up to his back. *Warm winds sound great.*

I maneuvered my legs into the two loops and buckled the straps securely. *Ready.*

Hold tight.

A great gust of wind came, collecting underneath us. The force of it formed a miniature cyclone, pushing us into the air. The white charms on either side of my legs lit up and blazed brightly, protecting me from the building cyclone. The force of the wind propelled us far above the castle, holding our weight until Rolf caught a southerly air stream with enough power to carry us.

I leaned back and admired the land stretched out before us. Moon Spire looked so small from here, one tiny piece of the puzzle that was the mortal realm. Smaller cities and towns were barely visible in the half-moon's light. The handful of flickering lights made them seem like toys.

But the people inside those towns were very real, and counting on me to save their kingdom from calamity—even if most of them didn't know it.

You're tenser than normal. What happened?

How sweet he was to worry. In all my years, only Ma ever cared so deeply for me. I had forgotten the feeling of unconditional love. *Our enemy is spying on us through Marcus. You can't speak with him anymore—not until this is over.*

Rolf's next words came with a wave of bitterness that cut right through me. *There's no way to stop her?*

They're connected through the plague. She can use that. I hated it, but Jacob VIII was right to hide things from his son. We couldn't expect a sickly twelve-year-old to protect himself against Kahri. *I'm sorry.*

Me, too.

The wind we were on slowed as we passed over the swamp. An orange glimmer near the centre caught my gaze. A ribbon of fire danced through the air, climbing toward the sky. Judging by the size, it had to be many paces tall.

A fire that big had to be using several weeks' worth of wood. Tonight's festival wasn't an ordinary event. What were they doing?

We need to go over there. I scowled at my own thought, but I couldn't ignore this. If Fiona had lied, and the telars were building an army, Moonshadow needed to know.

Rolf slithered into a west-moving air stream below us. The strength of this wind pushed us forward so fast that the world blurred around us. My stomach rose into my throat and I closed my eyes, bracing myself against Rolf's fur.

We fell out of the air stream and Rolf slowed, circling lazily in the sky.

I opened my eyes and leaned back again. The fire danced merrily less than a hundred paces below. Dozens of tents were clustered around it, packed tightly into Conall's main square. People danced in the narrow space between the fire and the tents. The faint sounds of drums and smells of meat wafted up toward us. Definitely some kind of celebration after all.

What could they possibly be celebrating? The Queen's death?

No, that felt wrong. They might celebrate that privately in their homes, but a gathering of this size? There had to be another reason.

They look like they're having fun, thought Rolf.

They do. Nothing bad about that. Still, something seemed off. *Can you visit again tomorrow night? Try to stay under cloud cover. I want them to act like nobody's watching.*

I'll do my best. Can we go now?

He started circling back into the sky before I could respond, but I didn't mind. I wanted to get away from here, too. *Let's find that southerly wind.*

Chapter Twenty-Nine

"This mission isn't like anything you've done before," I said, pacing the narrow patch of space available in the crowded inner courtyard. "Kahri is a powerful telar and an even more powerful mage. Nobody has seen her, or entered Riminira and lived to tell the tale, in over five hundred years. We have no idea what weapons she has, other than her magic. We have no real concept of her power, either, or its limits. If she has limits."

I glanced around the courtyard. The Slayers gathered around me listened with a mixture of grave and eager expressions. I could almost hear their thoughts. The older ones were honoured but terrified. The younger ones bristled with anticipation, excited for the fight of their lives. They didn't yet understand what the term 'fight of your life' truly meant.

I took a deep breath and went on:

"We do, however, know what we have. We have the complete backing of the royal family. We have a dragon. And we have you, the finest Slayers this kingdom has ever seen, carrying within your souls the same strength that allowed Moonshadow's first Slayers to push the dead back and reclaim their land. With this strength, we can overcome any enemy and win any battle, no matter how ancient or powerful the opponent." *I hope.* "We leave at dawn tomorrow. I trust that is enough time to set your affairs in order."

The recruits exchanged nervous glances as my words sunk in. Being told to "set your affairs in order" only ever meant one thing: you probably weren't going to live much longer.

I spent the rest of my day planning and packing. If I defeated Kahri, and Loki freed me, Jacob II would send the few belongings I cared about to an address on the island of Eidos, many miles south of Moonshadow. I would decide where to go from there.

If Kahri killed me, my possessions would be donated to the archives in the High Temple of Jaldan. The deity of knowledge wasn't worshiped the same way as Magdalene or Ashe, but Jaldan had always been my favourite. They, alone, believed in fair judgement for my kind. Even after the massacre at Eternia's wedding, they tried to lessen my sentence, arguing that I couldn't be held responsible for Eternia's actions.

Uneven footsteps and the distinct thud of a cane hitting the stone floor outside drew my attention. I grinned, bounding to the door and opening it before Jacob II could knock.

He chuckled. "Your senses are keen as ever, I see." His mouth tightened. "You'll need them to win this."

"She can't use the magic she used to end the battle of Riminira." At least, I hoped not. "She'll have to fight us, on our terms."

Jacob II ignored me, gesturing at the luggage trunks sitting open on my bed. "That's an awful lot of stuff for this journey."

"It's not for this journey." I gave him a sealed letter. "This contains instructions."

"You aren't coming back, either way, are you?"

I shook my head. "Loki and I have a deal. If I win, I earn my freedom. I get my own life."

Jacob II's eyes grew distant, wistful. "It's a great feeling, having your own life. Not being responsible for anything but yourself."

"I hope so." I placed the broken amulet Aldaen gave me on top of a pile of clothes. "I've waited a long time for it."

A slight shiver ran through Jacob II's body, small enough that a human might not have noticed it. His lips drew back, and his fangs lengthened, touching the tip of his bottom lip. They shrank again in an instant, and his mouth tightened into a thin line.

"Dawn."

"Time to go," I said, trying my best to sound cheerful. "Thank you for coming."

"No, thank you for saving my kingdom. Again." He hobbled to the door, then paused. "You never went to see him, did you?"

I looked away, unable to meet his eyes. There could only be one person he was talking about. Not a person at all anymore, really. A pile of ashes, in the deepest reaches of the Vonstone crypt. I grimaced. Even after all these years I couldn't bring myself to see him like that. I hadn't even considered it. Not even when we entered the crypt to create Isabella's shrine.

"It helps, you know," Jacob II said softly. "To see the shrine. You can't move through the pain until you acknowledge it."

"Maybe one day, I will." For now, I had to worry about the present.

"And so, we march to end this plague and save our prince!" I thrust my sword into the air and the Slayers around me cheered, raising their swords to salute mine.

I surveyed the group. One hundred men and women, devoted to Moonshadow, all with exemplary battle records and a fierce determination to save the royal line. The best of the best.

Why don't they make me feel more confident?

I shrugged the thought off and sheathed my sword. "Let us go!"

I pressed my horse forward, wishing that Andre rode beside me instead of in one of the wagons. The Slayers followed in three lines, their blue surcoats making them look like a river of people. Five wagons, including one specifically for healing supplies, and Andre's cot, brought up the rear.

We entered the city and turned onto Trader's Way, heading east. It was the widest road in the entire city, built to accommodate the once thriving trade with Shalinor. It had also been one of the busiest, lined with shops and bustling with activity well into the night.

Now, it was one of the quietest. Only a handful of shops remained, and only a single bar was open. Several people came to their windows to watch us, but the road itself was deserted.

Half an hour later we arrived at the city's outer wall. The Slayers by the gate stood at attention, pounding their fists against their heart and bowing as we passed.

I craned my neck to see the castle one last time. Captain Raldon had already closed the gate, making it impossible to see beyond the wall, but I didn't really need to. I saw it well enough in my head.

"Farewell," I whispered, and turned away from my former home for the last time.

Chapter Thirty

Kahri

I woke well before dawn and rolled around for hours, trying to go back to sleep. My body had barely recovered from resurrecting Caerwyn—my former stewardess and only true friend—a week earlier. A dull, throbbing sensation pounded at the front of my skull.

But there were worse things than pain, like the images that haunted me when I closed my eyes. The demon and the dragon, tearing my newly-restored friends limb from limb. Destroying my city, one building at a time. Shattering my orb, and with it, my life.

I gave up on sleep, slipped into a blue satin dress, and went to the garden.

The palace had three gardens once. Only one grew anything now. The last green space in my city, or perhaps, the first. Things had only begun to grow here again a few years earlier.

Either way, it became my favourite place in the world when I discovered the first weeds clinging to the stone planters. I spent years carefully tending it, summoning the hardiest seeds the telars could locate and filling the garden with them. Now it grew six different kinds of beans and several medicinal herbs. Enough to sustain my new friends, albeit barely.

I frowned at the lightening sky. Dawn was close, too close for me to go back to sleep. I had so many things to do before greeting our new arrivals.

I picked a leaf from one of the nearest herbs, checked it for bugs, and stuck it in my mouth. Wakara, most often burned as incense or smoked, but even more potent when absorbed through the tongue. The leaf cracked in my mouth, releasing juice that made my tongue tingle. A cool, calming sensation spread out through my veins, slowing the race in my mind.

"You're out early, Your Majesty," a woman said in a familiar sing-song voice.

Caerwyn stood in the archway leading back into the palace. A grass-stained white dress covered her voluptuous form, and she held a watering pot in one hand.

"I always water the plants before making breakfast," she said. "That way, the sun doesn't steal any of their drink."

I couldn't help but smile. Caerwyn cared about every living thing, however small. Her capacity for kindness stood in direct contrast to the politicians who had surrounded me in my old life. It kept me sane to know someone else cared as much as I did.

"You should get some more rest," Caerwyn went on. "They won't be here until midday, and breakfast's not for another hour."

"Sleep is a luxury I cannot afford. The enemy is closing in."

She rested her free hand on her hip and raised her eyebrows. "You said they're sending a war party. It'll take weeks for them to get here."

"Six weeks." My plan might delay them another several days, but I couldn't count on it doing more than that. Not with a dragon on their side. "It's not enough."

"You don't have to do everything yourself, you know? I can teach Fiona's people too."

"Yes, but—" I cut myself off. She was right. I had gotten too used to doing everything myself. A true queen knew when to rely on her people. "Yes, you can."

I watched them enter the city from my tower. They seemed afraid of Riminira, weapons drawn, as if something might attack them at any moment. A foolish notion. The city only harmed my enemies.

When they were halfway to the palace, I went to the entrance hall to meet them. Excitement and fear gnawed at my nerves in equal measure. My dreams rested on these six people. Fiona's six finest. But what did that mean, for the telars now? Would they be powerful enough to learn everything Caerwyn and I had to teach?

Someone shouted. The oak doors muffled the sound, so I couldn't hear what they said, but the words didn't matter. I tapped the centre of the doors lightly, opening them before the telars could get impatient and touch the doors themselves. The wards would kill anyone with unfamiliar blood.

The usual view of my grey city was obstructed by the wagon I had seen earlier and six frightened telars, wearing mismatched armour and carrying swords of several different sizes. Only one was a woman. She carried two sharply curved short swords. She had her weapons drawn, but she didn't look as frightened as the others.

"Welcome to Riminira," I said, stepping into the light. I heard the men's thoughts and smiled. They had imagined me to be an old woman, wrinkled from all my years alone. None of them truly understood the magic I had used. How could they? None but I had ever been given a spell of the gods.

The woman's thoughts lay beyond my reach, hidden beyond several mental walls. Breaking them would have been tiresome and pointless. The fact that she had walls at all was enough to tell me she would be my best student.

"You'll be training with me for the next several weeks," I said, looking each telar in the eyes as I spoke. "I will give you the knowledge you need to restore our people to their former glory."

Originally, I had intended for them to spend two years here, training alongside souls I rescued from the abyss. Forming an army. The plague would serve two purposes—keeping the kingdoms distracted by their own crisis, and allowing me to reclaim more souls.

Now I had only a few weeks before Moonshadow's people arrived to destroy my life's work. All because of my own softheartedness, my inability to kill Moonshadow's telar prince.

Fiona's people dropped to one knee in unison, digging their blades into the ground before them.

"I am Magda, leader of this expedition," the woman said. "We pledge our allegiance to you, Kahri, Queen of Telars. We shall follow you until the end, and restore glory to our people."

I swallowed hard and forced a smile. "I accept your service," I said, my tongue almost tripping over the words. I hadn't sworn anyone into service since a few weeks before the war ended, when I inducted the youngest soldiers in Shalinoran history, a battalion of desperate thirteen- and fourteen-year-olds, to protect my city.

Caerwyn bounced into the hallway, a welcome distraction. She grinned at our new guests, then at me. Somehow, even though my plan was falling apart before my eyes, even though the harbinger of our doom was already on the road to Riminira, I couldn't help smiling back at her.

"Should I show them to their quarters, milady?"

"Yes," I said. I turned back to the six. "I assume you wish to rest after your journey. We will speak at dinner."

Dinner was no feast, but it was certainly grander than anything held in this hall since the war. The telars had brought barrels of potatoes with them, and enough wheat to make loaves of bread for a month. They brought tea, probably farmed by mundane slaves in southern Estefar, and dried meats.

Tonight, we indulged in large servings of mashed potatoes and dried pork. We opened one of the wine bottles the telars brought. I savoured the taste. When the war ended, our cellars had been overflowing with wine, but the wine had been my only companion between Loki's visits. I only had a few bottles left, the finest bottles, stashed away, for my days of victory over the kingdoms who slaughtered my people.

Perhaps I would give them to my people, as a parting gift. After all, they would bring my victory. They could take over the minds of their politicians, overthrow the standing order, and conquer the continent with my training. They could finish the war for me. The other kingdoms would never see it coming. Even Moonshadow would return to ignoring my people after the plague ended. They had no reason to suspect the depth of my plans.

I didn't talk much throughout the meal, but our new companions made fast friends with Caerwyn and Galvan. Galvan had almost grown into a man now, and I could see the lust in his eyes as he spoke with Magda. She certainly was beautiful, her short blonde hair cropped to both frame her face and be convenient for battle, her features perfectly symmetrical. She carried herself well, too, like a woman who understood her worth.

One of the men—he had introduced himself as Elandil—sat beside me and started talking loudly about the events in Diseus before they left.

"They're sending an army to Moonshadow," he said. "To rescue Fiona. I would've gone, but we had to come here." He seemed disappointed, as though he'd been waiting all his life to be slaughtered by Moonshadow's army.

"How big is their army?" The words tasted bitter on my tongue. The real question was how many men would die? An army would attract attention—and swift retribution. A handful of highly skilled telars with the right disguises were more likely to reach Fiona.

"I don't know," Elandil said. "Most of the men in Diseus left to answer Allister's call the day we left. Every town sent soldiers."

Soldiers. Few people in the swamp had fought more than the occasional wild animal, let alone gone through enough training to be considered a real soldier. They were farmers, weavers, builders. To send such a force into battle was to condemn most of them to death.

"Damn it." I drained my glass and slammed it on the table. The others turned to stare, but I didn't care. My plans had already been ruined by Moonshadow discovering me; now what remained of my hope was to be crushed, killed along with hundreds of my own people. "The plague has weakened Moonshadow, yes, but not nearly enough. Allister's men are poorly trained and poorly equipped. Moonshadow's army will crush them."

Elandil recoiled as if struck, his eyes wide. I glanced at the others and forced a smile. This was supposed to be a celebration after all.

"Still," I said, "there is cause to celebrate. Your arrival marks the beginning of telar liberation."

This time Elandil grinned. His smile, at least, seemed genuine. One by one the others joined him, until I had ten eager faces beaming at me. I balled my hands into fists under the table, digging my nails into my hands so hard it hurt, and forced myself to smile back.

After dinner, I climbed the spiral stairs to the top of my tower. A magical ball of blue light floated above my head. I clapped my hands to make it disappear as I approached the top floor. At night, the protection runes carved into the stone floor around the orb glowed, giving off enough light for me to keep working. I had often worked through the night before I started restoring my people.

I sat in front of the orb and closed my eyes, reaching out to it with my mind. Its strength flowed into my veins and through me into the floor, and back toward the orb. I let it flow freely for a moment, became part of the flow, the river of power. Then I started shaping it to my will, pushing my desires into the air between me and the orb, giving them form.

I imagined her exactly like the harpies from my era: long grey feathers and tall wings, strong enough to carry their woman-like bodies across the sky. Sharp, curved claws in place of hands and feet. Teeth longer and sharper than a bear's, dripping with a yellow poison capable of crippling a demon, a poison even their magical blood couldn't overcome. Big, black eyes and eerily human features, even human hair sprouting from her head. I pulled pieces of her from my mind, drawing them all together. The body formed in my mind, then I took one deep breath and blew life into the harpy.

A bright light appeared. A shrill female voice cackled. A ball of feathers and claws tumbled out of the light. This bundle unfolded itself, revealing the harpy's full, grotesque body. She grinned, her lips stretching back to make every sharp tooth visible.

Yes, these creatures were perfect. Simple enough for me to summon without the full energy required for one of my people, but powerful enough to decimate Moonshadow's war party. They might even kill the demon, if one could sink their fangs into the right part of her.

"Two of your sisters are creating a nest one day's flight east from here," I said. "Go to them now. I will summon you when hunting season begins."

She shrieked with excitement, then flew out the eastern window, quickly disappearing around the corner of a building.

Chapter Thirty-One

I followed Eternia along the narrow crimson carpet, inclining my head to various noble guests as we passed them. Most didn't even notice me, too busy watching the princess.

And I couldn't blame them. Eternia had always been beautiful, but today she was a vision. She wore a dress the same deep shade of blue as the sea, with a wide skirt that rippled when she walked. Her hair was braided and pinned into a spiral atop her head. The low-backed collar of her wedding dress exposed the nape of her neck.

Everyone else in the temple garden, by contrast, wore only the simplest clothes, in blacks and whites. Only the bride and groom were allowed to wear colour at a Shalinoran wedding.

We were halfway to the prayer tree when Eternia's groom appeared on a second red carpet, extending from the High Priest's office. Lord Emaldus, a handsome fellow, despite being almost three times Eternia's age. He wore a lighter shade of blue than Eternia, chosen to compliment his darker features.

They arrived at the altar at the same time and joined hands. I moved to stand behind the priest, one hand always on the hilt of my sword. There had been another attempt on Eternia's life only a week earlier.

Queen Corinthia shot me a meaningful look, and I folded my hands behind my back instead. We might be on full alert, but nobody else needed to know.

I only caught it for the briefest of moments, the smile on Eternia's face, before—

Lightning struck the prayer tree, splitting it down the centre. Hundreds of people screamed, but nobody moved.

Another burst of lightning struck the prayer tree, and it exploded. Shards flew everywhere. Still, nobody moved.

Eternia's smile turned into a grin, more sadistic and monstrous than anything I'd seen on the Master's face.

The crowd became a flurry of movement, hundreds of nobles pulling knives out of hidden crevices, bringing those knives to their own throats.

"No," I shouted, finally finding my voice. "Stop, Eternia."

The first row of guests slit their own throats in unison. Blood spurted from their necks as they fell, twitching. The people behind them stepped away from the corpses, but their faces remained still. Their hands remained steady, holding their own knives to their throats.

Eternia laughed. My blood ran cold. The second row of guests slit their own throats.

I had to stop her, but my body wouldn't move. All I could do was scream, as—

I clapped a clammy palm over my mouth and kicked my way out of my bedroll. It tangled around my feet, but I hardly noticed, too busy gulping down mouthfuls of cool, precious air. Each mouthful slowed my heart, bringing it a little closer to its normal pace.

Four nights. I had slept on the road for four nights, without a single nightmare. I thought my soul had made peace with itself, that being away from my memories of Jacob III had restored my mental walls. *If only*. My soul wouldn't know peace as long as that memory lived in my head.

"I didn't do anything wrong," I told myself, for the millionth time. "She did it. She planned it. She killed them."

But I failed to stop her. I failed to protect her from herself. In the eyes of the gods—and in my own heart—that was the same thing. I was responsible for the massacre, and everything it did to Eternia's family.

Soon, I would be responsible for the complete destruction of their legacy.

No. I couldn't let myself think about that. Hesitation meant death, for Marcus and for thousands of others. I forced myself to focus on dressing, methodically putting on one piece of clothing and then another. The familiar movements comforted me, bringing me some measure of calm.

I emerged from my tent and squinted at the rising sun. Everyone would wake soon, providing a much-needed distraction from my past.

One woman from the nearest cluster of tents was building a fire. Imeni Byrne, the oldest Slayer in our war party, and our third in command. She looked nothing like the Byrnes of Jacob III's era, with deep brown skin and thick, curly hair, but she still followed their traditional family path of military service.

She straightened to salute me as I approached, bringing her right fist to her heart.

"I see you're up early," I said.

"I've always believed an officer should be up before her soldiers." She tucked a strand of coarse black hair into her lilandium helmet. "Keeps their spirits up, knowing their commander is at the top of her game."

I crossed my arms over my chest. "The circles under your eyes tell a different story. We have plenty of sleeping draught, if you need it."

"Can't take that stuff on the road. Too groggy waking up. What if we're ambushed?"

"Not sleeping is worse. If this gets too far, I will order you to take the potions."

She grimaced. "I'll make sure it doesn't come to that."

"Good."

Imeni returned to her makeshift fire pit and drew a symbol on one of the logs. It glowed orange, and a tendril of flame burst from the centre. According to her file, this was almost the full extent of Imeni's magic, but only our healers and I possessed more power.

"We'll pass Betham tonight." Imeni opened a small sack and produced a small silver pot, a pouch of dried beans, and a waterskin. "You sure we don't want to stop there? We're almost out of fruit."

"We'll restock at Amheld Fortress." This many Slayers entering Betham would only serve to create alarm. It might also show Kahri our exact location, if she could connect to every infected person the way she had connected to Marcus. "It's only three more days."

"Yes, ma'am." She dropped two handfuls of beans into the pot. "My uncle commands fortress Amheld."

"Commander Illius Byrne," I said, internally cursing myself. Something so basic should have been obvious the first time I saw their names, but I had been too absorbed in my own thoughts about how to defeat Kahri. I needed to pay more attention to my Slayers, if only to gauge their morale.

Imeni placed a thin metal rack over the fire. "I haven't seen him in ten years."

I tilted my head to the side. "Do you want to see him?"

Imeni's eyes narrowed. "I'm not sure. My father married a woman from the isle of Eidos, and I came out as a lesbian several years ago. Illius was quite—" She cast her eyes about, as if hoping to find the right words sitting on the ground. "Vocal about his disapproval in both situations."

"So he's a stalmit."

"A what?"

I stifled a curse. For a moment I had forgotten that Shalinoran was a dead language. "Stalmit is Shalinoran. It means 'person of small mind'."

"Oh. Well. He's just—"

I held up a hand to silence her. "I've read his file. You don't need to defend him. In fact, I'd rather you didn't. I need pure honesty from you. Especially when it's unpleasant."

She smiled, flashing a set of impossibly white teeth. "Thank you, ma'am."

Imeni returned to her cooking and I leaned back in the grass, watching the sunrise, its brightness blotting out the final stars.

I was amazed how something as simple as a clear day's sky could be so beautiful in the mortal realm. The demon realm had no clouds, no sun, no stars, only an eerie pulsing red light coming from its rocky crimson "sky." Nothing was beautiful in that light.

"Enjoy the sun while you can," Imeni said. "They say the sky is always overcast in the Wastelands, thanks to Kahri's curse. 'A curse so terrible, it scared both sun and rain away.'"

I bristled. I knew those words, or something like them, and not from any mortal song.

"A god word." How had I not realized it sooner? No mortal magic could kill so many demons in one shot. Or grant its caster immortality. "She used a god word."

Imeni straightened. "What's a god word?"

I ran my fingers through my hair. "God words hold great magical power, enough to bend the forces of nature to an individual's will. Each god word can destroy or create on a grand scale. The gods are forbidden from sharing them with mortals."

"But you think Kahri discovered one somehow."

"You don't simply discover a god word. One of the gods gave it to her."

"Didn't you just say that was against the rules?"

"This wouldn't be the first time they broke the rules." One god, in particular, enjoyed flaunting them.

Damn Loki, sending me to clean up his mess.

"Do you think they're helping her now?" Imeni's voice wavered on the last word. "One of the gods?"

"No. She won't be able to use the god word again either." I hoped not, at least. I didn't even know how her body had survived using it the first time.

"The god word didn't make her invincible, did it?" Imeni asked. "She can be killed, right?"

"She's still human."

Imeni scowled. "I hope you're right."

The telars are moving. Rolf's mindvoice entered my head, followed by a wave of worry. *All of them.*

I stiffened. *Where are they going?*

North.

Toward Moon Spire. The gathering had been an army, preparing to take advantage of the chaos Kahri's plague caused. The war between telars and Moonshadow's other citizens was about to begin, despite my and Fiona's efforts to avoid conflict.

Unless her attempted negotiation was a planned distraction. She had played us before.

How many are there?

Hard to tell. Four hundred? Five? An image of a dozen fires, strategically placed in a rectangle around a large group of tents, followed these words.

There had to be at least four hundred soldiers in a camp that size. Not enough to topple Moonshadow, but enough to destabilize it. *Get away from there for now. I will warn the king.*

"Are you all right?" Imeni asked.

"Pack my things. I need to report something to the king."

I took off at a run, heading for the supply wagons. Boxes of dried foods filled most of the space, but a black mirror dominated one corner, wrapped in several layers of cloth. I unwrapped the mirror, careful not to scratch it.

"Call Jacob VIII."

The mirror chimed four times before Jacob VIII responded. The circles under his eyes had deepened, and taken on the purplish-black colour of bruises. He wore his lilandium helmet and his neck was free of hand marks, but his skin had taken on a sickly grey shine. I doubted he had slept since we left.

He scowled. "What happened now?"

"I apologize for the interruption, Your Majesty." I bowed. "Rolf's discovered a telar army, roughly four hundred strong, heading toward Moon Spire."

He threw his head back and laughed. "Four hundred soldiers? Is that all they can muster?"

I balled my hands into fists behind my back. "It's enough to take out the smaller fortresses and devastate the southern towns."

"They won't reach those fortresses, let alone the town." He leaned forward, a sadistic gleam in his eyes. "You and your dragon will burn every last one of them to a crisp. Tonight."

My stomach churned as I remembered all those tents, all those people—

The smell of burnt flesh, as lightning struck Magdalene's High Priest and Eternia cackled.

The rows of corpses, still bleeding out on the temple ground—

I shook my head, forcing the memories back. "They deserve a chance to surrender. I can negotiate with them."

He slammed his fist on his desk. "You will not negotiate with these people. They've set a plague upon my kingdom, and now they wish to strike us when we're down?"

"All they want is to get their leader back." My voice rose with each word, but I stopped short of yelling. I didn't want the entire camp to hear me. "And to be full citizens of Moonshadow. To be considered people."

"You are the most belligerent servant I've ever had," Jacob VIII snapped. "I order you to take your dragon to burn that army alive, today. I order you to leave only enough survivors to let the story spread. The telars will discover what happens to those who threaten my kingdom. If they threaten it again, I will have you burn their villages next."

I opened my mouth to object but the compulsion was already heating my veins. The desire to leave immediately, to run to the swamp if necessary, overwhelmed my mind.

I couldn't disobey a direct order from my summoner, but I could convince him to change it. Or I could try, if I could push words out past the pain.

"The only thing they will learn is not to strike until they're ready to destroy Moonshadow once and for all." I spoke through gritted teeth as the heat in my blood increased. "Rolf and I won't be here to protect Moonshadow forever. When we're gone, they will strike back."

He stroked his chin. "Should we burn the villages now then? Make sure there's nobody left to start a war?"

My chest constricted. Did he really hate the telars enough to burn them all to death? Even the children? What about his own son?

I couldn't take the risk. "No, Your Majesty. Perhaps you should bring this issue to the council—"

Jacob VIII shook his head. "My advisors are simply that, advisors. I am the king. My word is final. I thought you, of all people, would understand the importance of permanently eliminating the telar threat."

I suppressed a shudder. "Perhaps the best way to eliminate the threat is to improve their lives, not end them. The telar curse isn't always hereditary, after all. We can't ensure their permanent destruction."

The king's neutral expression contorted into a scowl. "You aren't even one of my advisors. You have your orders."

He disappeared. I stared at the mirror for several long moments, the hollow shock in my chest dulling the pain of Jacob VIII's compulsion.

Meet me at today's campsite in one hour. I sent the thought to Rolf, trying to keep the emotions behind it steady and warm. To give him the same comfort he gave me. *We have orders. To destroy the telar army. With fire.*

I made it halfway back to my tent before Rolf responded, his mindvoice trembling. *He wants us to kill all those people? They haven't done anything.*

They're an army. They only want to do one thing. Well, three things. Raping, killing, and looting. This was an army formed out of spite, not any real plan to destroy the royal family. If that plan existed, another army existed for it too. Fiona was too smart to count on a few hundred soldiers. *He used the compulsion. It will kill me if they aren't dead by sunset.*

A surge of searing heat burst through my veins, as if the spell could hear my thoughts. I wiped a wave of tears away with my sleeve and broke into a jog. The heat receded, my body satisfied that I was working toward my given objective.

"Rolf and I must run an errand for the king," I said, skidding to a stop beside Imeni. "We'll be back tomorrow."

"Why? What's more important than stopping the plague?"

She's starting to distrust the king. How long would it be until his madness became apparent to everyone?

"I'm not permitted to tell you. The war party will follow your orders in my absence."

"Shouldn't we wake Andre up?"

I shook my head. "We need to minimize his exposure to sarentin." More importantly, I didn't want to get caught in an argument about Jacob VII's sanity with the compulsion still burning my veins. "It won't take me more than a day. I'll be back before you reach Shalinor."

"I hope so." Something in her voice told me she didn't believe the group would survive if I didn't.

"I'll find your campsite tonight. I promise."

Rolf arrived half an hour after the war party set out, coiling himself in a loose circle around me. *We don't have to do this, you know. We could return to Dragon's Keep.*

You can. Loki had made it clear that he didn't care why I wanted to abandon this contract. All of this was part of my punishment. *My life ends if I disobey this order.*

I guess I'm stuck too, then.

I balled my hands into fists. How could I make Rolf do this? He was a kind soul. A true friend. An innocent. How could I take that away from him? *Maybe—maybe death is better.* In death, I would be nobody's pawn. I would be nothing at all, without pain or guilt. *But not free from the compulsion. It needs to be—*

A surge of blistering heat burst through my veins, searing through my rebellious thoughts. I doubled over, gasping for air.

I won't let you suffer like this, and I won't let you die. Rolf's mindvoice rode a wave of cool, steadying calm. *Those aren't innocent people, right? They're an army.*

They're still people. You don't have to do this. I whimpered as the heat increased, the first blisters breaking out on my arms. *Kill me instead, I'm only one person—*

You're my friend. I'll burn them for you, alone, if I have to.

I gaped at him. *But why?* What had I done to earn such a true friend? If anything, I had ignored him for the past few weeks, too wrapped up in my memories and this damned job.

You introduced me to the world. And there's still more for you to show me, right?

I smiled. I did have more to show him, when this was over. Someday we could explore things even I hadn't seen. *Yes.*

So let's do this, and we'll be one step closer to exploring.

All right. I pushed myself off the ground and stumbled toward Rolf. "Dramlech."

The belt-like flying contraption appeared around Rolf's middle, and my body cooled. The pain dissipated with the heat. I leaned against his side for several moments, waiting for my muscles to stop shaking.

I climbed up to his back and then strapped myself into the flying belt. *Ready.*

Rolf called a spiral of wind, and it hurled us into the air, connecting us to a powerful southwestern wind stream. The force of it howled and screeched against the flying belt's magical barrier.

This wind carried us all the way to the telar army before midday. They had made impressive progress for such a large group.

Rolf maneuvered into a lower air stream and circled slowly, making slight adjustments to the circle to stay behind cloud cover. *There's really no other way to break the compulsion?*

Only my death.

A deep sadness accompanied Rolf's next words. *Then I choose your life.*

He swooped down toward the camp, catching an easterly air stream to carry us from one end of the army to the other.

Heat pulsed through Rolf's body, collecting in his scales until it burned my skin, even through his fur and my clothes. I yowled, but Rolf's roar overwhelmed all other sounds as he released the first stream of fire. The fire claimed two rows of soldiers with a roar of its own. They panicked, several bolting through the crowd, spreading the flames as they ran. Others dropped to the ground, rolling around in the damp to extinguish themselves. Screams filled the air, the sounds puncturing my head.

Rolf let out a second burst of flames, lighting a chain of supply wagons. The fire spread and the world below us turned orange, the roar of the flames overwhelming the human screams. I stared at it, wondering how many men we had killed, whether they had women fighting too, whether they had sent children. What kind of blood was on my hands now?

Tears streamed down my face, but these weren't caused by physical pain. My body felt cool and light, free of compulsion. My heart, however, hung heavy in my chest. Was this the cost? Was it worth it? Was *anything* worth this?

It had to be. *That's enough.*

Good.

We flew up into the cool night air and fled the scene. After a while, Rolf circled down toward a clearing in the northeastern woods of Moonshadow.

I'm sorry I asked you to do such a terrible thing, I thought to Rolf.

Neither of us had a choice.

You did. I wiped the latest set of tears away with my sleeve. *You could have gone back to Loki.*

That's not a real choice.

I chuckled. *You're sweet, you know that?*

We sat in this clearing for a long time, lost in the silence of mourning. The sun passed overhead, and the shadows grew long. I buried my face in Rolf's fur, dreading the day's end. Soon I would return to my army, as promised. This time I would face Andre, and questions I didn't want to answer.

We won't have to do anything like that again, will we? Rolf asked.

Kahri is the only person living in Shalinor. We'll fight her alone.

Are you sure?

I wasn't sure about anything anymore, but I did know where to find answers. I clambered up Rolf's side and clipped myself back into the flying belt. *We should inform the king, in person.* And while we were in Moon Spire, I needed to speak with Fiona.

Chapter Thirty-Two

We arrived in Moon Spire an hour after sunset. Jacob II greeted me in the castle's entrance hall, wearing grey mourning clothes and a grim expression. The stone in my stomach grew to fill my entire body. I opened my mouth, but no words came out.

Had I killed all those people for nothing? Was Marcus—

"Marcus is alive," he said.

Guilty relief flooded my body. There was still time to save Moonshadow. "Who?"

"We still mourn Isabella, at the king's insistence." He adjusted his weight to lean more heavily on his cane. "He told me of your task."

"I'm here to report it completed."

He looked away. "I'm sorry."

I forced myself to shrug. "Killing is part of the job."

"I never would have condoned such a cruel plan."

"There's a reason he didn't ask you." Jacob VIII wanted vengeance for his wife, and he held the entire telar community responsible. The army was merely an excuse.

Jacob II sighed. "Watching Marcus grow worse and Isabella die is tearing him apart. It's hard to be a king and completely powerless in the face of disease."

His grip on his cane tightened until his knuckles seemed to pop out of his hand. He stared into the middle distance over my shoulder. I knew where his mind had gone. His wife's final weeks, as her body was torn apart by an illness nobody could even recognize, let alone cure. The debilitating illness his daughter-in-law suffered decades later. The madness that claimed his mother's mind. The Vonstone family was no stranger to suffering.

"A king doesn't have the luxury of letting such things drive him mad," Jacob II said. "I convinced him to take a hefty dose of dreamless sleep draught. He'll be out until past dawn."

"Good, he needs it." He needed a lot more than a single night's sleep, but it was a start.

"Kenneth is taking over the courts, at my insistence," Jacob II went on. "I will be handling most of the king's other duties."

"Aren't your kind supposed to let the living govern?"

"This is an emergency. But you're right. Neither of us likes it. We're hoping when Marcus recovers—"

"*If* Marcus recovers."

He frowned. "Yes, if. We hope the king will stabilize then."

"What if he doesn't?"

Jacob II shook his head. "I have no idea."

I went to my chambers on the pretence of taking a bath and changed into a nondescript grey dress instead, one of several designed to help me get around the city unrecognized. I added a thin black cloak, clasped it with a plain silver pin, and pulled the hood down over my head.

My next stop was the kitchen. I warped my face as I went, pushing my nose into a crooked line and extending my jaw forward.

The castle kitchen was immense, with half a dozen wood-burning stoves, three ovens, and enough counter space for twenty servants to work comfortably. Only two servants were here now, a pair of elderly women scrubbing pots and pans from supper.

The closer woman caught sight of me and grinned, revealing a set of wooden teeth. "Hello, dearie. What do you need?"

"I—tea for the king."

She gestured at a narrow stove with a cast iron kettle on it. "We keep that one ready for him. You new?"

"Started last week, ma'am." I hurried to fill the kettle, hoping the woman would return to her task. I hadn't created a story to go with my temporary face.

"The Vonstones are scary at first, but they're good employers." The toothless woman started on another pot, scrubbing with a ferocity that would frighten most Slayers. "Been working here my whole life. Wouldn't trade it for anything."

I stuck three pieces of wood in the stove, closed the grate, and pushed the flame-shaped button on the side. A fire rune flared to life under the wood. All three pieces caught at once. The fire rune went dark again, but the wood continued burning.

"Well, maybe I would trade it in, to actually be one of them."

The other woman scoffed. "Wouldn't want to be one of them now; they're all nuts."

"The king is grieving," the toothless woman said. "Not insane. Right, dearie?"

"I don't know, ma'am. I'm new here." I grabbed a tray, a teapot, and a single mug from one of the upper cupboards.

"Well, you'll see. This plague will run its course, and everything will go back to normal."

The other woman rolled her eyes and wrung out a wash cloth. "Must be nice having such a simple view of things."

My kettle whistled and I grabbed it, steam burning my hands as I poured the water into a pot. I cursed and hurled the half-empty pot across the room. The other women stared at me. Heat of an entirely different kind rushed to my cheeks.

"I'm sorry, madams, I—"

"Don't worry about it, dearie," the toothless woman said. "You just get that tea to the king before he has a fit, all right? We'll clean everything up here."

The other woman made a face. "You will, you mean."

The toothless woman put her hands on her hips and glared at her companion. "It's the right thing to do, missy."

I bowed deeply and grabbed the tray. "Thank you, madams, I won't forget this."

I bolted out of the room and made my way to Fiona's cell with a little extra bounce in my step. Maybe the toothless woman was right. Maybe when I defeated Kahri—if I defeated Kahri—everything would go back to normal, including the king.

Two Slayers in full battle armour, complete with lilandium helmets, guarded Fiona's cell. They drew their swords when I entered the hallway.

"Who are you?" The Slayer on the left stepped forward, lowering himself into a fighting stance. "Only Maerin is authorized to serve this prisoner."

Damn. But there might still be a way out of this without violence. "Maerin sent me. She isn't feeling well enough to come herself."

"She was here less than two hours ago. Why are you really here?"

"Doesn't matter," said the Slayer on the right. "She knows what's in here. Arrest her."

So much for the easy way. I threw my tray at the first Slayer as he lunged for me. The teapot shattered against his face, soaking him in boiling water. I followed it with a palm to the throat, cutting off his scream. My other palm pressed into his stomach, pushing him into his friend. Their helmets banged together, and they fell in opposite directions, the second one impaling himself on his sword.

I cursed under my breath and knelt beside the impaled man. Spurts of blood soaked his sword as he twitched and gasped for air. He panicked and flailed, gutting himself in the process. He let out a high-pitched squeal and went limp. The dead weight knocked the sword over, smearing blood all over the nearest wall.

Not what I wanted, but at least I didn't hear footsteps. Nobody else needed to die tonight.

I found Fiona staring blankly at the green light charm painted on the white ceiling, hands clasped together so tightly her knuckles were white.

I forced my face back to its normal shape. "Your army has been defeated. A pitiful force, really. Why send them at all?"

She tore her gaze from the charm on the ceiling to stare at me. She looked so regal, her auburn hair flowing about her shoulders, her eyes blue as the sky, framed perfectly by the white lilandium wall behind her. Her expression was regal, too, the practiced emotionlessness of a noble entering a negotiation.

I control nothing from this cell. If you saw a telar army, it was my brother's doing.

The auburn-haired man from the council. Allistair, or at least that was what Aldaen called him. At this point, I doubted even the names these people gave me.

"Don't lie. You used your brother just like you used Kahri to get to the negotiation table."

My control over my brother is more direct. It's also impossible here. She gestured at the white stone walls.

She used outright mind control on her brother? What kind of heartless woman was I dealing with?

"What would you have him do, if you could control him?" I asked, pushing aside the rest of my questions. Only one thing mattered right now.

Her left eyebrow twitched upwards. *Are you offering me freedom?*

"Jacob VIII will execute you if I leave you here," I said. "If you want freedom, or life at all, you need to swear another blood oath. Swear to stop your brother from going to war with the Vonstones."

She smiled. *That, I'm happy to promise.*

Her lack of hesitation bothered me, but I didn't have time to think about it. The unconscious guard would wake any minute now.

"Good. We'll get out of here first."

Chapter Thirty-Three

I found the war party camped a short ride from Betham and asked Rolf to deposit me in a clearing out of the horses' sight. Even Moonshadow's war horses didn't much like being around a dragon.

Someone had taken the liberty of pitching my tent near the supply wagons. Andre sat a few feet away, drinking from a bottle of blood.

His head snapped up as I entered the camp, and his eyes narrowed. "I hear my brother sent you on an errand. With the dragon."

"I am here to serve the king, and Rolf allows me to cross great distances quickly."

"What else does he allow you to do? What did my brother want?"

My hands curled into fists. "What is this, an interrogation?"

"I'm your second in command. I need to know things."

"Not these things."

I strode to my tent and ducked inside, closing the flap before Andre could ask more questions. For once, he didn't attempt to follow me.

The solitude and darkness of my tent brought immeasurable relief. I yanked off my boots and stretched my feet, but I didn't open my bedroll. After last night's events, the last thing I wanted was sleep. How much worse would my nightmares be now?

I stuck with my waking nightmare instead. I polished my boots, sharpened my sword and daggers, and listened to the Slayers' banal conversations as they prepared for sleep. Even the sound of the healers counting supplies was a welcome distraction.

The night progressed at a snail's pace. I ran out of things to polish, clean, and sort not long after midnight. The camp was silent, most of the Slayers resting for the next day's journey.

I wandered around the camp, counting the tents to keep myself occupied. One hundred tents, lined up in rows of ten. Two Slayers on watch at either end of every row of tents. Nobody—alive or dead—would sneak up on this war party.

Braiden Cowell watched the northern edge of camp, his eyes probing the darkness beyond the circle of light created by his watchfire, as if he actually hoped to see an enemy. He hummed a familiar tune as he did so, one foot tapping the same rhythm into the dirt.

"Another quiet night," he muttered.

"You should be grateful," I said, approaching the stump where he sat. "We'll need all our strength for the battle ahead."

His eyes lit up. "It's going to be the battle of the century, isn't it?"

"We should hope it isn't." I was betting everything on the theories that creating the plague had used most of Kahri's power, and that she couldn't use the god word again. If either was wrong, we didn't stand a chance.

He slumped. "I know. Everyone else joined to protect people, to preserve order. They don't really want to fight."

I tilted my head to the side. "And you?"

"I want to inspire Aislin," he said. "She's a bard back in Moon Spire. Before that, she lived in my home town. She's the most beautiful woman I've ever seen, with a voice to match."

"So, you want her to write a song about you?" I couldn't decide if that was the sweetest thing I had ever heard, or the stupidest.

"It's all I've wanted for years—the whole reason I became a Slayer."

I stifled a sigh. "Maybe you should think about being alive to hear it, too."

"But if she writes the song, I'll always be alive, in a way."

"It's not the same thing at all. I'm sure she'd agree." At least, I hoped she would.

He looked away. "You're probably right."

Dawn came at last, and we set out again. I rode with the war party but kept my stallion well ahead of the main group, eager to continue my solitude. Imeni hadn't asked about my errand for the king, and I wanted to keep it that way. I already had no idea what to say to Andre when we made camp for the night.

The journey, at least, gave me something else to think about. Sometime tomorrow we would pass through Amheld Fortress, a grand fortress at the border between Moonshadow and what used to be Shalinor. A day after that we would enter Shalinor itself, or the Wastelands as it was now known.

And I still had no better plan than setting the whole place on fire and hoping Kahri burned. What else could we possibly do against a woman powerful enough to use a god word?

Imeni brought her horse up to ride beside mine. "We'll need to stop on the other side of the hill to let the horses drink." She gestured to the sloping path ahead.

"Of course."

"You seem distracted."

"It's..." I paused. "A lot of things."

"The soldiers are worried about entering the Wastelands. Some think the whole country is cursed, that anyone who enters it will be cursed too."

If we survive long enough to get cursed.

"They might be right."

She grimaced. "Still, you can't let them believe it. We need to keep their spirits up. You need to be fully present, for their sakes."

She's right.

This was the part of leadership I hated, the reason I preferred to work in the shadows. Taking responsibility for other people's emotions never sat comfortably with me. "I'll be fully present when we reach the border. Don't worry about me."

Imeni scowled, but she didn't say anything more.

We made camp around the curve of a small lake a half hour before sunset. I ran through Imeni's words for the thousandth time as I pitched my tent. Jacob II's words, too, echoed in my head. *You have to acknowledge the pain before you can move on.*

Maybe this flood of memories was a sign. My own mind telling me to move on, to immerse myself in this moment before distraction killed me.

I sat cross-legged in front of the fire Imeni had built, watching the flames, hearing the screams of the telar army.

How was I supposed to move on from that?

Andre joined me by the fire, a bottle of blood in one hand. "Are you all right? You seemed upset last night."

I tensed. What did I say? That I killed four hundred people the night before? That his brother was a maniac? "Just—caught up in some memories."

"Of Shalinor?"

No, but Shalinor provided the perfect distraction. Even if it did take me to another part of my unpleasant past. "I lived there once, you know. Before Moonshadow even existed."

He raised his eyebrows. "How old are you, exactly?"

"After a few centuries it ceases to matter. You'll understand someday." If we survived.

He fell silent, and I let the conversation end. I didn't want to talk about Shalinor any more than I wanted to talk about last night.

"What was it like?" Andre asked.

"What?"

"Shalinor." Andre gestured at the eastern horizon. "Riminira."

I hesitated. How much should I tell him? The memories were beautiful, but tainted with the wrongness of Eternia's final act of cruelty.

Stick with the easy things.

"Back then, Vandemor was the capital. We only went to Riminira once." To conduct Princess Eternia's engagement ceremony. The beginning of the end.

"We?"

"My first job was to guard Shalinor's eldest princess." My first failure was letting her brother abuse her right under my nose. "When she turned thirteen, we toured the queendom, so she could assess potential suitors." Only she wasn't doing the assessments. Queen Corinthia was, because the royal family needed allies.

"You sound like you miss it. Like you miss her."

I glared into my horse's mane. "When you get to be my age, you miss a lot of people. I miss her especially."

But not who she became at the end, the moody young woman desperate to talk her mother out of an arranged marriage. I missed the sweet child who smiled every time she saw me, who danced as often as she walked, who brought light into every room.

"What happened to her?"

"I—" My throat constricted, and it took all my strength to get the next words out. "I failed to protect her."

Andre fell silent again, and I was grateful. I needed to give the words some space before I went on. Enough that the stabbing sensation in my chest faded.

"She lost herself," I said, so quietly I wasn't sure he could hear me.

Eternia and Lord Emaldus reached the prayer tree at the same time. They bowed to each other, then clasped their hands together. Eternia's expression remained calm. None of her recent moodiness showed through.

The Princess, despite months of arguing, would go through with the wedding and cement her mother's alliance with the Emaldus family.

Queen Corinthia, standing at the edge of my vision behind the priest, relaxed.

I, on the other hand, stayed alert, counting the guests, watching for signs of trouble.

A movement from the prayer tree caught my attention. Eternia's smile widened as a heavy black cloud formed above the temple garden. Lightning burst from the sky, striking the prayer tree. It split right down the middle, all the way to the base, splinters flying.

Screams filled the air, drawing my eyes to the crowd. Row after row of guests, holding their daggers to their own throats. Some cried, others trembled, but all held their blades in place, ready to end their own lives.

Queen Corinthia's hands remained at her sides, pinned either by Eternia's will or her own blind panic.

Eternia cackled. "You all think you can control my life. Now, who is in control?"

The first row of guests slit their own throats, without a moment's hesitation. They collapsed at the feet of the second group, bodies twitching as they bled out.

I gaped, my body frozen with fear. Was this the true power of telars? Not to kill, but to make others kill themselves? How could Eternia, the princess I adored, do something so heinous?

Eternia laughed again. The second row of guests drew their blades across their own throats. One woman's skull shattered when it hit the ground, blood and bone flying everywhere, soaking the petrified row of guests behind them. The stench of urine filled the air as dozens of people pissed themselves, their bodies shaking with fear, unable to break Eternia's hold.

"Stop!" I heard myself yell. "Stop, Eternia, please stop."

"Oh, Riana." She jerked her head to the side.

Another row of guests slashed their own throats, cutting their own screams short as blood spurted from their necks. Their bodies fell onto the row of guests behind them. Corpses upon corpses upon corpses. Warm and twitching and dead.

Somewhere inside me a spark lit, and I could move again. I drew my sword and raced toward—

"I order you to stop moving now," Eternia said.

My blood boiled, bringing me to the ground. I screamed as agony filled every inch of my being, but I forced myself forward, pushing through the pain.

"I order you to watch."

Blisters broke out all along my skin. I screeched and let go of my sword. I curled my body into a ball and lifted my head enough to see the crowd.

The compulsion receded, the heat fleeing through the cold stone beneath me.

"And I order—no, I want—you to understand that this is your fault. You failed to protect me. First, from my brother."

The fourth row of guests stabbed themselves in the chests. Their screams filled the air, making it almost impossible to hear Eternia's next words.

"Then, from my mother."

Queen Corinthia yelped and crashed to the ground, falling into my line of sight. A dagger stuck out of her left eye, blood and vitreous fluid pooling around it. My eyes blurred with tears, this time from sorrow instead of pain.

"Or, finally, from a wedding to one of the most monstrous men alive."

Lord Emaldus let go of Eternia's hands, and raised his own to cup his jaw and the top of his head. He twisted with all his might, breaking his own neck with a mighty crack.

"I'm sorry," I said, the words escaping between sobs. "I never realized—"

"Too late now." Eternia gestured at the remaining guests, covered in blood and shaking with terror. "You're going to watch me kill all of them, and then I'm going to kill you."

"I failed her." I wiped a stray tear away with my sleeve. "Her brother abused her for years, right under my nose. And then I let Queen Corinthia sell her to a cruel, awful man."

"You might have failed her," Andre said, "but you're not responsible for what they did to her. Or what she did."

He sounded so certain, as if he had seen the whole thing himself. As if he could really understand what happened from my words.

"Maybe not in your mind," I said. "The rest of the world disagrees." The gods themselves disagreed. Magdalene had threatened to destroy me outright, and Kalum agreed with her, for once. Even Jaldan had believed I deserved punishment, albeit a mild one. Only Loki considered me blameless.

The only one Loki couldn't convince was me. "My failure led to Eternia's massacre and the end of Shalinor's golden age." The dragons left after Eternia's massacre, leaving Shalinor's royal family vulnerable. Centuries of back-and-forth civil wars ensued. The queendom only stabilized three generations before Kahri's time. Even then, Shalinor remained a shadow of its former self. "Shalinor might still be standing, if I protected her properly."

"Or Princess Eternia might have lost her mind and massacred everyone anyway," Andre said. "You were bound to follow her orders, by a blood oath. You couldn't have stopped her."

"Yes, I could have. If I had been willing to give my life for theirs." Instead I capitulated, submitting to Eternia's will to make my pain end. I'd thought only about the momentary agony, not what came next.

"This is where you say something heroic, right? Something like 'we always have a choice?'"

I raised an eyebrow. "It's not heroic, it's true. We always have a choice. Even if the choice is death." A choice I was prepared to make, now.

Andre shook his head. "That's not a real choice. Everyone wants to live."

"Then why did you come back to Moonshadow?"

His expression darkened, and he turned his attention to the fire, staring into the middle distance. His horse sped up, putting several paces between us.

"I'm sorry," I said after several moments of silence. "I shouldn't pry into your past."

He sighed. "I didn't think I was choosing death. I underestimated Alexis's spies."

So, she caught him the second time. No wonder he hated her so much. "Still, you knew it was a risk."

"A minor one." He took a deep breath. "At least, compared to the risk of breaking my son's heart."

I tilted my head to the side. I didn't know what I expected him to say, but it certainly wasn't that. Even Jacob II hadn't told me about Andre's son.

"Calder. We celebrated his eleventh naming day the night before Isabella's funeral." Andre spoke with all the warmth of a proud father. A brief smile crossed his face. "I promised to take him to the spring festival. His mother's a barmaid. My brother wouldn't let us marry, and she won't accept my money, so she still works."

"And the spring festival is one of the busiest nights of the year," I said. "Did you get to take him, at least?"

Andre scowled. "No. They caught me too fast." His hands balled into fists around his reins. "Calder forgave me, though, when I did see him. Said he forgave me, anyway."

"You don't believe him?"

"When our parents betray us, some part of us never forgives. We certainly never forget."

I didn't ask what infractions he was trying to forget.

Amheld Fortress was built to impress the Shalinoran dignitaries who passed through its gates, and it showed. Both the outer wall and the keep were built of the same gleaming black stone as Ashe's temples. White marble gargoyles guarded either side of the steel-reinforced wooden doors.

Two towers also guarded this entrance, their crenellations carved to look like flower petals. A middle-aged Slayer wearing a lilandium helmet poked his head out between a pair of these stone petals.

"Who goes there?" he shouted in a raspy voice.

"Riana of Moonshadow and the Seventy-First Slayer Contingent," I yelled back. "On the king's business."

"Riana of Moonshadow," the Slayer echoed. "Open the gates."

More shouting ensued, followed by the screech of metal scraping against stone, likely the portcullis rising behind the gate. Four Slayers, all middle-aged men wearing lilandium helmets, pushed the doors open, two to each door.

I nudged my stallion forward and we rode into the courtyard, a wide green space hemmed in by a series of towers. Narrow steps led to the keep, guarded by another pair of towers on either side of the entrance.

Commander Byrne, a big man with red cheeks, stood on a landing halfway up the stairs. Eight Slayers, all either fresh young faces or men almost ready for retirement, stood around him in a diamond-shaped formation.

"Welcome, honoured guests," Lord Byrne said, once the entire war party had entered the courtyard. He shot Imeni a quick, dirty look, but kept his gaze mostly on me. "Your supplies are already prepared. My men will load them into your wagons while you rest. And tonight, a feast! We've spent weeks preparing."

Imeni and I exchanged looks. She shrugged. We weren't here to celebrate, but it might do our soldiers some good. There certainly wouldn't be much to celebrate once we entered the Wastelands.

"So long as the festivities are short," I said. "The king's business cannot be delayed."

He frowned, but nodded. "Of course. For now, you must be eager to eat and rest. My men will take care of your horses."

Chapter Thirty-Four

The room provided by Commander Byrne was small but well furnished, with a simple wooden wardrobe, a bedside table holding an oil lamp, and a surprisingly comfortable bed. I stripped to my underclothes and crawled in between the linen blankets, relishing their softness on my skin.

After so many nights on the road, this bed felt divine. I sank into a heavy sleep within moments.

And for once, there were no dreams.

Several hours later, a distant scream jolted me awake. My heart pounded in my chest as I leapt out of bed, straining my ears. More screeching, and the sounds of metal clanging against metal, filled my head.

Hurry! Rolf called. *There's too many of them.*

Of whom? I asked, pulling on my breeches.

Harpies.

Harpies?

Bird women. Rolf's thought rode a wave of panic so strong it almost knocked me off my feet.

I strapped my sword to my waist. *But they've been extinct for centuries.*

They're here now.

Oh, gods. I shivered. Harpies were wild, vicious beasts, the scourge of humanity before they died out. *Get into the air now.*

Already up.

Good. I stepped into my boots. *On my way now.*

I slid my chainmail shirt over my underclothes and pulled my coat on, tying it shut as I dashed through the halls. Left, right, down a flight of stairs, out the main door and—

I came to an abrupt halt, shielding my eyes from the midday sun. A harpy squealed, dragging an archer off of the battlements by his scalp. The archer screamed and flailed until his body came loose, falling onto the steps in front of me. He exploded, blood and guts filling the air. Warm, wet spray covered my boots and breeches.

The harpy cackled and rejoined her sisters, thirteen other harpies, their awful leathery faces drawn back in sadistic grins that revealed rows of sharp teeth. They were pushing a line of Slayers, mostly Commander Byrne's men, toward the keep, their long talons already soaked in blood. Corpses littered the ground around the outer wall. More archers were dragged off of the battlements as I watched, their horrified yells filling the air as they were dropped onto the stone foundations of the fortress.

A silver shimmer caught my eye.

I swivelled to see Rolf streaking across the sky, harried by four harpies who screeched with delight as they closed in on their prey.

Rolf's head whipped around, and his mouth opened. Flames burst from his throat, a wide stream that engulfed all four harpies. The stench of burning flesh and feathers filled the air as they fell from the sky, their bodies smashing against the outer wall.

Another harpy appeared behind Rolf. One of her talons caught on a crevice between his scales. She yanked. A fur-covered scale came free, followed by a stream of reddish-black liquid.

Rolf roared and slammed his body against her, hurling her into the nearest tower. Bones crunched against stone and she fell, twitching as she tried to force air into punctured lungs.

But the damage was already done. Blood poured out of Rolf's wound at an alarming rate. More harpies turned toward him, excited by the scent. They were going to kill him.

I screamed, pouring all my frustration into an anguished roar. *Get away, Rolf. You're faster than them.*

You need me. Rolf's mindvoice sounded strained, as if even those words took an enormous amount of effort.

The nearest line of harpies broke away from the Slayers they were fighting and charged toward me. I drew my sword.

Go, damn it. The nearest harpy swung her clawed feet at my face. I ducked, and thrust my blade upwards. A talon grazed the base of my neck, breaking the skin. My sword scraped the harpy's spine, shuddering as it hit one vertebrae after another. Blood and feathers rained down on my head, sticky and stinking.

My blade sank into the joint of the harpy's left wing. A spasm wracked her entire body as she tried to free herself. I yanked my blade free, and she spiralled toward the ground with an awful, guttural yell. Slayers rushed forward to finish her.

Two new harpies filled my vision, claws swinging at my face and arms. I stumbled backward and ducked. One of the claws sank into the door behind me. I chopped through the leg attached to it. Hot, dark liquid spurted from the wound, covering my face and eyes.

I stumbled back, trying to wipe away the blood with my sleeve, but it was soaked too. My foot hit the edge of the platform and I scrambled back toward the door. The muscles in my back frantically stitched up my wound as I moved, the area tingling as new skin stretched over it.

Two rows of four sharp teeth clamped down on my ankle, crunching bone. My leg gave way and I tumbled down the steps, sword flying out of my hand. The harpy clamped down further, clinging to me as we hit one step and then another. I screamed and kicked at her head with my other foot, but couldn't land a single blow.

The force of smashing against the second landing knocked her free, catapulting her into the sky above me. A volley of arrows from the towers on either side of the steps filled her body. Blood poured from her mouth, her body sinking below my range of vision. I leaned back and gulped down as much air as my lungs could fit.

Pain hit then, searing, burning agony that shot outwards from my ankle and consumed every part of my being. Skin and muscle tried to pull itself back together, but the damage was too great. It would be days before I could walk again.

Riana, no! Rolf's mindvoice forced me back to consciousness. *Hold on, I'm coming.*

A wave of magical energy followed these words, filling my body, pushing it to heal faster. I opened my eyes and pushed myself into sitting position. *You've helped enough. Find a safe place to heal. That's an order.*

You don't command me.

I cursed. Loki sent Rolf as a companion, not a subordinate, and now Rolf was going to use his freedom to get himself killed.

Please go. I'll be safe. I unclipped the dagger from my right arm brace and stood, clenching my teeth as agony rippled outwards from my ankle. *The battle's almost done anyway.*

The last part, at least, was true. Corpses, a mixture of harpy and human, littered the courtyard. Piles of guts glistened in the sun. The sounds of battle had mostly been replaced with the sounds of death.

A glinting movement caught my gaze and I leaned forward to see Braiden Cowell fighting one of the remaining harpies. She kicked at his head. He moved back, pressing up against the wall, and raised his sword. She swung again, one talon catching on his sword, knocking it out of his hands.

Braiden grabbed a hunting knife from his left boot and drove it into the harpy's other foot. She screeched and yanked it away, taking the knife with it and leaving Braiden unarmed.

I tried to stand, but my leg wouldn't even move, let alone support my weight.

The harpy dived again, this time head first, her jaws open impossibly wide. Braiden's eyes widened and the colour drained from his face, his legs locking together at the knees. He knew fear now, and would die afraid, whimpering for his life.

No. I hurled my dagger at the harpy with my remaining strength, aiming for the small of her back, right below the wings.

The harpy knocked Braiden's raised arms aside and clenched her teeth around his neck, tearing his head off.

My blade sank into her back and she collapsed, her body landing in a pile with Braiden's, their blood mixing together in a terrible, disgusting pool of feathers, skin, and death.

I leaned over the edge of the platform and let the contents of my stomach loose. A war horn sounded somewhere, three short blasts. *We won.* The harpies were dead.

Dark spots filled the edges of my vision. I rested my head against the steps, hardly noticing the sharp edges or the hardness of the stone.

Riana? Is it over? Rolf's anxious mindvoice filled my mind.

Yes. Maybe even all of it.

I closed my eyes, letting the darkness carry my mind away.

I woke in Amheld Fortress's healing hall, a narrow chamber with forty beds lined up along either wall, spaced four paces apart. Slayers who stank of death and infection filled most of the beds, emitting the occasional groan or whimper. Several rattled with each breath, the sound grating on my nerves.

Pain consumed the rest of my thoughts. My head throbbed. My stomach churned. Searing agony shot up and down my right leg.

The only thing that didn't hurt was my right foot. No feeling came from that foot at all. Only the crude cast around it told me it still existed at all.

Memories flooded my mind, overwhelming my still-foggy mind. Harpies. One bit my ankle, right through the bone. *But I* am *magic.* I should have healed. Or at least be healing.

I shifted my weight. Sharp pain shot up my leg, growing more intense as it traveled up my leg before subsiding. I gasped, my eyes watering. *It's still attached.* For now.

"You're awake," a familiar voice said from somewhere to the right of my head.

I looked up to see Andre sitting beside the bed, his mouth pressed into a tight line. He held his arms crossed over his chest. There wasn't even a hint of his usual carefree attitude.

"What—" That wasn't the word I wanted. *Think, self, think.* I had survived worse pain before. I would survive this, if only I could focus.

"Harpies—"

I held a palm up to stop him. I needed quiet to focus. But when Andre paused, other sounds filled my ears. The sounds of the dying.

"Get me out of here," I said. The words sounded strange and tore at my throat, but they were the right words. "I need silence."

"I don't know where your room is," he said.

I cursed. Of course not. This was Fortress Amheld, not the castle of Moon Spire. I didn't really know where my room was either. "Take me to yours. Anywhere's better than here."

"The healers won't like it. You're not to be moved."

"Too bad." I clenched my teeth and swung my legs over the side of the bed. "I'm not staying here. They don't know anything about healing demons anyway." They didn't have to. Normally we healed on our own.

Andre chuckled. "I see your injuries haven't diminished your spirit." His expression grew solemn. "Stay still, and I'll help you."

His tone was warm and genuine, with a gentleness I didn't know he was capable of. I stilled, letting him place my arms around his neck and lift me, one arm supporting my back and the other wrapped around my thighs. He pressed me close to his chest and straightened as he carried me out of the room.

I closed my eyes and leaned into him. I had forgotten how good it was to be held, even if it was out of necessity, not love. And he smelled nice, for a vampire. Like clean soil instead of the usual blood-magic stench.

A shrill voice interrupted my thoughts. "Sir, her leg shouldn't move for at least—"

One of the Vonstone healers who had accompanied us from Moonshadow, an elderly man with thinning white hair, stood between Andre and the door. His brow was furrowed and his mouth curved downwards, his overall expression halfway between worry and condescension.

"Have you ever treated a demon before?" Andre asked, a warning edge in his tone.

"No, but—"

"I will take care of her." Andre stepped around the healer and strode out of the room.

The healer followed us for several paces, giving Andre an endless litany of instructions. Call for broth and water, make sure both get into my system. Wash and re-wrap the ankle wound every six hours. The ankle wound that should have healed.

Why wasn't I healing? What was happening to me?

"I slept through the battle," Andre said as we turned a corner. "By the time the servants woke me, the fighting was over. I couldn't do a damn thing to help."

"Even your kind has limitations," I said. "They attacked during daylight. You weren't capable of fighting back. That isn't your fault."

He frowned. "But it *is* my fault. I chose to return to Moonshadow. I let you convince me to wait until we crossed the border to start taking the sarentin."

The harsh edge of self-hatred in Andre's tone stunned me into silence. Clearly I had misjudged him. He was nothing like Loki. His lighthearted nature was a mask. The same way my confidence was.

Andre didn't speak again until we reached his room, a carpeted chamber twice the size of my own. Probably one of the rooms intended for Shalinoran nobles passing through.

"I thought harpies were extinct," he said, lowering me onto the bed.

"So did I." I ran a hand through my hair, cursing as my fingers caught on a series of knots. "The past few weeks have shown many things I thought I knew to be lies." And many things I assumed were lies to be true.

"Do you think Kahri sent them?"

"Where else could they have come from?" If anybody in the mortal realm had the power to restore an extinct species, it was Kahri. Besides, she was the only one who wanted us dead.

Andre's voice dropped to a near-whisper. "Magdalene. Only the gods can create life, right? And she always favoured the telars."

I bit my bottom lip. The gods rarely intervened on a mortal's behalf, but they had done it before, for Kahri. Would they do it again? Magdalene did love vengeance.

But this wasn't her style. "No. It wasn't Magdalene or the other gods."

He raised an eyebrow. "How can you be so sure?"

"If Magdalene wanted to stop us, we would be dead or trapped in another realm. She doesn't leave things to chance."

"That means Kahri can create life using nothing but magic." He stared into his lap, balling his hands into fists. "How are we supposed to fight an enemy like that?"

"She's still human," I said. "She can still die." *I hope.*

I spent the next several hours drifting in and out of consciousness. Andre remained by my side, accompanied by a different person every time I woke. A pasty-faced serving boy with a tray of soup and tea, which I downed so quickly that the boy gaped. Commander Byrne, whispering news into Andre's ear. All bad, judging by their expressions. The elderly healer from earlier—Jayr, that was his name—pushing a cart full of medical supplies.

This last visitor dragged Andre out of the room for several moments, arguing with him in hushed tones. I didn't need to listen to know what they were talking about. The healer wanted me back in the healing ward, with the injured Slayers. Andre wanted me comfortable, and that meant staying here.

Eventually they returned, Jayr's face twisted into a scowl.

"I'll show you how to tend her wound," he said. "I can't be running back and forth across this fortress constantly."

"What about the other healers?"

"Resting." He brought his cart in line with the bed. "They've healed most of the wounds that weren't poisoned. They'll need to sleep through most of tomorrow."

"Poisoned?" I asked, propping myself up on my elbows.

The healer grimaced. "Harpy saliva is poisonous. Everyone who got bitten is dead, except you."

Was that why I couldn't heal? Poison made injuries harder to heal, but I had always recovered within a few days. Maybe all I needed was more time. "How long has it been? Since the fight?"

"Two days," Andre said.

"Two *days*?" That was plenty of time for my ankle to heal.

Jayr moved the blankets away from my leg. "People with a poisoned or infected injury often lose time. I imagine it's the same for your kind."

"Yes, but—"

"This is going to hurt." The healer grabbed a short wooden stool from the lower half of the cart and propped my leg up on it. "I brought pain reliever potions, but I'm not sure what they'll do for you."

"Not much."

He sighed. "That's what I feared. I need you to stay still, no matter how much it hurts."

Andre moved to the other side of the bed and held a hand out. "If it helps, you can squeeze my hand."

I took the offered hand with a bleak smile. "Thanks."

The healer untied the top of the bandage that held my cast together. He unravelled the first layer with three quick movements, revealing a second bandage soaked in green and yellow puss. It stank, too, like my leg was already rotting.

Panic swelled in my chest. What if it was already rotting? What if I was going to lose my leg? Growing another one would take years of meditation and rest. Years neither me nor Moonshadow could afford to lose.

"I'm going to pull this free on the count of three," Jayr said.

"Just do it," I growled.

His eyebrows lifted slightly, but he followed my command, ripping the bandage away in one swift yank. Healing skin tore away with it, exposing the wound to cold air. Itchy, cold pain spread outward along my skin. The veins around it were swollen and green, the poison trying to force its way into the rest of my body.

The wound itself was a deep cavern, layers of infected blood and muscle cut away to reveal bone. Its stench caught in my throat, making my stomach do somersaults. Andre wrinkled his nose and his lips tightened into a thin line.

"No change," Jayr said, frowning. "The bone healed within a few hours, but everything else, well—"

"My body has stopped the poison's spread, but can't kill it." From the discolouration in my veins, I doubted my body would even be able to slow it for much longer. "We need the antidote."

"That's going to be a problem," the healer said. "The virum root was never cultivated outside of Shalinor. It died out when Kahri cursed the land."

So *that* was Kahri's plan. Kill the human soldiers. Poison me and Rolf.

Rolf. I hadn't heard from him since the fight. I closed my eyes and forced myself to concentrate, using all the strength left in my mind to call for him.

I'm here. His voice was weak, but warm and comforting all the same. *Sleeping on the other side of the wall. Healing.*

At least one of us was healing. *When will you be able to fly again?* If I couldn't fight, our only option was to send Rolf alone, and pray that his fire was hot enough to melt Kahri in her palace.

I could fly now, but I shouldn't for another three days. Irritation tinted these thoughts, like the impatience of a child waiting for a storm to end so they could play outside.

Damn Loki, sending Rolf into this. He deserved better.

Wait. Loki. That was it.

"Riana?" Andre asked. "Are you all right?"

I laughed. "All right? No. But I do have an idea. Bandage me up and get me a communication mirror."

My stomach growled, awakened by the need to power my healing processes. "And something to eat."

Two bowls of soup, half a dozen pastries, and one painful re-bandaging process later, Andre propped me up into a sitting position for my meeting, aided by half a dozen pillows. Commander Byrne's full-length communication mirror stood three feet away, facing me. I was grateful for the pure darkness of its obsidian surface. I didn't want to see what the poison had reduced me to.

"Are you sure you don't need anything else?" Andre asked. "More water?"

I shook my head. "Just privacy."

"I'll stay in the hallway. Shout if you need me."

I couldn't help but smile. I rather liked this new, kinder side of Andre. "I will."

He smiled back, though it didn't reach his eyes, and left the room. I waited until his footsteps stopped—exactly halfway down the hall—before turning my attention to the black mirror.

Loki appeared before I finished forming his image in my mind. He sported a red beard and was bald for the day, but his face otherwise remained the same, including that damned grin.

"What can I do for you?"

"You already know the answer," I said.

"Well, you could be contacting me for any number of reasons. You might want to know about the prince's failing health, or that the king is mad, or—"

"I could want to find the virum root." Though if *Loki* was calling Jacob VIII mad, Moonshadow might not be worth fighting for, after all. A mad king could do a lot of damage in the year before Marcus became old enough to rule in his own right.

"Oh," he said, screwing up his face in mock confusion. "Why would you want to know that?"

I rolled my eyes. "Why do you think?"

"Well, I suppose you might want to keep your ankle. And the foot attached to it. But I thought you knew. It grows in Shalinor, mostly around Vandemor."

The city where I lived with Eternia. A place I had hoped to avoid on this journey. "But nothing has grown there in centuries."

Loki sighed. "That you know about. You really should have flown, you know."

I blinked. He almost sounded concerned. "I can't fight Kahri alone."

"Nobody has to fight Kahri if you can destroy her power source."

"Her power source?" Was he talking about the relic she must have used to channel her power? I assumed there had to be one, of course, but what if it did more than just channel her power? What if it was the source of that power?

"Tut-tut." Loki's brow furrowed in an attempt to look stern. "You can't expect me to figure everything out for you."

He disappeared before I could respond. I stared at the blank mirror for a long time, willing him to reappear, but nothing happened.

I cursed and hurled one of my pillows at the far wall. The thin fabric holding it together ripped and the stuffing fell out, the case drifting to the ground behind it. Falling apart, like everything else. And my only hope to fix myself hinged on trusting Loki's words and finding the virum root in Vandemor before amputation became necessary.

Somehow this job had gotten even worse.

Chapter Thirty-Five

At sunset the next evening, Andre half-carried me to a meeting room. Imeni was there, tapping a nervous rhythm on the table with her fingertips. A blood vessel had burst in her right eye, turning half of it pink.

"Shouldn't you still be resting?" She gestured at my wounded leg. "Healing?"

"Rest won't heal me." I hobbled into my seat, wincing as my wound brushed against a chair leg. "Only the virum root can help me."

Imeni's fingers stilled. Her next words were weighted with the same defeat I had heard in Andre's voice the night before. "The virum root died with Shalinor."

"Not according to Loki."

Imeni's eyes widened. "You've spoken to—"

"He *is* the one who sent me here." I grabbed a stone pitcher and filled a tankard with ale. The drink was nothing like the king's brandy, or even the ale served to castle servants, but it quenched my thirst well enough. "He says the virum root grows again, in Vandemor." The last place I wanted to go.

"And you trust him? The god of mischief?"

"He's the god of more than mischief," Andre said, his tone low and threatening.

I had almost forgotten about Andre's past in the Midnight Order. I knew why he left, but why had he joined in the first place? What did Loki mean to him?

Questions for another time.

"We can either trust him, or give up." I met Andre's eyes. "That's not a real choice."

He smiled. "I'm with you. We'll head to Vandemor and find the virum root. Even if we have to search every nook and cranny."

"We only have thirty soldiers left," Imeni said. "We should wait for reinforcements. My uncle can send search parties into the Wastelands. They can scout ahead, too, for other enemies."

I leaned forward, resting my forearms on the table and folding my fingers together. "In other circumstances, I might agree. But Marcus is dying. We don't have time for search parties to leave, find the root, and come back."

Imeni stiffened. "With all due respect, the prince could die any day now. Rushing into this only increases the odds that *we'll* die."

"This isn't only about my nephew," Andre said. "Thousands of others are dying, too."

"Waiting for reinforcements increases our odds of saving those people."

"Waiting gives Kahri more time to prepare," I said, in the most commanding voice I could summon through my exhaustion. "New soldiers won't mean much if we've given her the time to build a whole army of harpies. We'll take reinforcements from Commander Byrne's men."

Imeni scowled. "Half of his men died. He doesn't have the numbers."

"We don't want his soldiers either," Andre said. "Ours are handpicked, elite warriors in their prime. The soldiers here are old men sent to enjoy relative peace in their final years, or green brats sent to learn patience."

"They're better than no reinforcements at all." I straightened, letting my arms fall to my sides. "You will choose twenty-five of Commander Byrne's Slayers to accompany us."

"Twenty-five? That still only gives us fifty-five soldiers total."

I bit back a groan. I didn't have the time or the energy for this. "Fifty-five soldiers, a demon, and a dragon. Seems like plenty against one woman."

"What if she has more harpies? Or other monsters?" Imeni's voice shook, though I couldn't be sure whether it was from fear or anger. "We need an army, not a handful of soldiers."

"There are limits to her power." Even if I had no idea what they were. "We must assume that if she could summon more monsters, she already would have."

"What if she's waiting for us to enter Shalinor so she can pick us off with ease?" Imeni spat out the words, anger overriding her fear. "Drawing your enemies out is basic strategy."

"Rolf's already outside the fortress walls. No monsters have come for him." And I could think of no better strategy than attacking a dragon while he was injured. "My decision is final. We leave at dawn."

Chapter Thirty-Six

Kahri

I brought the bowl to my lips and gulped down the last of the broth. Caerwyn beamed as I returned it to the tray on my bedside table. This was the second full meal I had managed in twice as many days. Chewing even the mushy vegetables in my soup required too much energy.

"Do you want me to bring something more substantial for supper?" Caerwyn refilled my glass with water. "Perhaps some wine?"

I shook my head. "I'll come downstairs tonight. I feel well enough."

"Excellent. I'll be sure to set a place for you." A suspicious look crossed her face and she rested her hands on her hips. "You're not going back to work, are you? You must save your strength."

"My harpies died." I felt their deaths as they happened, one small tug at my heart after another. "I must prepare to defend Riminira."

"By gathering your strength. We'll help, too. Tell us what you need."

"I need you to focus on teaching the others." I climbed out of bed. "And I promise, all I'm doing today is looking. We need to know what we're up against if we hope to fight them." She wouldn't be anywhere near the fighting, but I was saving that piece of information for later. I didn't have the energy to argue about it now.

"Why can't I look for you? Teach me how to use the orb."

I shook my head. "Only those bound to the orb by blood can use it." If I died, or the orb was destroyed, anyone bound to it would die with us.

Caerwyn grimaced. "I see." She lifted my meal tray. "I'll check on you in two hours."

"I won't be working that long, promise." I did need to conserve my strength, as much as I hated to admit it. My harpies might have defeated, or at least disabled, the demon and the dragon, but Moonshadow would send an army next. I had only earned a temporary delay.

I sat cross-legged in front of my orb and rested my hands on my knees, palms facing the ceiling. A deep calm washed over me, and my eyelids drifted shut. My lips curved into a slight smile as I leaned into the soothing darkness behind my eyes. There was something calming about returning here, to the chamber where I had spent most of my life, no matter the circumstances.

I took a deep breath and focused on the core of my being, a bright blue ball pulsing with magical energy. A silver chain held it together. One end of this chain connected my soul to my orb.

This bond, forged when I spoke the word of power, kept me in the mortal realm and preserved Riminira. It turned my connection with the orb into a strange kind of synergy, giving me access to magic beyond anything my ancestors could have imagined.

I focused on this connection. The chain between us glowed. Crimson shot out from the orb, turning half of the chain red.

My spirit floated out of my body and an image of a grey, rocky plain dotted with black tents formed below me. The tents were built in a series of half circles with cooking fires between them. Blue-coated Slayers ate around these fires, while others kept watch at the camp's edges.

There was no sign of the demon or the dragon. Perhaps my harpies completed their job after all. I could defeat ordinary humans while protecting my city and its people, and keep those I'd brought back to life here a little longer, to teach them more of my ways.

A silver shimmer caught my attention and I swivelled to see the sky serpent flying toward the camp.

I cursed and willed myself back to the observatory. My eyes snapped open and my palms flipped, my fingernails digging into my legs as I stared at the orb.

My harpies had accomplished nothing. The dragon seemed uninjured, and if he still followed the humans, I could only assume the demon was alive. In ten days, they would enter my city. On the eleventh day, Riminira would be no more, and neither would I.

I began private lessons with Magda, the most skilled telar among the group Fiona had sent me, after breakfast the next morning.

"Caerwyn tells me you're learning well," I said.

Magda broke into an ear-to-ear grin. "Fiona taught me, when she had time."

I gestured for her to sit in the armchair on the other side of my desk. "You are Fiona's first disciple. She trusts you."

Magda's expression grew solemn and her back straightened. "Yes, your Majesty. She helped father raise me."

I raised an eyebrow. Fiona had mentioned apprentices, but she never mentioned raising a child. She certainly didn't have any of her own, unless she had gone to great pains to hide them from me. *Why would she hide such a thing?*

"What about your mother?"

"She stayed in Moonshadow, with my sister. They didn't have our gift, so father thought it best they remain there."

"Do you miss them?"

Magda shrugged. "Not really. Sometimes I wonder about my sister though, what she's like now. What she'd do if we met. Has Moonshadow made her hate people like me? Would she even want to meet me again?" She flushed. "I'm ranting, aren't I? Sorry."

"It's all right." Every piece of information helped me confirm that I had chosen the right pupil. "Your name, is it short for Magdalene?"

She beamed. "After the goddess herself."

"A bold choice, comparing one's children to the gods. My people once forbade such names, declaring them the ultimate act of ego."

"That wasn't their intention." Her voice grew thick with the fervour of complete devotion as she went on. "They wanted me to honour the goddess. To remember who created life, even when I lived in the ignorant land of Moonshadow."

By the end of her speech, there was a fire in her eyes. I had carried the same fire in my soul once, the same undying loyalty to Magdalene. When she abandoned me, that loyalty fell to Loki, who had put the pieces of my shattered soul back together with a gentleness entirely unlike him.

Now he was gone, too. All of the gods had deserted our people. But faith and hope carried people through the darkest times in their life, so I let Magda keep hers.

"Can I count on the same loyalty you offered Magdalene, the devotion you extended to Fiona?"

"Without question." She gazed into my eyes. "Always."

"Good." I unrolled a map of Shalinor and stretched it across my desk. "I have a task for you."

Chapter Thirty-Seven

The main garden of Magdalene's high temple stretched out before me, its stone paths cracked and discoloured by patches of old blood. At the far end stood the prayer tree, blackened and split down the middle. A patch of spiky purple leaves poked out between its roots.

My heart soared. The virum root had spiky purple leaves. Loki had told the truth after all.

I hopped across the garden, sticking to the main path. Even with the damage it was smoother than the surrounding ground.

My left foot caught on an uneven cobblestone and I fell face-first. My arms instinctively moved to block the worst of the fall, but the stone tore chunks of my skin away. Blood poured out of the wounds, but I felt no pain, only shock.

A heavy wave of exhaustion washed over me. I rested my head on the ground, staring at the purple leaves. If only they weren't so far away. I stretched one arm out, but the tip of my longest finger fell far short of the nearest leaf.

A woman behind me laughed. I rolled onto my back and propped myself up with my still bleeding arms.

Eternia stood over me in her blood-soaked dress, her head thrown back in laughter.

"You'll never reach it."

"I will," I said, trying to sound confident. "I'll heal, and I'll end Kahri's plague."

She laughed again. "You won't do anything. You'll fail, like you did before."

She vanished. The garden disappeared too, leaving me in complete darkness. Darkness, and an unbearable cold that made my body ache.

A new face appeared above me. Morgan's face, smiling, as he knelt beside me. I reached out to touch him, but my hand went right through him. The familiar ache of loneliness filled my chest.

"Why?" I asked. "Why could you not choose living death? We could have had eternity."

His mouth drooped at either end and he shook his head. He ran a ghostly hand down the side of my cheek, his fingers a cold, thick fog. I shivered, but pressed my face into his hand anyway. It passed through me, and the fog lifted me, brought me closer to him. Icy tendrils wrapped around me, pulling me in a demented, yet graceful, dance. My body was frozen all the way through, but I said nothing. I wanted him too much, wanted to enjoy this beautiful moment, the comfortable silence.

When we finished our third circle, he kissed my cheek with cold lips, smiled sadly and let go.

I plummeted to the ground. My Morgan vanished. I screamed but only wind came out.

Eternia kept laughing.

Someone pressed a cool, damp cloth against my forehead. I smacked their hand away and swung my legs out of bed.

My right leg hit the corner of the bedframe and I yowled as sharp, invisible needles jabbed into my calf.

"You mustn't move like that." Jayr grabbed my shoulders and attempted to push me back down onto the mattress. "You'll aggravate the damage."

I shrugged him off and waved at a pair of crutches lying across one of the boxes that dominated the left side of the wagon. "Bring those here. I'm going for a walk."

"Didn't you hear what I said? You're going to make it worse."

"I'm *going* for a walk." I gritted my teeth and pushed myself off of the mattress, putting all of my weight on my left foot.

Jayr frowned. "Please, Commander, you need rest."

Rest was the last thing I needed. "We've been on the road five days. I spent most of those days confined to this bed. I need air." I hopped over to the box with the crutches.

He frowned, but helped me get the crutches down and under my shoulders. I leaned heavily on them and propelled myself forward, wincing with each step.

"You really shouldn't," Jayr said. "We can move stuff into the other wagon, make a path for you to walk in here. It'll be crammed, but it'll fit."

"No." This wagon didn't have nearly enough space. Or open sky.

He sighed. "Very well. I'll come with you."

"I need solitude." My memories were more than enough company.

I reached the edge of the wagon and lifted the canvas curtain. A Slayer on watch several feet away caught sight of me. She straightened, brought a fist to her chest, and bowed.

I smiled. I preferred working alone, but being in charge was kind of nice.

"Help me down," I said, gesturing for the Slayer to come forward. "And make sure nobody follows. Especially Jayr."

The Slayer's mouth tightened, but she saluted me with a "yes, ma'am." After three attempts and twice as many curses, we got me out of the wagon and back onto my crutches. My infected leg burned and itched and ached, the pain flaring into agony as I moved away from the wagon.

"You sure you don't want the healer to come with you?" the Slayer asked.

"My orders stand. Don't even let him leave the wagon until I return."

"But, Commander—"

"Thank you for your assistance." I swivelled on my left toe and hobbled into camp.

Our camp remained in the same formation we used when traveling in Moonshadow— several semi-circles of tents all facing a large common area. At Andre's insistence, he and Imeni now rested in the semi-circle closest to the supply wagons. This allowed him to check on me every day before the march began. It also gave me a safe place to walk without the main army seeing the severity of my condition.

The sheer effort of moving with crutches provided a welcome distraction from my memories at first, but eventually I fell into a comfortable rhythm and the memories returned, more vibrant than ever. Eternia's wedding. The sentence the gods handed down to me, a sequence of tortures, each worse than the last.

My recent batch of nightmares—ten of them in half as many days—were different though. Rooted in the future, not the past. And the virum root was there. Were my dreams trying to tell me something? Did the virum root grow in the bloodstained soil of Magdalene's garden?

My infected ankle slammed into one of my crutches and I collapsed. Dark spots filled my vision. My stomach churned.

I rolled onto my back and closed my eyes, breathing slow and deep. The memories racing through my mind slowed and eventually stopped, giving way to blessed nothingness.

"What in the five realms?" Andre's worried half-shout penetrated the darkness of my mind. "Riana, are you all right?"

Cool arms encircled my shoulders, lifting me off the ground and bringing me close to someone's chest. Andre, from the smell. I smiled and shifted my head to rest against his shoulder.

Imeni sprinted over, her footsteps punctuated by a string of curses.

"She's alive," Andre said.

My ankle flared back into agony and I groaned, digging my nails into Andre's chest. His arms tightened around me. I forced my eyes open. My vision was clear again, without a single dark spot to mar Andre's handsome face. My smile returned, despite another wave of invisible needles pushing themselves into my veins.

"Riana? What happened?"

My throat was drier than a desert, but I forced words out as best as I could. "Tried to go for a walk. Fell here. Went to sleep."

"You can't be out of the wagon on your own like this," Andre said, tucking a strand of hair behind my ear.

"We should send her back to Fortress Amheld," Imeni said. "She shouldn't be on the road like this. Her dragon can fly her to us when we've found the virum root."

"No. I must enter Vandemor." I pushed Andre away and grabbed the crutches that had fallen on either side of me. Jacob II, Andre, Loki, they were all right. "I must face my memories." Or I would never be free of their weight.

Imeni's eyebrows shot up almost to her hairline. "You'll never survive like this. The ghosts of Vandemor—"

"I know."

Vandemor had been destroyed with a series of relic-enhanced spells that incinerated its inhabitants, leaving empty buildings to crumble into dust. Those spells also cursed the people, trapping their spirits. Now they waited, watched, and devoured the souls of anyone foolish enough to stop in their city for longer than a moment. If I fell, they wouldn't hesitate to take mine.

"Riana will travel with us," Andre said. "Even into Vandemor. I will keep her safe." He glanced at me. "For now, let's get you back to the wagon."

Chapter Thirty-Eight

Our war party arrived at Vandemor's edge at sunset two days later. We made camp outside the city limits, and I gathered the strength to meet Imeni and Andre in the centre of the common area. We divided our soldiers into groups of five, assigned them to different areas, and sent them out.

"Andre, you and I—"

"You aren't still thinking of going out there," Imeni said.

"I called Vandemor home once. I must see the destruction for myself."

"We'll be safe," Andre said. "I can handle a few ghosts."

Imeni scowled. "Vandemor's cursed with more than a few ghosts."

"And I am more than an average Slayer," Andre said. "If we want to cover much ground tonight we should leave now."

I threw him a grateful smile and followed him into Vandemor.

The city stank of old blood, an overwhelming stench that filled my nostrils the moment we crossed Vandemor's border. Pale, dead faces watched from the windows of crumbling houses. Some doorways held only one ghost. Others held entire families, eagerly watching us as if we had come to save them from their prolonged suffering. None moved, beyond turning their heads to watch us go, hundreds of dark eyes tracking our progress.

"This place is even creepier than the stories," Andre muttered.

"In Eternia's time, this was the heart of human civilization, with the liveliest market in the world." I had fallen in love with it—the colours, the music, and the strange customs. The more familiar I became with its people, the more my love grew, filling my mind and my vision. Blinding me to the abuse going on right under my nose.

The city's decline, perhaps the entire kingdom's failure, began with Eternia's madness. By the time war struck, most of the city's inhabitants lived in poverty, and the university had all but closed.

"We won't be here long," I said.

"Of course not. There's only two hours until sunrise."

"Not because of that. Because—"

The words dried up in my throat as we entered the city's market square. The wooden market stalls had long since rotted away and become dust. Only the ruined fountain in its centre was familiar. Once upon a time, a stone Magdalene poured water from a jug into a great basin, and wealthy children played in it. They stomped around until their mothers scolded them and pulled them out. I had dragged Eternia out of there several times myself.

Now the fountain had dried up and the basin was stained with blood. Magdalene's stone hair was crumbling. Her eyes were black with dirt, her feet caked in long-dried blood. I always hated Magdalene, but seeing such a beautiful statue ruined still tore at my heart.

"Are you all right?" Andre asked.

"I will be." I gestured to the staircase leading to Noble Row. "Once we get up there."

"Is that a good idea?" He gave my leg a pointed look.

"That's where the memories are." The worst of them, at least. "It's also where I believe the virum root is."

Andre frowned at the stairs, chewing on his bottom lip. "I can carry you up those stairs, but I can't carry your crutches at the same time. Or fight."

"We'll leave the crutches here." I swung myself toward the bottom of the steps. "And we won't see many ghosts up there."

"What makes you say that?"

"Most of the nobles abandoned it after—" I looked away, staring at the cobblestones beneath us. "After the massacre at Eternia's wedding."

Andre winced "Sorry. I shouldn't have asked."

"It's all right." I rested my crutches against a nearby wall. "I'm here to face the memories."

Andre gathered me into his arms, shifting my weight several times until I rested comfortably against his chest. "I'm honoured to help."

I wrapped my arms around his neck. "And I'm grateful you're here."

"Hold tight."

He began his way up the stairs. My calves bounced together with every step. I gritted my teeth and braced myself for the pain, but it didn't help. By the time we reached the top, my body was in total agony and my stomach had twisted itself into a knot.

But we were on Noble Row now, the road that led to Magdalene's temple, and beyond, to the first Shalinoran palace.

I couldn't help but smile. This part of the city had hardly changed. The ruins were magnificent, manors three or four stories tall. Gargoyles glared down from the corners of roofs, their hideous faces twisted into menacing expressions. In my time, the houses had been many different colours—blue and green were the most common—but the paint had peeled in several places, revealing grey stone. The stone itself was only now starting to crumble, its layers of magical protection finally fading away.

We rounded a corner and the temple came into view. My chest constricted, but not for the reasons I expected. None of my memories returned. My mind was too overwhelmed by the sight before me.

Magic hadn't protected this place. Magdalene's statue remained regal at the top of the ruined stairs, but it was the only part of the temple left undamaged. The building had crumbled around her. Its once-great archway had caved in, leaving only a narrow entrance.

"This is it." The one place in the mortal realm I had hoped to never see again.

"Where the virum root is?"

"Yes." I had to believe my dreams sent me here for a reason, something more than forcing me to relive my worst memories. There had been too many of them, all too similar to be a coincidence.

He redistributed my weight again, bringing my face closer to his so he could look into my eyes. "You sure about this? You want to go in there?"

"We don't have a choice. That passage leads directly to the main garden."

Andre grimaced, but he carried me into the temple.

The temple consisted of a series of narrow passages bordering and separating two gardens, one for public prayer and one for growing medicine. Most of Shalinor's rituals had taken place outside, at the base of a prayer tree. Priests, priestesses, and servants had lived in a manor behind the temple.

Now there was only one passage, a narrow path to the main garden. Debris blocked the rest of the hallways. A thick layer of dust covered everything, speaking to thousands of years of disuse. Andre's feet kicked up several clouds of it, coating us both in dirt. I attempted to wipe my face with my sleeve but only got more dust on myself.

Nineteen steps later, we entered the garden. It looked exactly as it had in my dream, its paths cracked and stained with ancient blood. The prayer tree at the end remained split, its halves hanging almost parallel to the ground. Its blackened husk and the blood-stained ground were the only hints that life had ever been here at all. Not a single ghost lingered, though there was a coldness to the yard that suggested proximity to Ashe's realm.

A tiny sliver of purple caught my attention. I leaned forward a bit, tilting my head to see the rest of the purple leaf.

Relief flooded my body as I pointed at the herb. "It's over there."

Andre grinned and strode forward, bending as low as possible, with me in his arms, to examine the plant. There were three of them, growing in the spaces between broken path stones.

"I'll need both hands to dig these up." Andre set me down several paces away from the tree, propping my back up against the temple wall. "If anything moves—"

"I'll scream."

He chuckled and returned to the base of the prayer tree. I watched him work, admiring the subtle grace and confidence in every movement. The markings of his training as a warrior.

I yawned. Preventing the poison's spread sapped most of my energy. The walk here had drained what little I had left.

Perhaps I should catch some sleep before we set out again. Yes, that sounded lovely. Even a brief moment would do me some good. I shifted my body lower and rested my head on my dust-covered sleeves.

Darkness came, the kind that could only mean I had slipped into a dream. It didn't matter how wide I opened my eyes or what direction I faced. Light never penetrated this realm.

I returned to my original position and brought my knees up to my chest. My ankle didn't hurt here. A welcome change. I rolled the leg of my trousers to reveal a perfect ankle, with the same unblemished skin as the rest of my body.

A flash of light drew my gaze to the left. A ball of bright white light floated roughly level with my head, growing as I watched.

Eternia emerged from the ball. She seemed older, but still wore her ruined wedding dress.

She smiled at me. "Welcome, Riana."

I recoiled and punched myself in the leg, trying to wake myself. "You're not real."

"I am, here," Eternia said, carefully arranging her skirts so she could sit, cross-legged, in front of me. "This is no ordinary dream. I brought you to my realm."

"Your realm?" Surely that wasn't right. The gods promised her punishment, not a realm of her own. I was there.

"You didn't see their final decision," Eternia said.

I flinched. Did she guess what I was thinking, or could she read my mind in this place?

"They confined me to a pocket dimension." She rearranged her skirts as she spoke, strategically folding them to hide most of the blood. "Connected to but separate from both the mortal realm and Ashe's. In the temple, those realms are closely connected, easy to pass between. This linked you to my realm in three ways, allowing me to pull a piece of you through."

"A piece?" So, I still existed in the mortal realm. That meant I could return, if I could figure out how.

"I'll send you back, don't worry." Eternia met my eyes for the first time. Hers were an even brighter blue now, glowing like miniature lamps. "I couldn't count on getting another chance."

"A chance to what?" I winced at the bitterness in my own tone. Eternia was little more than a child when she hurt me. She didn't deserve my venom, no matter what she put me through.

"To apologize, and forgive you." Her lips tightened, as if saying the words physically hurt her. "You didn't cause my pain."

"I didn't stop it either. That was my job, to protect you. I failed." At every opportunity I'd failed, through a combination of self-obsession and the foolishness of youth.

"Nobody could have protected me. Not from my family." She looked away. "Not from my brother."

Silence, thick and heavy with sadness, filled the space between us. Sparkling tears flowed from Eternia's eyes. I wanted to comfort her, but couldn't bring my body to move to her side. Too much sadness lay between us now.

"You've really been alone all this time?" I asked.

"Loneliness is my punishment. To live here, alone, for the same number of lifetimes I stole." Her eyes grew brighter. "Soon those lifetimes will end, and I will be allowed to die."

"You sound excited."

She tilted her head to the side, the same way I always did. "Don't you wish for death sometimes, Riana?"

My heart twisted painfully. "Every immortal does, at some point. Each new lifetime is another century of pain."

Her expression brightened. "I knew you would understand. It's nice, talking to someone again."

"I—" I broke off, unsure what to say. I dreamed of a moment like this so often, for so long. A chance to speak to Eternia again, to say my apologies and my farewells. To ask why, the real reason why all those people had to die. But now the words died in my throat.

"You don't need to lie." She lowered her head, letting her black hair fall across her face like a curtain. "I understand if you hate me. I probably would, in your shoes."

Do I hate her? *The idea startled me, but what startled me even more was how right it felt. Eternia forced dozens of people to kill themselves. She blamed me for it, and, in turn, the gods blamed me. I spent three hundred years being torn apart and put back together in the most painful ways imaginable. All because of her.*

Yes, I hated her. Almost as much as I despised myself for failing her. But nobody deserved to be alone like this, not for so many years.

More tears burst from Eternia's eyes. I crawled over to sit beside her and put an arm around her. Neither of our sins mattered now. We had suffered enough for our crimes.

"I'm sorry," Eternia said. "So, so sorry." She wrapped her arms around my middle.

"Me, too."

We held each other for a long time, taking solace in each other's sadness.

A rough, bouncing motion woke me. Andre carried me on his back, running through Vandemor. The city passed in a blur as we raced the sun, which had begun to turn the sky pink.

Sunrise. Had I spent that long with Eternia? Did Andre spend the whole time trying to wake me? Did he even know I was alive? He must have, if he was bothering to bring me back.

We entered the camp and he slowed, approaching the wagon. Jayr cursed at the sight of us, loud enough to pound a spike of pain into my head. I groaned and closed my eyes.

Two people lifted me off Andre, onto a stretcher, and into the wagon. Imeni Byrne and Jayr himself, whose strength was impressive for such an old man. They lowered the stretcher beside my cot. The other healers helped roll me in. I wanted to help, too, but everything hurt too much to move.

"The poison is spreading," I said. "My ankle, cut it off."

Jayr cut away the right leg of my breeches and gasped. All the veins below my knee were bright green. "I'll get the saw."

"Don't." Andre held three ugly yellow plants with purple leaves up for inspection. "We have the cure."

Jayr frowned. "We may be too late."

"Try," Andre spat.

"Yes," I said, head swimming, "try."

Chapter Thirty-Nine

I drifted in and out of wakefulness as Jayr ground the virum root into powder and mixed it with water and honey, creating a thick yellow salve that smelled strangely appealing. He rubbed this first into my wound, then up my entire leg. The salve mixed with my blood and entered my veins, replacing my pain with a cool tingling sensation.

Andre hovered at his shoulder the entire time, alternating between anxiety and excitement. He was still pacing along the length of the wagon when Jayr went for dinner.

I snatched Andre's hand out of the air as he tried to pace around the room for the hundredth time, pulling him to my side.

"I'll be back on my feet tonight." I gestured at my leg. Most of my veins were already back to normal and the gaping wound where the harpy's teeth had sunk into my leg had begun filling itself in. A gruesome sight and process, but one that would restore my ability to walk within a day or two. "We did it."

"Have you forgotten something? We still have to fight Kahri."

"Maybe not."

"You have no idea what her power source is," Andre said. "Besides, she'll protect it. She'd be a fool not to."

"We'll figure it out." I squeezed his hand. "For now, I want to relax. You should, too."

He sat on the edge of my bed and folded his other hand around mine. "I will, now."

With my ankle healed, we set out on the last leg of our journey: a five-night ride to Riminira. The clouds thickened above us and a stench permeated the air, growing stronger as we approached the ancient city. Our soldiers acted as if they didn't notice, but their pace slowed and their posture slumped.

Imeni, Andre, and I ate together each night, but we didn't speak. We still didn't have a plan, and the closer we got to the city, the harder it became to think.

At the end of the fourth night, Imeni brought out a thin wooden pipe and a bag full of wakara. The circles under her eyes had grown so dark they looked like bruises, and she had lost weight since entering the Wastelands.

"Have you figured out what Kahri's power source is yet?" she asked, filling her pipe.

I ran my fingers through my hair. I hadn't thought about Kahri much at all in the past few days, too busy reliving my visit with Eternia. Wondering how many more years she still had to spend alone in that awful, dark place. Wishing I could have stayed with her, that I had no ties to the mortal realm. Perhaps also hoping she would spend another thousand years in that terrible place, because she had ruined my life.

"Riana?" Andre asked.

"No."

Andre and Imeni exchanged dark glances. I stared into the fire, unable to look either of them in the eyes.

"It's been hard to think since, well." I pointed at my ankle, unsure what else to say.

"The king knew he was sending us on a mad quest, didn't he?" Imeni stared into her pipe but didn't light it. "That we couldn't possibly defeat someone as powerful as Kahri."

Andre shook his head. "He knew there's always a way. If anyone can find it, we can."

"The power source is a relic strong enough to allow its wielder to speak god words," I said. "It would have taken a lifetime to create."

Andre straightened. "So Kahri didn't create it. She was only twenty-eight at the end of the war."

"That's not enough years, even if she started working on it at birth. It would take at least fifty years to make something like this." I clapped my hand to my mouth. "That's it. Fifty years."

Queen Corinthia scowled at me. "I told you to stay with my daughter, even when she's asleep, didn't I?"

"Yes, Your Majesty." I hung my head, doing my best to act ashamed. "I was only curious about the sounds."

She sighed. "If I show you what I'm working on, will you promise to never enter this workshop again?"

I barely managed to suppress my grin. "Of course, Your Majesty. I would be honoured."

"Very well."

She led me deeper into the workshop, past several strange inventions and a handful of assistants who pretended they didn't know me. All the way to the exact centre of the room. Magic hung in the air here, so powerful that it crackled against my skin as I moved. Someone had carved a circle of containment into the floor, almost identical to the one my mother attempted to use to contain my demonic transformation.

At the centre of this circle stood a stone pedestal topped with a silver cushion. A black orb sat on the pillow. Raw power emanated from it, unlike anything I had felt in the mortal realm.

"My mother created this," she said. "With a mixture of demon blood and her own."

Judging from its strength, the orb had absorbed the blood of several demons. How many people died to summon those demons? How much death had gone into the creation of this relic?

"She died before completing it." Queen Corinthia entered the containment circle. "I have spent the past ten years refining it. Soon, it will be ready."

I swallowed hard. What could she want with this kind of power? She said herself that she didn't want to rule the other nations, or to fight a war of any kind.

"What is it for?"

"It channels and amplifies magic." She rested a hand on the orb, her mouth twitching as the current flowed into her body. "With this, we will be able to watch over our entire queendom without leaving this palace. We'll be able to protect our people from any danger, anywhere in the queendom, within days."

I wanted to believe her, but it didn't make any sense. "This type of magic is rarely used to protect people."

"So are demons, but that is why we summoned you." Queen Corinthia moved away from the orb. "The dragons might leave someday. They weary of humanity, and I do not blame them. But we need a way to protect ourselves if they leave." She smiled at the orb. "This is it."

"She died before finishing it," I said. "Someone else must have completed it."

"Do you have any idea where in Riminira they might keep it?" Andre asked.

“Its original purpose was to watch the whole queendom of Shalinor. There’s only one sensible place to keep an object like that.”

I described the observatory, a room atop the palace’s highest tower with more windows than walls. “The view stretches for miles in every direction. Even without the orb, she could watch us entering the city from there.”

Was that why Loki told me to fly?

“It’s also the most logical place for her to be,” Imeni said. “If she sees us, she can destroy us with magic.”

“If she has enough. She hasn’t sent any attacks after us since the harpies. Creating them must have weakened her.”

Imeni took a long drag from her pipe and blew the smoke toward the sky. “So, how do you propose we get to the orb?”

I leaned forward. “Rolf will carry me and Andre to the tower. I’ll fight Kahri. Andre can destroy the orb.”

Andre’s eyebrows shot up into his forehead. “How am I supposed to destroy something like that?”

“Stab it. The orb is powerful magically, not physically.” I rubbed my temples, wishing I had more of the king’s brandy to smooth this conversation over. “We’ll leave one hour after sunset tomorrow.”

“What about the rest of us?” Imeni asked. “Did we come all the way here to do nothing?”

“You’ll distract Kahri,” I said. “Enter her city on foot. If she’s watching you, we might be able to surprise her.”

“This woman’s smart enough to create a telepathic plague as her means of vengeance.” Imeni filled her pipe again. “I doubt she’ll be fooled.”

“It’s worth a shot.”

Chapter Forty

Kahri

I stared, for a long moment, at the pile of books that lay before me, carefully stacked upon one another for easy wrapping. They were written in Shalinoran, a language Galvan and Caerwyn would return to my people, and told of how my ancestors built humanity's first true civilization. A handful also taught the mental control techniques Fiona's people needed to create a new telar nation.

For most of my life, the stories in the royal library were my only solace, their characters my only companions. These were my favourites, the ones I returned to time and time again. I ran my fingers lovingly along their spines, whispering my farewells, as though they were people.

"It's time," I said.

Magda grabbed the corners of the cloth under my books. She pulled them up and tied them together carefully, to keep the books safe within. My heart ached as the cloth hid my treasures, my babies. I wanted to spend my last nights with them, to enjoy their words and lose myself in their stories.

But those stories didn't belong to me anymore. They never really did. They belonged to my people. The time had come to return them.

"Our people will study every word. We should meet the others." Magda cradled the pile in her arms, the same way I used to.

I nodded and followed her outside. Our people were gathered around the wagon they had brought with them, wearing durable travel clothes and armed to the teeth. Galvan held Caerwyn in his heavily-armoured arms. She flailed when she saw me, trying to push Galvan away from her, to come to my side.

"You can't make me leave," she shouted. "I will stay with Queen Kahri"

"No," I said. "I will defend this city alone, as I always have. You must teach our people. Show them the truth of their heritage. Give them the strength to reclaim their lives."

She gestured toward Galvan. "He can do it."

"Not alone." I went to her side and rested a hand on her shoulder. "His task is more difficult than mine. Galvan needs you."

She deflated, her jaw setting in the way that told me she didn't like this, but she would listen. "I wish you had told me sooner."

"And given you an entire week to yell at me about it?" I forced out a laugh.

She flashed me an equally forced smile. "I suppose that would have been silly."

"It would, wouldn't it have?" I kissed her tenderly on the cheek and returned to the top of the palace stairs. Time to offer my people what little hope I could, and send them on their way. I had spent all week preparing for this moment, writing snippets of my speech in stolen moments between lessons.

"You have all been witness to something amazing," I said, speaking the words slowly to keep my voice from shaking. "The first living souls to enter Riminira in centuries, you have reclaimed the old ways. You must go, spread this knowledge among our people, so it might never be forgotten again.

"If I may ask of you any one thing, it is this: build a new sanctuary for our people, one as glorious as Shalinor in its golden age. And if I could ask for only one more thing, it would be that you remember me as I am, not as a monster who destroyed her kingdom, but as a woman who gave her life to rebuild it. A woman who would give her life a thousand times over to offer any one of you a chance at a better life.

"Do not look back. Do not fear for me when you go forward. These might be the last days of my life, but I have waited a long time for them. Now is your time, not mine. Go forth with happiness and bring a new era of wealth to our people."

I stopped there, unable to go any further. I wanted to promise them prosperity, peace, but I could promise nothing more than hope. Anything more would be a lie.

"It's time," I said after a moment. "Go, before the sun falls. Head due west. Don't turn south until you've been on the road for four days." I wanted them far away from Moonshadow's war party.

Magda's people saluted me and led the wagon away. Galvan and Caerwyn lingered, watching me.

"You could—should—come with us," Galvan said, his voice shaking like a leaf on the wind. "Don't stay in this dismal place."

I shook my head. "I am bound to this city. I cannot leave. Not today, not ever." Riminira and I would die together.

"Then I could stay—"

"Me, too," Caerwyn interjected.

Oh, how I wished they could. How I wished we had more time together. But I wouldn't let them pay for my mistakes, not again. "No. You will have a future in the telar lands, maybe even a family."

"You are my family," Galvan said.

Caerwyn nodded. "My future, too."

"Don't make me call the others back. They will drag you away if I order it."

"You wouldn't," Caerwyn said, pulling free of Galvan and resting her hands on her hips.

"If it means saving your lives, I will do anything."

Galvan gazed into my eyes. "You're certain?"

"More certain than I have been of anything in a long time." If they survived, all my suffering, all those years of loneliness, would at least have meaning.

"Then we'll go." Galvan grabbed Caerwyn's hand and then paused. "Thank you. For everything."

"No," I said. "Thank you, for restoring my hope."

A moment later he walked away, half-dragging Caerwyn behind him. She didn't so much as turn to the path ahead, too busy watching me. I watched her, too, gazing into her eyes until they disappeared into her face, watching her and Galvan walk until they turned into black dots on the horizon.

Only when they disappeared completely did I turn away, permanently locking the palace doors behind me.

Engulfed by the silence of an empty palace once more, I made my way to the vault. Most of my family's great artifacts were on display in the great hall or the relic room, but a handful were hidden away in a basement vault. My family's darkest secrets.

The chamber's magical locks reacted to my blood, glowing brilliantly and then receding back into the stone door. It rolled out of the way, revealing an enormous chamber covered in five centuries' worth of dust.

I moved through the room slowly, revisiting my family's hidden history. The bracelets my mother used to spy on her servants, and eventually her own family, as her paranoia grew. The skin-binding necklaces used to ensure complete loyalty during the dark times, after the dragons left, considered a "kinder" option than outright mind control.

At the far end of the chamber, the Demon Slayer stood. The sword Princess Eternia used to kill the demon who, summoned to protect her, abused her instead. Only she didn't stop with the demon. She killed every guest at her wedding, throwing Shalinor into chaos.

This was my family's most shameful secret, one hidden by an extensive series of executions, book-burnings, and lies. A revelation only passed down to the heir of each generation, so we might know the truth about our family, and the true consequences of summoning demons.

The sword, however, might have been our greatest achievement. If the legend was true, it killed a demon with a single stroke. It was the only human-made weapon to ever kill a demon without fully decapitating it. And in Shalinor, the legends were all true, if a little twisted.

I opened the display case and gingerly removed the sword. The silver blade pulsed with power. Tiny purple runes along its edge glowed at my touch, the regular runes for strength and sharpness, plus a hundred more, all designed to sap magic from the blood. A painful experience for any mage, but a deadly one for a demon.

I would fight the demon, but on my terms. I clipped the sheath onto my belt and made my way to the observatory.

A flood of new power surged into my body when I connected to the orb. Another wave of Moonshadow's people dead, their souls absorbed. Energy crackled through my veins. I pressed my palms into the ground, letting the power connect my soul to the tower, the palace, and the city itself.

I brought this power into the air, raising a magical dome around Riminira. A dome made of pure magic, ready to burn anyone who tried to enter my city.

Near the top, parallel to my tower, I created a hole in this dome. An entrance for the dragon. An invitation.

Let us all die together.

Chapter Forty-One

The soldiers fell eerily silent as we approached Riminira, like men who believed they were already dead. Even Andre went quiet as the outline of the city took shape before us. I rode ahead, unable to tolerate the air of dread hanging over the war party, but equally unable to boost their morale. Our plan gave me no comfort. Imeni was right. Kahri would expect diversion tactics, even if she didn't think we knew about the orb.

We chose to march through the night, eager to end this once and for all. The despair building in our hearts could not be allowed to grow for another day. Besides, Andre was a more reliable ally during the night, even with sarentin.

My horse's nose smashed into something invisible, and he reared. I flew through the air and my left shoulder crashed against the ground, pain lancing down my arm. I winced and rolled away from the road. Whinnies and shouts came from every direction as my stallion squealed, its nose red and swollen.

Most of the Slayers managed to remain seated, calming their horses, as I attempted to soothe my own. Andre and Imeni dismounted and walked their horses forward, meeting me a few paces from where my stallion panicked.

"What in the five realms was that?" Andre asked.

"I don't know," I snapped. "My horse hit something invisible and threw me."

"It was visible, for a moment," Imeni said. "A blue wall, stretching around the entire city. Well, the parts we can see."

A magical shield, the largest one ever created, if it really did cover the entire city. I cursed. Kahri must have recovered the magic she spent to create the harpies.

"What about the sky?"

"What do you mean?"

"It can't go on forever," I said. "Rolf, Andre, and I can still get in."

"It's curved." Andre glared at the now-invisible wall. "Like a dome."

"There still might be a hole. Kahri might still be weak." It could be a challenge. Or a trap. Probably the last one, but we needed to take the risk. Our journey had already been delayed too many times. "Imeni, set up camp. Andre, gather stones and then meet me at the far edge of camp in half an hour. We'll be flying from here."

Rolf, it's time.

Half an hour later, Andre and I met at the edge of the hastily-constructed camp, each of us carrying a bag of small stones on our backs.

"Come with me. I don't want to risk scaring the horses again." I had instructed Rolf to land half a mile back to avoid this.

"What, exactly, is your plan?" Andre followed me away from the war party.

"Drop the stones on the city. If they hit the wall, we'll see it."

"And if nothing happens, we'll know it's a safe place to enter the city."

"Exactly."

For several moments neither of us spoke, the air between us heavy with a strange tension. Andre's mouth moved rapidly, but didn't open, as if he was forcing his own words down. I didn't pry and kept my gaze focused on the road ahead.

"Riana," he said at last. "We're probably going to die tonight, for real, so—" He absently scratched at the back of his neck. "I wanted to say that you're the most amazing woman I've ever met. If we survive this—"

"My contract with your brother will end." All my contracts would end, forever. I could take on a new face, start a new life somewhere. As desirable as Andre was, especially when he dropped his persona, I didn't think I wanted him to be part of it. Or any Vonstone.

His face fell. "Right."

A distinct pang of sadness cut through my chest. Few humans had ever been as kind to me as Andre, even when they believed I was human. He didn't deserve such abrupt treatment.

"I'm sorry," I said. "I didn't mean..."

He shrugged. "It's all right. Some things are simply impossible."

This time I didn't respond, letting the silence drag out until we reached the top of a hill. Rolf lay at the bottom, his body stretched out along the road. He pulled his lips back in his usual gruesome smile. *I've never had two riders before. It'll be fun.*

It'll be short. When we find the entrance, the battle begins.

You sound afraid.

I am. I didn't know what frightened me most, the idea of fighting Kahri or the idea that we might not be able to enter Riminira at all. *But we have to do this.*

For Marcus.

Yes, for Marcus. And the kingdom of Moonshadow. Most of all, for my freedom from all of it.

Then let's go.

All too soon we were circling up into the sky, Andre's arms wrapped tightly around my waist. His grip grew tighter as the world expanded beneath us. Soon our camp became visible, an oval outlined by a series of dark blobs. Riminira expanded, too, its blue and white buildings shining in the full moon's light.

"It's beautiful," Andre said in my ear.

"Flying is the best feeling in the world." I glanced up at the stars. "But we're not here to have fun."

I grabbed a handful of stones from the bag, now tied to my waist, and then dropped them on the city below. The blue dome flared into life, burning the rocks until they glowed and cracked, crumbling to dust. I grimaced. *No wonder my stallion panicked.* This was powerful, painful magic.

We circled the city several times, each time doing a smaller loop. The dome flared and fizzled, the rocks cracking faster each time.

I was almost out of stones when one fell into Riminira without touching the dome. "Found it."

"Let's test the size," Andre said.

I'll tighten the circle. Rolf curled inwards, almost coiling in on himself.

Andre and I threw the last of our rocks at random intervals, hollering as each one landed on the city below, untouched by Kahri's magical wall.

Bring us down. I thought to Rolf. *Take us to the tallest tower in the city. Kahri's power source will be there.*

Rolf obeyed, his body sliding through the hole without issue. We flew low over the city to avoid the rest of the dome.

I gaped at the remnants of Riminira, the empty but perfectly preserved buildings and streets. Statues of Magdalene stood on almost every corner, still covered in perfect coats of green and gold paint.

The only hint of the city's corruption was the stench of blood magic. It permeated the air, clinging to the inside of my nostrils and collecting on my tongue. The closer we got to the palace, the worse it stank.

"It's incredible," Andre said as the palace came into view.

I couldn't bring myself to speak as I stared down at the familiar building. Most of the structure was built with white stone. Alternating series of decorative animals and magical protection runes were carved into each one, making it both beautiful and almost impossible to destroy. All were in perfect condition as if they had been cast the day before.

One tower, built from rocks the colour of the morning sky, rose out of the back of the palace. It stretched far above any other building in Riminira, high enough to see most of the city from its uppermost chamber. The windows on this uppermost floor stretched from the floor to its ceiling, giving us plenty of room to jump through.

"This is it," I said.

"Our final destination," Andre said, his voice cold as steel.

Stay level with the window until we've jumped, then get out of here. I leaned forward and kept my eyes on the window. Looking down wouldn't help. *We don't know what will happen to the city when Kahri dies.*

What about getting you out?

I've survived worse. I could only hope I sounded more confident than I felt. I had no idea how Kahri's death would impact me. "Let's do this."

Good luck.

"Was that your dragon?" Andre asked. "Did he just—"

Damn it, Rolf.

"We'll talk about it later." Those kinds of questions were the last thing I needed to deal with right now.

I pried Andre's hands away from my waist and jumped, rolling as I hit the tower's stone floor. The impact stung, but I stood and turned back to Andre as if it hadn't. I couldn't afford to show vulnerability now. Andre needed to be confident in me, and Kahri had to fear me.

Andre stared at me for a moment before edging over Rolf's back. He closed his eyes and hurled himself forward. He barrelled into me with so much force, we both fell backward. I pushed him off and rose to my feet, taking in the room around us.

Rows of dummies marked with the magical plague hung from the ceiling, their faces pointed at the room's centre. Defensive runes had been painted on the floor around the orb. Some of them glowed, giving off an eerie light strong enough to see by, even on the night of the new moon.

Kahri's black orb stood on a marble pedestal at the centre of the circle. Clouds of crimson energy swirled across its surface. The source of Kahri's power—and the city's stench. Andre doubled over and puked blood. He pulled himself up with help from one of the dummies, then recoiled from it as if he'd been struck.

"This place is disturbing," he said, drawing his sword. "Let's make this quick."

"Those runes—"

Andre stepped forward and his left foot landed on one of the runes. A ring of fire sprung out of the floor with a terrifying roar. He screamed and rolled away from the flames, closer to the orb. I wanted to run to him, but the fire stood between us now, crackling angrily.

Andre gingerly rose to his feet and tried to step over the next set of runes. The edge of his heel landed on the corner of a round symbol. Large metal spikes burst from the ground, digging into his foot. He screamed and yanked his foot off. Blood poured from the wound. He hopped toward the orb and fell on his knees, narrowly missing another trap rune.

Somewhere below us a door slammed shut. *Kahri's coming.* I inched my way toward the exit, following the edge of the room to avoid stepping on more trap spells. I positioned myself in front of the stairwell, then lowered myself into a fighting stance.

Andre screamed again. I clenched my teeth, trying to force the sound out of my mind. I needed to focus. If I went to help Andre, we would both die. I had to distract Kahri and hope Andre still had enough strength to destroy the orb. He was sobbing now, the sound drowning out the footsteps below me, even the sound of my own heartbeat.

I didn't turn around, not even to check if he was still moving forward. I just had to believe he was.

A ring of bright blue light appeared on the stairs. Kahri came around the bend a moment later. I held my breath, unable to look away. She appeared not to have lived a day over twenty-five, with an air of adulthood but not a single wrinkle to be found. Only a sadness in her eyes spoke of all her centuries alone.

Kahri stopped a few steps below me. She wore a long baby blue dress, impractical but beautiful. Something proper for a queen to die in. An ornate silver sheath with a golden handle above it hung from a sash tied to her waist. Her expression was solemn, her eyes staring at me as if they saw deep into my soul, even though her gift couldn't penetrate my mind.

"You've come to end me." Her voice boomed with magical power.

"We've come to end your plague," I said. "You don't have to die if you stop the killing." I knew it was hopeless, but I still had to say it. Had to offer her a chance for survival. For her and for Riminira.

She laughed. "I've spent too long planning my revenge to abandon it now."

I took a step forward, blocking the chamber's entrance. "Then I must kill you."

"You can try." She gestured for me to come closer.

A strong wind pulled me off my feet and whipped me down the stairs. Spine connected with stone and pain shot through my whole body, knocking my sword out of my hands. I smashed into the next landing, cracking the bones in my right arm as I caught myself.

My body began to heal, the bruises fading even as I jumped to my feet. My bones pulled themselves together as my gaze darted around the stairwell. Where in the five realms had my sword gone?

There. A glint of silver at Kahri's feet. She would strike me down the moment I came within arm's reach.

She drew a familiar longsword edged with purple runes and spells to kill anything in the mortal realm, even demons. The sword I wore once, all the way back in Eternia's day. The sword Queen Corinthia made especially for me.

Kahri intended to kill me with my own weapon. How fitting.

She hurled herself at me. I dove under her, smashing my ribs against the stairs with another crack of sharp pain. My left hand closed around the hilt of my sword and I stumbled down to the next landing. I forced air into my lungs in quick, sharp gasps. Dark spots appeared at the corners of my vision.

No, I can't give up.

I gritted my teeth and raised my sword, forcing the metal to grow long and narrow. I needed more distance between us.

"I see why Loki chose you," Kahri said. "Strong, but foolish."

I pushed her words out of my mind and lunged for her, driving my sword into her calf. She yanked her leg free as if it didn't hurt at all. Blood poured from the wound, soaking her dress, my sword, everything. She hardly noticed.

Maybe she wasn't human after all.

Maybe I was the one who would die here.

Riana, I can't get out. Rolf's panicked mindvoice filled my head. *The hole in the dome is gone.*

I leapt away from another blow, teetering on the edge of a step. *Are you sure you're in the right place?*

The exact spot we came in. The wall grew. I tried to push through, but—it hurt so much. Too much. His panic overwhelmed my thoughts.

I doubled back, falling another three steps. Kahri followed in a single leap and pinned me to the wall, pressing her blade to my throat. The metal was cold, so cold it burned my skin. My throat constricted. I gasped for air, eyes watering.

"You see it now, don't you?" Kahri asked triumphantly. "There's no escape. No survival. For any of us."

The blade dug further into my skin, sending trails of fire up and down my body. Darkness gathered at the edges of my vision. Rolf was still screaming in my head, but it seemed distant now. Everything was distant now.

I'm going to die. The freedom I had fought for, the life I was planning in the mortal realm, the life that had seemed only days away a few moments ago, none of it was going to happen. I had failed.

My heart sank into my chest, heavy now with realization but still pounding with adrenaline, tearing me apart. I closed my eyes, tears trailing down my cheeks, not from the pain but from the sorrow of a life stolen.

There would be freedom, though, of a different sort, the clean oblivion of a demonic death.

I lifted my head to smile at Kahri. "Thank you."

A triumphant shout bounced down the walls toward us.

"So we'll die together," I said, in a whimsical tone that sounded delirious even to my ears.

Kahri stared at me, then up at the tower, her expression of triumph crumbling as her skin turned grey and started falling off her bones. She dropped the sword and collapsed, staring at her hands as the dead skin flaked away, piling up on the ground like so many ashes.

She raised her eyes to me, her face a gaunt shadow of its former self, her expression frozen in fear.

"What... "

Her jaw fell away from her face, clattering to the floor. The rest of her followed, bones turning to dust as they struck the ground. I scrambled away from the dust, using the far wall to pull myself up.

Andre appeared on the stairs above me, his forehead burnt almost completely away, his eyes blackened from fire, a bloody hole in his left hand.

"Riana? Riana? Are you—"

A brilliant light filled the air behind him and blew the world apart, sending me into darkness.

Chapter Forty-Two

I woke to darkness and pain, and something heavy sitting on my stomach. Everything hurt, but I was alive. And I could hear things. Voices. Familiar voices. At first, I only heard muffled sounds, but as they grew closer, and I grew more conscious, I could make out words.

"There's nothing left of it," someone said. "Not a single building."

"There might still be bodies," said a voice that could only be Imeni's. "The King will want to see his heroes buried."

"Have you seen the size of these rocks? Even the smallest chunks of rubble will take all night to move."

"You will find the bodies," Imeni's voice hardened. "They will have proper burials."

"But—"

"That was an order."

Then the voices drifted away. Soon, the only sounds were shouts and grunts of effort as the Slayers sifted through the rubble of the palace ruins.

My mind wandered through a landscape of pain. I envisioned the piles of rubble all around me. I remembered Kahri's body falling to pieces, five centuries of decay catching up to her in moments. The panic overwhelming my mind as Rolf tried to get away from the city.

Oh no.

Rolf. Rolf? Rolf? I put all the power I could muster into my thoughts, begging him to answer. Human voices came and went above, but no thoughts. Not even his comforting presence.

A sharp pang tore through my heart and stomach.

Rolf had promised he would always answer. Loki had promised he could always hear me.

He's gone. The city had taken him with it, not just Kahri. My sweet, childlike friend who only wanted to save Marcus so they could fly together. The one soul in the mortal realm that was purely, absolutely good.

The one good thing Loki had ever given me. My truest friend. Gone. I wept, as much as was possible with dry eyes and a scorched throat.

"Hey," a man's voice said. "I think I heard something over here."

"Like what?"

"Someone in pain."

"Let's hope it's one of them," Imeni's voice echoed down to me.

I let out one last mourning sound, then darkness claimed me.

One of the Slayers tripped over a rock and almost fell, throwing me half out of the makeshift stretcher. My rib cage drove painfully into my elbow before I pushed myself back in, bracing myself as we moved toward the wagon. I had ended up in almost the exact centre of the rubble. Every rock we climbed over was another series of painful bumps, making my head throb and my stomach churn.

Finally, Imeni smiled at me as she grabbed the top of my stretcher and lifted me into the wagon. Jayr appeared behind Imeni, his mouth twisted with a mixture of irritation and concern.

"We're still looking for Andre," Imeni said as she set me down. "But there's something you ought to see."

The wagon moved underneath me, wheels catching every few feet on the small pieces of rubble littering the road. Every bump jarred my bones painfully. Were most of them broken? How I survived at all was beyond me.

"Where are we going?"

"Not far. I didn't want to walk you there," she said. "But you should get to say good bye."

"Good bye? You said you were still looking for Andre."

Imeni frowned. "I—"

Memories rushed back into my mind. The dome. Rolf trying to escape, his panic throwing me off balance and under Kahri's mercy. My desperate calls for him when I woke. The silence that echoed in my head.

"Rolf," I said.

Imeni nodded as we turned a sharp corner and pulled to a stop. I forced myself to sit up. Every muscle in my body came alive with fiery pain as I did so. Imeni's hand rested on the small of my back, supporting me.

A pile of white rubble with flaking green paint rose before me, perhaps thirty paces tall. Something glimmered near the top. A chunk of silver fur.

"No," I whispered.

But the rest of the rubble confirmed it. Bloody clumps of fur and scales dotted the ruins. A fang stuck out of one stone. So many pieces, too many pieces.

"I'm sorry," Imeni said. "The dome contained—well, we're not really sure what happened—but it also contained him."

His panicked screams filled my head again, throbbing against my skull. I hadn't even comforted him in his final moments. I let the pain overwhelm me instead, let myself fall into weakness and shock.

"I'm the one who should be sorry," I whispered.

Chapter Forty-Three

Darkness, as complete as the darkness in Eternia's realm. Only there was no Eternia here. Nothing at all. I spun in every direction and saw nothing, until I turned back to the first direction had I faced.

Andre lay before me, not moving. An angry red scar covered his left eye and most of his forehead.

"He's... dead?" I asked, though I didn't know who I expected to answer.

I ran my fingers through his hair, delicately removing flakes of dust and dried blood. His skin was cool, but that was to be expected. The lack of movement, too, could have merely been a result of the sun rising outside the dark cavern where we were trapped.

But the terrible cold feeling in my chest told me otherwise. Andre was dead. He followed me to the end, destroyed the orb and guaranteed my freedom, and what did he get? Rejection and death. He truly cared about me, and I didn't appreciate it. Not the way I should have.

"I've been terrible," I whispered. "Terrible to everyone who mattered. Please, Andre, live so I can show you."

Show him what? That I appreciated how much he cared about me? That I was grateful for him destroying the orb? No. That wasn't right, wasn't enough.

"Show you that I love you." Yes, that felt right. "Give me a chance to be with you, like we talked about."

The hand in mine twitched, and his lips curved into a slight smile. Warmth emanated from his hand now, and it comforted me. It flowed from his hand into mine, through me and back into him through my other hand. Our life forces merged together, heat filling my limbs. My mind grew lighter, as though I were floating. A wave of comforting energy washed through me, filling me with joy.

Then darkness came again.

I woke staring at the black canvas roof of a wagon. My entire body ached, but not so much as before.

"Awake at last." Jayr handed me a wineskin.

I took the wineskin but didn't open it. "Andre?"

He nodded and gestured to his other side, where Andre lay, his left eye and half his forehead covered by a mound of pink scar tissue. His chest rose and fell slowly, but peacefully.

I wept tears of joy for the first time in centuries—wept until my eyes were dry and I drifted back out of consciousness—this time on my way to a peaceful slumber.

I spent most of the journey home passing in and out of consciousness. Each time I woke, I expected Loki, but I'd open my eyes to see only the healer, and Andre's motionless form. Each day I grew healthier than the last, but Andre's condition remained unchanged.

When we finally returned to the castle, Andre was immediately carried to his room by a fleet of royal healers. I went with them, holding his hand the whole time. I stayed, clasping his hands, while they drip-fed him bottle after bottle of blood. His hands twitched occasionally but he still didn't open his eyes. He didn't speak, didn't do anything.

"We can't do anything more," Jayr said eventually. "Even here. He's—"

"I won't believe he's dead until he starts rotting," I said, all but spitting in his face. "You saw him move. You will bring him more blood."

He frowned. "I don't think more—"

The door flew open and Jacob VIII strode into the room. He cleared his throat and the healer hurried away, letting the door fall shut behind her. Jacob VIII looked a dozen years older than when I had left, but slightly saner, or at least cleaner.

"Marcus still sleeps a lot," Jacob VIII said. "But the marks are fading, and he can walk—even run short distances. Thank you."

"Andre's the one who destroyed Kahri's power source. She would have killed me."

Jacob VIII gave his brother a long, considering look. "Did he?"

"He's a better warrior, and man, than you give him credit for." He was a better man than I had given him credit for.

If only he would wake up, so I could tell him how sorry I was. So we could start over.

"I see. I'll be sure to thank him if he wakes up."

"When he wakes up."

Jacob VIII scowled. "If he wakes up. In the meantime, you will work with Generals Alexis and Cornelius—"

My hand tightened around Andre's. "I will remain here until Andre wakes."

The king's face reddened. "You will do as I command. If you don't report to General Cornelius's office tomorrow by noon, I will use the compulsion. Do you understand?"

I froze, remembering the pain shooting through my veins like a thousand tiny knives. Loki hadn't given me freedom, hadn't even appeared. Our deal, it seemed, was no deal at all. I was still bound to this madman, betrayed by my own blood.

"I understand."

"Good."

He stormed out, leaving me alone with the deafening sound of my own thoughts.

Prince Marcus strode into the room shortly after dawn the next morning, truly looking the part for the first time since I met him. He wore a green velvet doublet with silver trim at the collar and the ends of each sleeve, fitted black trousers, and shiny leather shoes. The bags under his eyes were gone, and he had already started growing again. Looking at him, at the young man he was now becoming, made my sacrifices feel almost worthwhile.

"I wanted to thank you," he said.

"Don't. It's enough to see you well."

He sat in the chair beside me. "You deserve much more. I am only alive because of you."

I said nothing, returning my attention to Andre's sleeping form. His eyes were moving under his eyelids now, as though he dreamed, or perhaps understood our conversation.

"Father agrees. He's hosting a feast to celebrate the plague's disappearance in one month's time. Nobles from all over the kingdom are coming."

I raised an eyebrow. "Wasn't the nature of the plague meant to be a secret?"

Marcus flushed and stared at his feet. "Father's decided to announce the truth. He also believes the people deserve to know the reality of the telar threat."

"The telar threat?" The words tasted rotten on my tongue.

"So long as the telars continue to exist, there is danger that this might happen again."

So it comes to war anyway.

"Does he really believe that? What about you?"

He bit his lip, still staring intently at his feet. "I—I don't know."

I put three fingers under Marcus's chin and lifted his head until his eyes met mine. He didn't resist, but his eyes darted in every direction, unwilling to meet mine.

"You don't believe that," I said. "Because it's not true. Kahri used special magic, magic nobody else alive can use, not even me. Nothing like this will ever happen again."

His eyes shone with tears, but they didn't fall. "Are you sure?"

"Yes. Most telars are good people, like you."

"Father doesn't believe that. He wants to kill them—all of them. He says it's to eliminate the threat, but—" He lowered his voice. "I don't really believe that, either."

My heart twisted. Even at a whisper, the pain in his voice was audible. He understood his father's madness now.

"Please change his mind. I don't want anyone else to die."

Or perhaps he saw the madness but didn't understand it. He was still too young, too sheltered for that. He had never tried to argue with a madman before. His father had been sane once, after all.

"I will do everything in my power to stop him."

Marcus relaxed. "Thank you, again. We don't deserve you."

"You are not your father," I said. "Never let yourself feel guilty for his crimes. I spent too many years feeling guilty for other people. Don't fall into the same trap."

"I'll try." He smiled, or at least his lips did. His eyes remained clouded by pain and worry. "Oh, and I'm ready for those flying lessons now, whenever Rolf comes back."

My heart twisted further, taking the breath out of my lungs and making me aware of a deep, burning hole in my chest. Like the one I had carried for Jacob III for all of those years, the one that was only now beginning to heal. It took my words away and brought tears to my face. They streamed down my cheeks. Marcus stared, his expression wavering between pity and fear.

"He's not coming back, is he?"

I shook my head. "He's—he's dead."

Marcus's hands balled into fists. "Because he tried to save me."

I wanted to shake my head again, to comfort him, but I couldn't. He was right, and I was angry at all of us for dragging Rolf into this. For making my sweet, innocent friend commit terrible crimes and ultimately sacrifice his life for a single mortal boy. I might have done it for the kingdom, but Rolf did it for Marcus.

"I'm sorry," Marcus said.

I opened my mouth, but nothing came out. Marcus's head drooped, and he shuffled out of the room, tears starting down his cheeks as well.

I tightened my grip on Andre's hands as one sob tore itself from my throat, then another. Andre's eyes moved faster beneath his eyelids, but he didn't wake. I was alone with my sadness, with the terrible certainty that not only had I sacrificed the sweetest friend I ever had, I had also set the telars on a path toward complete annihilation.

"Please don't leave me alone like this," I whispered. "Please wake up. I don't know what to do without you."

Chapter Forty-Four

Loki appeared soon after Marcus left. He wore a rugged red beard and scraggly red-and-grey hair today, for once, choosing to appear older than twenty-two. He offered me a wrinkly grin, and rage bubbled up in my chest.

"You took long enough," I said coldly. "Almost twenty days since we completed the job."

He shrugged. "You didn't look like you were in a hurry to leave."

I stared at him. "Freedom does include the freedom to stay here, does it not?"

"Of course, but it does come with a price."

I yanked my hand out of Andre's and stood. "What kind of price? I finished the damn job. And sacrificed the best friend I've ever had to do it."

"Best friend?" Loki asked.

I glowered. "Rolf died."

He shrugged. "He only lost his first life."

The words hit me like a punch in the stomach. I stumbled back into my chair. "You mean—Rolf's still out there somewhere?"

"Ashe returned his spirit to me," Loki said. "He will know life again."

"What about me?" My voice came out smaller than intended, like a child's. "Will I get my friend back?"

"You can return to Dragon's Keep, and see Rolf when he is reborn," Loki said. "Or stay here, with Andre. But, if you wish to live freely in the mortal realm, you must give up your powers, your immortality."

A chance to live a true human life. The life my blood denied me.

But—

"I've spent over two thousand years enslaved by my curse, and I only get one human lifetime of freedom?" Was that what I suffered for, what I killed so many people to get? One measly human lifetime?

He chuckled. "You're never satisfied, are you?"

I wrinkled my nose and stared at Andre's sleeping form. "He'll get an eternity."

"If he wakes up." Loki took a round, golden device out of his pocket and looked at it, clicking his tongue. "Look at that time! You're going to make me late for dinner."

"Bind me to Moonshadow." The words burst from my mouth before I could stop them.

Loki blinked. "Excuse me?"

"The rules say all demons in the mortal realm must be bound into mortal service, right?"

"Yes. One of the conditions of your survival."

I suppressed a grin. "If I'm bound to protect Moonshadow, I serve all of its people, but I'm still free. The land itself can't give orders."

"And if Moonshadow falls?" Loki asked.

"Then I'll fall with it." This was my home now, and I didn't want another one. Especially if it meant leaving Andre behind.

"If you're certain." He snapped his fingers and a contract appeared, written in the demonic language, a series of violent scratches of ink. "Sign with a drop of blood."

He waved his other hand and a small silver knife appeared. Demonic runes of binding were carved along the length of the blade. The leather handle pointed in my direction, bouncing slightly as if the knife wanted me to use it.

I grabbed the knife and examined it closely. How long would Loki let me put off the decision? If I delayed long enough, maybe Andre would wake up before I made up my mind. I didn't want to be stuck watching him sleep for centuries, watching the kingdom crumble around his sleeping form, for all kingdoms must eventually crumble.

Loki cleared his throat. "My dinner is growing cold."

I rolled my eyes. "You're a god. You can summon another hot meal any time you want."

"I could also revoke the offer and make you mortal—or dead—on the spot."

I swallowed hard and grabbed the contract.

Our next visitor, Jacob II, arrived less than an hour after I signed Loki's new contract. He sat beside me, without speaking, for a while, watching Andre sleep. I examined my friend's face carefully. He looked as young as ever, but he slouched as if the kingdom literally weighed on his shoulders now.

After a while, he looked up and met my gaze. A sad smile spread across his face.

"You know," he said. "I saw you like this once, at a man's sickbed."

My heart constricted as my Morgan's sickbed appeared in my mind, surrounded by bouquets sent by noble ladies from all over the kingdom.

"I loved that man. And I love this one."

He smiled. "I thought you might say that. You know, my son died a long time ago. Andre is a Vonstone too, but he's a different man."

"Our love is different, too."

Morgan loved me only with conditions—the death of his wife, boredom, loneliness—but Andre loved me from the start. With Morgan, it always felt unreal, being unable to marry or even to acknowledge our love in public. But things were different with Andre. He wasn't the king, and he was already a vampire. Our love could be both public and eternal.

"I'm glad. I wish I could love again." Jacob II said, turning back to watch Andre sleep.

"Maybe someday you will."

"No. I thought so once, but I will only ever love one woman. Someday, perhaps, I will be reunited with her. Although I doubt Ashe would let me have a second life after so many years of this one."

A long silence fell between us. Andre rolled over, but made no sound. I leaned closer and peered into his face, hoping against hope that his eyes would open.

"I suppose," Jacob II said, "I should leave you two alone."

"No." The last thing I wanted was more time alone with Andre's unconscious body. "I—I have to ask you something about Jacob VIII."

His expression darkened. "I thought you might."

"Marcus says his father wants to exterminate the telars."

Jacob II drew a flask from one of his trouser pockets. "Jacob VIII believes it's the only way to prevent them from causing more chaos." He opened the flask and took a generous gulp. "Generals Cornelius and Alexis are organizing mental defence boot camps as we speak."

The screams of the telar army filled my mind, the smell of burning flesh searing my nostrils. "Hasn't he done enough? Haven't *we* done enough?"

"Not until they're all dead. Cameron was murdered. The king believes telars killed him."

My chest constricted. *So he was the spy.*

Fiona probably had him executed before he could be arrested. "Does he have any proof?"

Jacob II shook his head. "He doesn't need it. I doubt the people will, either."

No. They hated the telars enough to kill them without question. "There's got to be some way to stop him."

"None I can think of." He sighed. "Perhaps you'll find a way to guide the king, and Moonshadow, back to peace."

I snorted. "Because I've done such a great job so far."

"You've done better than I have."

I tilted my head to the side. "What do you mean? You've guided this kingdom for centuries. You've had lifetimes more time than I have, spent in this land."

"Does Moonshadow look like a better place than it was six centuries ago?" Jacob II shook his head. "My aid has stifled this kingdom. And when I left? I left Moonshadow in the hands of the mad king. My descendants were fools to listen to me."

"Even if that's true, what makes you think I can influence Jacob VIII? He despises me." To him, I was only a tool.

"There are ways to influence a kingdom without the king's ear. Even without his knowledge."

I blinked. "What exactly are you suggesting?"

"Only that I know you will do the right thing for Moonshadow." He smiled sadly. "I, however, must go."

"Go?" No. I must have heard him wrong. "You love this kingdom."

"Sometimes the greatest act of love is letting something—or someone—go."

I fingered the brooch pinned above my heart, the words reverberating through my memory and returning in a different voice...

I leaned forward, tightening my grip on Morgan's hand. "You can't die. I—"

"You lived for thousands of years before me," he said. "You will go on for thousands of years after me. It is your nature."

"Your father and grandfather live. You *have a choice to join us in eternity, to experience life beyond kinghood, to be—" I flushed, ashamed. "To be with me, for real."*

The Vonstones' head healer, a round man with several white streaks in his black hair, entered with a solemn expression. My chest constricted. His downcast eyes, the way his hands were folded together, those could only mean one thing.

"There's nothing we can do, Your Majesty," he said in a thin voice that made it sound like he was dying, too. "Your body is too old to accept our magic."

It's over. *I bit my lip, willing my tears away.*

Morgan nodded, his eyes sad but his jaw set. "Fetch the High Priest. We must make arrangements immediately."

The healer bowed and hurried out of the room, the door slammed behind him.

I doubled over, tears streaming down my face. A sob burst from my throat. "You can't—"

Morgan caressed my cheek. "I must. And you must let me go, so you can be free to live the life you are meant to."

"Riana?" Jacob II asked gently.

I clutched the brooch to my chest, feeling the points of the flower dig into my hand. "Where will you go?"

"Everywhere." He smiled, and this time it reached his eyes. "I want to see the world again, Riana. One last time."

"Last time?" I knew what he meant, as I had known what the healer's expression meant on that other terrible day, but I couldn't help asking.

"I've lived more lives than any man has a right to. I am tired, and soon, I will rest." He removed an obsidian ring from one of his fingers. "Keep this, to remember me."

I opened my mouth to say—what? What right did I have to stop him? If any man was worthy of so many extra lives, it was Jacob II, but he also deserved peace. He deserved the rest he sought, after all the suffering he had seen.

"And this." He handed me a green pin with silver stripes, shaped like an A.

I stared at it, my emotions a jumble of pride and despair and joy. His advisor's pin. "This is—"

He pressed it into my palm, on top of the ring. "I officially appoint you, Riana of the Demon Realm, to my place on the advisors' council, until such time as I return."

"But—"

"You will be an excellent advisor, even if it takes the king a while to see it." He pushed himself up with his cane. "I really must go now."

I sighed, folding my fingers around his gifts. "I suppose that makes this farewell."

He inclined his head. "Goodbye, even."

My heart sank. "So you won't ever be back?"

"If I come back, I'll never truly let go."

I glanced at Morgan's brooch, remembering how the memories flooded my mind as soon as I returned to Moonshadow. "I suppose I'm living proof."

He squeezed my shoulder. "You've shown me the path I must take. Thank you, Riana."

He hobbled to the door, leaning on his cane more than usual. I slipped his gifts into my pocket, then unclipped my brooch.

"Wait," I said, leaping out of my chair. "There's one last thing I would ask of you. Take this to your son's resting place."

He paused, one hand on the doorknob. "Isn't this something you should do yourself?"

"I said goodbye to Morgan over five centuries ago." I looked at Andre's unconscious form. "Looking back will only stop me from moving forward."

Jacob II accepted the brooch with a slight bow. "I understand. It will be done."

"Thank you—and goodbye." My voice cracked on the last word, but I held the tears back and forced a smile. "Safe travels, my friend."

Chapter Forty-Five

Jacob VIII stormed in, less than half an hour later. "Jacob II resigned from the council. He tells me he's passed his position on to you."

I fished the advisor's pin out of my pocket. I didn't feel right wearing it, no matter what Jacob II said. "He gave me this."

The king's eyes narrowed. "How dare he do such a thing without consulting me?"

"You wanted me here," I said. "With the plague ended, what better purpose could I serve?"

He opened his mouth, then shook his head. "Perhaps you're right. And there are certain—advantages—to giving you a council vote." His lips twisted into a sadistic grin. "Yes, many advantages. As your first official duty, I order you to meet with Generals Cornelius and Alexis and inform them that the plan will be accelerated."

I waited for the familiar heat in my veins, but nothing came. A smile spread slowly across my face. Loki kept his promise after all. "No. I will not be part of your extermination."

"I order you—"

"It won't work." Nobody would ever compel me to slaughter innocents again. My blood only demanded that I protect the land itself, and that, I was happy to do.

"But you're still here, still bound to me."

I laughed. "Loki didn't tell you? We have a new contract. You're not part of it."

His rage turned to shock, then fear. He backed away, his hands in the air and his eyes wide. "Then why are you still here?"

"For him." I gestured at Andre's unconscious form. "So, I suggest you leave me here, with him, and we'll forget all about this incident."

"I—very well. Stay here. The war will begin without you."

He strode out of the room, muttering a stream of curses under his breath. I relaxed, feeling lighter than I had in years, or ever, really—except maybe for the childhood I barely remembered. Freedom, of a sort, was mine. For the first time, my choices were my own.

"And I choose you," I said to Andre. "If you ever wake up."

In the meantime, I needed to think up a way to stop Jacob VIII's invasion.

On the fourth night, I grew desperate. Jacob VIII was campaigning for genocide, and I was stuck here, powerless, at Andre's side. I needed him back so we could stop his brother.

I shook him. I yelled in his ears. His hand grew tighter around mine, but he didn't wake. The healers came and went, perplexed.

Around nightfall, he grew restless. His hand gripped mine properly for the first time, pulling it to his chest. I leaned forward and begged him to wake. His legs twitched, and his grip on my hand stayed tight. I remembered my dream, the way our power mingled.

Maybe human blood wasn't strong enough. Maybe he needed something stronger, like the magic running through my veins right now. Maybe, just maybe, I could save him.

I unclipped the dagger from my arm brace, rolled up my other coat sleeve, and slashed my wrist open. I gasped at the pain, the first real thing I had felt since Jacob II's disappearance.

Blood spurted from my wound, a veritable fountain of power for a vampire. I pried open Andre's mouth, letting it pour down his throat. His grip tightened on my other hand as blood flowed into him. His neck throbbed as he swallowed one mouthful, then another, then another.

I pulled my healing arm away after the seventh swallow and waited, holding my breath.

Nothing happened. My wound closed, but Andre didn't stir. Eventually, I had to let my breath go and the sobs began. My final, desperate move had failed. Andre would be like this, unresponsive but still trapped in his body, forever. Tears streamed down my cheeks, making my lips taste like salt.

I had rested my head on his stomach to cry when I heard movement from the bed. I jumped up, tightening my grip on his hand and pulling it closer to me. Andre shook his head first, then tried to open his eyes. The scarring kept his left eye mostly closed, and the other eye was fogged over.

"What happened?" He brought his hand to his face. "Why can't I see?" His voice raised with every word. "Where am I? What's—"

I put a finger to his lips. "It was the explosion. You've been out for almost twenty days. It's a miracle you woke up at all." If I didn't know better, I would think the gods themselves had intervened on our behalf.

"Twenty days?" Andre tried to sit up, flinched, and fell backward onto his mattress. "No wonder I feel so strange. What about Marcus?"

"Alive and well." For now.

Andre smiled. "Thank the gods."

"No, thank you." I kissed the top of his forehead, above his scarring. "You saved Moonshadow."

He shuddered. "I've never seen anything like that orb. The evil—"

"Don't think about it. It's over. The orb and the city are gone."

"What about the others?"

"All made it home. Except for Rolf." I winced at the familiar pang of sorrow in my chest. "He was caught in the explosion." If Loki told the truth, Rolf's spirit would live again, but I would never know him. For us, he was gone forever.

"I'm sorry." He squeezed my hand. "I know how much he meant to you."

"Thanks."

"I'm still tired." Andre closed his eye, sliding down the headboard to fall asleep. I pulled off my surcoat and climbed into bed beside him. He put his arms around my waist. We held each other in silence for a long time. He stroked my hair and I tightened my grip around him. I closed my eyes and a strangely familiar warmth spread through my limbs. Joy.

"I guess," he said, "this means you want to give us a chance after all."

I smiled and squeezed his hand. "I guess so."

About the Author

Dianna Gunn has wanted to be a writer since she was eight years old. She wrote her first novel for Nanowrimo at eleven years old, but quickly discovered that writing books is not an easy way to make a living. So she decided to broaden her horizons, seeking another way—any way—to build a career in publishing. Her career began in earnest when she became a marketing intern at Musa Publishing in September 2011, and quickly became a staff writer, in charge of multiple imprint blogs.

In April 2017, Dianna's first book, *Keeper of the Dawn*, was published through Book Smugglers Publishing. She went on to fund her second book, *Moonshadow's Guardian*, on Kickstarter in March 2018. The sequel, *Moonshadow's Champion*, will be released to her Ko-fi members (https://ko-fi.com/diannagunn/tiers for details) in October 2022 and published to all ebook stores in early 2023.

To learn more about Dianna's creative process, and when the next book comes out, visit her at www.authordiannagunn.com.

ACKNOWLEDGMENTS

There are hundreds of people who have contributed in some way to this book, whether it be through encouragement and support, feedback and editing, or funds for my Kickstarter campaign. I can't fit everyone into this acknowledgments section without making it a book of its own, but I'll do my best to mention the most important people.

First, to the people who actually worked on Moonshadow's Guardian in its various incarnations. My beta readers, Jasmine Fahmy and K. J. Harrowick. All of my editors, Jade Benjamin, Cait Gordon, and Sloane Taylor. The incredibly talented Reiko Murakami, who illustrated my original cover, and Eric Desmaris, who did the original formatting. And, last but certainly not least, Mato Steger who created a brilliant new cover for this book & an even more brilliant cover for book two.

Second, to all my Kickstarter backers. In particular, thank you to everyone who donated $10 or more: Arne Radtke, Brian Fitzpatrick, Bunnyhero, Cait Gordon, Christina Gale, Christy Eichenberger, Dana Lawrence, Daniel Lyn, David Zimmerman, Dylan Madeley, Eliane Mullen, Eric Oulster, Fiona Nowling, Hylke, Jade Benjamin, Jen & Eric Desmaris, Katy Van, Katrina Allis, Krysta Rhiannon, Mekki MacAulay, Miriam Goldman, Nicki BH, Rhel, Saylor, Shael Hawman, Steven Wolfman, W.L. Munn, and Zeynep Sıray.

An extra-special shout-out goes to those wonderful souls who contributed more than $100 to this campaign: George Woodruff, Tanja O'Hanlon, and Wanda Aasen.

Third, to the authors who contributed rewards to my Kickstarter campaign: Amelia Smith, Brian Rathbone, Chris Pavesic, Crystal Collier, Martin Bolton & David Pilling, L Taylor, and Meredith Katz.

And last but certainly not least, to my grandmother, Victoria Roth, and my fiancé Astrid Flannery, for giving me the space and love to grow into the person I needed to be to finish this book.

Made in the USA
Monee, IL
04 May 2023

33021403R00142